Avalon Found

by

E. M. Hanzel

Cover Design by E.M. Hanzel
Background artwork by Michal Marek, used by permission.

This book is a work of fiction. Names, characters, places, and incidents either are products of the author's imagination or are used fictitiously. Any resemblance to actual persons, living or dead, events, or locations is entirely coincidental.

E. M. Hanzel
Visit my website at https://emhanzel.com

First Printing: June 2022

ISBN: 979-8-9861659-0-5

This book is dedicated to my family who believed in me, helped me, and encouraged me to write my heart out.
Special thanks to my wife, I wouldn't be who I am today without you.

To Nathan Lowell for being a great mentor.
To Scott Bartlett and M.R. Forbes for their insight and assistance.
To David Wimsett and Greg Johnson for your last-minute contributions. Your input at the eleventh hour made this book that much better.

Shout out to the Gateway Foundation for permission to use their concept of the Voyager Station. This was the inspiration for the generation ship.

CHAPTER 1

Jocab pointed the telescope toward the darkness overhead. A lone candle burned on the table beside him giving a small glow to see by. He made sure to stay hidden from view. If one person spotted what he was doing, he was sure the temple guards would break down his door. The fear weighed heavily on him like a millstone around his neck. His emotions and anxiety threatened his ability to focus. He took a deep breath to calm himself and peered through the eyepiece, drawn to his discovery like a temptress in the night, a siren calling his name.

Avalon's two moons were waning, giving him the perfect viewing conditions. With luck, he would have several hours to study it. He needed this time to copy the finer details in his sketchbook. A large wheel hung in the sky, with four large spokes running from the center to the outer edge. Jocab observed the sun reflecting off its surface, making him believe it was made of steel, beautiful, glorious steel. Steel was both rare and extremely valuable on Avalon and from the gods themselves.

Jocab remembered a childhood story of some lucky soul that had found iron. They had an abundance of coin and never worked again. He continued to gaze through the telescope, as he daydreamed about a life with a purse forever full of coin. A big house, his future children's education, and a few colorful dresses for his wife.

Jocab sighed as he grabbed his sketch and quill to painstakingly draw the object circling overhead. It fascinated him as it slowly rotated in the night sky. He wondered what it was. How did it get there? Did the gods make this too?

The temple preached the gods created man in their image and was never kind to those that professed anything different. Jocab was unsure what to believe but kept his thoughts private. Voicing his opinion or asking too many questions could bring persecution. He wondered how to reconcile the temple's teaching and this recent discovery. The view through his telescope was throwing everything out of order. Jocab knew it was of great importance. He could feel it to his core.

Excitement coursed through him as he yearned for understanding. The temple priests must have the answers. They could give him that knowledge. All he needed was to show them. But would showing them his discovery brand him a heretic? He feared their reaction since it didn't line up with scriptures. His feelings swung back and forth as he continued to draw.

After several hours, Jocab closed his sketchbook and placed it on the table. He rubbed his eyes as he stood, stretching his aching back. His thoughts drifted to joining his wife and falling asleep under the warm blankets. He smiled at the thought as he fastened the attic window and headed down the ladder.

USSF CALYPSO

Steven settled in his chair, a small speck of light from the system's primary, visible in the distance. "Captain, we have completed the bend. We went further than expected, so we are well within the Heliosphere."

"Not bad," Captain Danielle Yasser replied. "I'd rather be a little closer than further out. What were you expecting?"

"On target would have been just outside the heliosphere."

She focused on the pinprick of light through the forward glass. "You were close. Please scan the system for any radio transmissions or signs of life." She marveled at how humanity had recently discovered how to bend space. They could now travel several light years at a time, thus expanding their colonization efforts. Prior to this discovery, the colonization of distant planets required generation ships to travel hundreds of years before arriving.

"You still there, Sar?"

"Huh? Sorry Steven. I was just thinking."

He punched commands into the console in front of him. "I thought you might be. I'm starting scans now, Captain. Do you think any survived?"

Danielle blew out a breath. "That is the question of the century."

An hour later, the console chimed. Steven acknowledged the alarm before scanning the results. "No activity, Sar. Nothing viable on any frequency bands. If they survived, they aren't using any common methods of communication."

AVALON

The rooster crowed outside, announcing the morning. Jocab buried himself deeper in the covers to muffle the sounds. He pulled the pillow over his head as the rooster crowed again.

His wife, Ayleth, turned to face him. "It won't work."

Jocab felt like he had just closed his eyes minutes ago. "I need more rest."

"You're the fool that stayed up all night. Serves you right that you're tired."

Jocab rolled over, refusing to give up. "I just need another hour of sleep."

"Not happening. You promised Wilton you'd finish installing the grommets on his boat before noon."

"Please don't remind me," he whined.

She sat up, laughing. "You made the promise, not me. And... I don't need you running around being grumpy all day either, mister. You tend to bark at everyone when you don't get enough sleep."

"I promise Ay, I won't."

She leaned over and kissed him. "Good!" She climbed out of bed and pulled on her wool robe.

Jocab dragged himself to a sitting position. "I can't wait to show you what I saw last night. I'm almost finished drawing it. I can show you tonight if the skies are clear."

"I'm not sure I want to. What you found is not in the scriptures. It might be best to leave it alone."

Jocab crossed the room and pulled her into a hug. "It will be fine. They must listen to the truth. They can bury their heads in the feeding trough, but they can't deny it's up there."

Ayleth tried to stop a small shiver from traveling down her

spine. "I'm just scared, that's all. I have a bad feeling about it, and I can't bear the thought of you being arrested."

"It will be fine, I promise."

It was late afternoon when Jocab wandered down the path. Anxiety coursed through him as he thought about how to start the conversation. His only hope, the temple priest Donav would be receptive to his findings. Images of temple guards tossing him in a prison cell threatened to overcome him. Jocab reigned in his thoughts as he continued walking. He knew Ayleth was fretting at home, fearing the worst. The sooner he returned, the sooner he could relieve her fears.

He spotted Donav sweeping the stone walkway as he broke into the clearing. He was a short man with broad shoulders and looked more like a stonemason than a priest. He had a quiet demeanor that helped put people at ease. A large, manicured lawn surrounded by a few shade trees spread out on both sides of the pathway before reaching the temple.

Donav stopped and smiled as Jocab approached. "Jocab, what a surprise. What brings you to the temple in the middle of the day?"

Jocab looked around before answering. "I found something the other day."

Donav laughed. "That's rather cryptic."

Jocab dropped his gaze. "Yeah, I know."

Donav raised an eyebrow, his curiosity peaked. "Would you feel better if we discussed this in private?"

Jocab relaxed a bit. "Could we?"

Donav guided Jocab to a bench under a shade tree a short distance away. "Certainly. We can talk privately over here."

CHAPTER 2

Donav knelt before the image of the goddess. His heart thundered in his chest as he bowed his head to pray. He tried to relax and calm his breathing before the meeting. Nothing worked as he lifted his eyes to heaven. This was his first time here. The vast temple overwhelmed his emotions. Donav yearned for the simplicity of presiding over the villagers back home.

"Why did Jocab have to show me his drawings and looking glass? A telescope, he called it! If he had not told me, I would be home doing what I love. Donav took his priestly vows to help people, not to have face-to-face meetings with the High Priest himself." The meeting both terrified and excited him. Not everyone met with the holiest of holies. Donav prayed, calmed his thoughts, and gathered his courage before heading for the large wooden door along the back wall. He maneuvered his way across the sanctuary, being careful of the surrounding worshipers. Several stopped him and asked for his blessing, which he gave willingly. Finally, he stood before the door that led to the inner sanctuary. Donav closed his eyes and prayed for wisdom before reaching for the doorknob.

He entered the lobby and noticed several people sitting behind a long, curved counter. A young man in an acolyte robe looked up and asked, "Can I help you?"

"Yes, I'm Donav and I have a meeting with the High Priest."

The acolyte looked down, reviewing a piece of paper on the desk. "Ah yes, here it is. We've been expecting you." The acolyte reached into his top drawer and pulled out a small map of the building and handed it to Donav. "You will go through that door over there and follow the map to his office. It's on the third floor, end of the hall," he said, pointing to the map.

"Third floor end of the hall. Got it."

Donav opened the door, and it looked as if he'd entered another world. He left the Temple Sanctuary, with its tall stone pillars and carved wooden ceiling, and into a hallway with steel walls, decorative paneling, and carpeted floors. Power and wealth emanated from everywhere. He felt air blowing on his face as he closed the door. Donav raised his hand toward the small vent above him. He could feel the air flow between his fingers like a cool springtime breeze. He stood in awe, wiggling his fingers in front of the vent a few times before heading for the stairwell. It took him a few minutes to gather himself and find his courage before climbing the stairs. As he climbed, his thoughts wandered to how the gods created such a building. Scripture taught the building was a gift from the gods. A monument to their worship. Donav admired everything, including how the corners of the walls and roof came together so perfectly. It was an amazing work of art. He reached out and ran his hands and fingers along the smooth metal, feeling the coolness on his fingers. He reached the top and headed down the corridor, stopping at the last door. "I can do this," he said under his breath as he opened the door.

He stepped in and looked around. A clerk sat behind a small wooden desk along the wall. Behind her was a double door that Donav assumed led into the private office of the High Priest himself. Donav observed an antique couch, coffee table, and two sitting chairs against the far wall. His gaze brought him back to the clerk who said, "You must be Donav."

"Uh, yes, ma'am. I have an appointment."

She stood, reached over the desk, and offered her hand. "Of course, Donav. May I get you some water? You must be quite parched from your long journey."

"No, thank you. I freshened up prior to my appointment," Donav replied, letting go of her hand. "I'm sorry, I didn't get your name."

"No apologies, Donav. It is I that must apologize. My name is Sanara."

"Pleased to meet you, Sanara."

"Pleasure is all mine, Donav. Now, please excuse me. I will let His Excellency know you have arrived."

Donav sat as Sanara stepped into the next room. She returned within seconds. "He will see you now."

Donav stood and followed Sanara through the double doors to meet the High Priest.

The High Priest, Athels, was sitting behind a metal desk. As soon as Donav entered, Athels stood and came over to greet him. "Donav, please come in. I hope your journey was uneventful."

Donav knelt before the High Priest. "Ah, yes, Your Excellency."

Athels placed a hand on Donav's head and blessed him before stepping back. Donav rose, his eyes taking in his surroundings. The office was not what Donav expected. Truth be told, he realized he did not know what to expect. A deep red carpet covered the entire floor, where it clashed with whitewashed metal walls. Wall hangings adorned the walls, and a long metal bookcase took up the wall behind the High Priest's metal desk. A small metal conference table sat next to the desk with four matching metal chairs. The open display of such wealth threatened to overwhelm Donav and set him on edge. It was almost too much to bear. He continued to peer around the room, eyes wide as saucers. Athels noticed Donav's distress and came to his rescue. "It is quite a sight, isn't it?"

"Yes, Your Excellency!" Donav gushed, eyes still moving from one piece of furniture to another. "How do you handle the power of this place?" he asked without thinking.

Athels chuckled and guided Donav toward the conference table. "One must continually be strong and live the life the gods ordained. Come, let us sit and you can share with me the reason for your journey."

Donav sat and attempted to compose himself. It was more difficult than he thought. His eyes darted back and forth as he took in his surroundings. After several deep breaths, he focused on the High Priest. Athels was a middle-aged man with a little gray on his temples. Deep brown eyes looked back at him, radiating confidence and patience. Donav took a deep breath, relaxed a little more, and started speaking.

Donav completed his story with only a few interruptions from the High Priest, usually to clarify some minor detail. Once finished, Donav looked at the High Priest, trying to gauge his thoughts. He waited patiently till Athels leaned forward and spoke. "I wonder if your Jocab would travel here and show us this marvel himself."

"I am sure he would. He was quite excited to share his findings with me."

Athels stood and straightened his robe. "Great! I will have

Sanara help you make it happen."

"Thank you," Donav said, lifting himself from the chair and kneeling before the High Priest. Athels blessed him with a prayer of safe travels before opening the office door.

Donav stood and followed the High Priest out of the office. "Donav will need help to retrieve a member of his village. Please see to it that he has everything he needs."

Sanara gave a slight bow before replying, "Yes, Your Excellency."

Athels smiled at Donav. "I look forward to your return."

Donav overheard the High Priest as he closed his office door. "This is most interesting. Most interesting, indeed."

Donav shaded his eyes as he stepped into the afternoon sunlight. He smiled and stood aside to allow a few worshipers to enter the temple, each of them hoping the gods would show them favor for the small offerings they carried.

Donav always appreciated the villagers' gifts back home. The gifts helped sustain the temple priests. While Donav received a stipend from the temple, he understood the true blessings came from the worshipers. Every evening, an acolyte would gather the offerings and catalog them. If they didn't use offerings locally, they would send them on to Avalon.

With his eyes finally adjusted to the sunlight, Donav started down the stone steps, eager for a meal. He remembered spotting a place that showed promise on his way to the temple. With plenty of coin from Sanara, he figured an enjoyable meal was certainly in order.

Donav walked along the cobblestone street, keeping clear of the wagons, carriages, and horse dung. He noticed most of the buildings were stone instead of the wooden structures of his village. Then he remembered the High Priest's office. Metal and steel were everywhere. Everything in the Priest's office had been metal. Donav figured the desk alone was priceless, let alone the tables and chairs. Donav smiled, remembering that he had sat in one of those metal chairs during his meeting.

Donav's feet led him to a small wooden sign announcing the "Broken Fork". He stepped across the threshold and headed to an empty table. An attractive young woman exited the kitchen. She had her dark black hair pulled back into a ponytail, accenting her dark brown eyes and high cheekbones. "Can I help you?" she asked.

Donav smiled and looked at the rotisserie chicken cooking behind her. "One of those chickens and some ale, please."

"Coming right up. Please find a seat and I'll bring it over."

"Thank you very much."

Donav sat at a small table in the corner to enjoy his meal. He had just settled in when the food arrived. "I'm Estellia, and I'll be your server. Please let me know if you need anything further."

"Thank you very much, Estellia, I'll do that."

Donav sipped his ale and settled into his meal. He was gnawing on bones when Estellia wandered over with a fresh glass of ale.

Donav gave a happy sigh and smiled. "Delicious and very filling. What do I owe you?"

"This is on the house, sir. Please allow us to bless you."

"Why, thank you. I've been thoroughly blessed. My name's Donav."

"Hello Donav. Are you new to Avalon?"

"I'm from Cumber, it's a small village west of Avalon."

"Cumber? You're a little far from home."

"Just a little, but I'll be heading back tomorrow."

"Well, it was a pleasure to serve you."

Donav took a sip of ale before speaking. "Pleasure is all mine."

Estellia smiled and picked up the dishes, leaving him to his ale.

She returned shortly with a small sack. "Here's a little something for your trip home. If you find yourself in Avalon again, please stop by."

"I will and thank you again. May the gods bless you for your hospitality."

Estellia gave a small curtsy before heading back to the kitchen.

Donav finished his ale and stood. He fished out a few coins and left a generous tip on the table.

CHAPTER 3

The afternoon sun was setting as Donav strolled along the road. He was looking forward to the evening with Jocab and Ayleth. They had invited him to discuss their trip to Avalon over dinner.

Their home was just off the main road at the end of the village. Donav rounded the corner in the road and saw the modest home in the distance. As he walked, he could see the smoke from the chimney rising in the air and wondered what was for dinner.

A few minutes later, he knocked on the front door. He heard footsteps approaching and a petite young woman answered and smiled at him. "Come in, Sire. Please, come in. Dinner is almost ready."

"Why, thank you. Please call me Donav. No need to stand on formality here."

"Thank you, Donav. Can I get you something to drink? Ale, water? We also have some fresh goat's milk."

Donav stepped in and removed his coat and scarf. "An ale, please. Thank you."

Ayleth hung his coat on an empty peg behind the door.

Donav let his gaze wander, taking in a good sized living room with a small kitchen in one corner. He felt that the artisan who built the house knew what he was doing. A bedroom door shared a wall with what looked like a dual fireplace that heated both the bedroom and living area. Between the bedroom door and fireplace was a ladder, leading to a loft or attic above the bedroom. While Donav had visited in the past, he had never stayed more than a few minutes.

Just then, Jocab entered from the bedroom and gave Donav a warm welcome. "Donav, thank you for coming. Ayleth has made some wonderful meat pies with fresh vegetables from the garden."

"It smells delicious too."

Jocab led Donav toward two reclining chairs. "Please come sit. Ayleth has everything almost ready."

Donav lowered himself into a chair next to Jocab as Ayleth

handed them two tall steins of ale. "Here you go, but don't fill up before dinner."

Jocab smiled up at Ayleth. "We promise to leave plenty of room. It smells divine."

Ayleth's smile widened at the compliment. "Thank you, dear."

Jocab and Donav enjoyed their ale while watching Ayleth put the finishing touches on the evening meal. Donav finally broke the silence. "The High Priest seemed genuinely interested in your discovery."

Jocab was excited. "The High Priest himself?" He leaned forward in his chair. "That's great. What did he say?"

"He has requested your presence in Avalon to share your findings with the high council. All expenses paid, of course."

Jocab raised his eyebrows and looked at Ayleth. "Did you hear that? Avalon! He wants me to travel to Avalon."

Ayleth placed the pies on the table and looked up. "Really? That is quite a trip."

Donav took another sip. "About four days' travel. We will spend a couple of days there before we return and another four days back. Have either of you been to Avalon?"

Ayleth shook her head. "I grew up here in Cumber my whole life. Farthest I have been was to visit Jocab's parents' farm outside of town. You follow the creek up a good day's journey, and you run right into it. The creek runs right through the farm."

"Same here," Jocab replied. "I lived on the family farm before settling here in Cumber with Ayleth."

Ayleth pulled off her apron and announced. "Dinner is served."

Jocab and Donav stood. "Donav, would you take the seat of honor?"

"Why, yes. Thank you."

Donav took his place at the head of the table and blessed the meal. The three of them settled into eating, with some occasional small talk between bites. Donav finished his pie first and sat back with a contented sigh. "That was delicious!"

Ayleth beamed. "Thank you, Donav."

Jocab tucked in his last bite and washed it down with a sip of ale. "She's always made a mean pie. They are so good; I swear I'll never tire of them."

"Oh, stop it, you two. So Donav, you're saying ten to twelve days max to Avalon?"

"Might add a day or two, depending on the weather."

Ayleth stood and picked up the empty plates. "When do you plan to leave?"

Donav drained his ale and set the stein down on the table. "I would like to leave as soon as possible. Summer's coming and I'd like to be back before the heat kicks in."

Jocab looked over at Ayleth for approval before speaking. "Give me a day to get everything settled here and then we can leave."

Ayleth nodded her approval. "I think you only have to fix the wagon wheel for Paterson."

"I finished it this afternoon. I can deliver it in the morning."

"Oh, wow. That was quick," Ayleth replied.

"I just had to straighten it after he scraped it against the wall near the dock. Was a little wobbly, that's all."

Ayleth turned to Donav. "Then it's settled. I'll pack Jocab a travel bag tomorrow and you can leave first thing the next morning."

Jocab finished his ale and placed his empty glass down. "Will we be walking?"

"No, we can use some horses from the temple. We always keep one or two for trips to Avalon."

CHAPTER 4

Donav and Jocab were sweating in the afternoon sun. Jocab could tell they were close to Avalon. Villas, small farms, and vineyards dotted the landscape. "A few more hours until we reach the temple stables. We'll have time to eat and wash off the road before evening."

Tired, hungry, and beyond saddle sore, Jocab commented, "I need a day of rest after all this riding."

Donav laughed. "I'm with you. My backside needs a rest too. I hitched a ride in a wagon last time."

They rode along for another hour before the city opened in the distance. Jocab stopped his horse and just stared. His eyes bounced from one place to another, taking everything in. Avalon sat along a river where fishing boats hugged the docks along the river's edge. A stone bridge directly ahead provided a crossing point into the city proper. Brick, wood, and stone buildings several stories high filled his vision. "I heard the city was large, but this is huge. It's bigger than a hundred villages."

Donav gave a low chuckle and urged his horse forward. "It's that and then some. You think this is amazing, wait till you see the temple."

Jocab proceeded to rubber neck, not even realizing his horse had followed Donav's mount. He continued to take in the sights, trying not to miss anything. Before he knew it, they had arrived at the temple stables just inside the city.

Donav and Jocab dismounted and handed their horses off to a stable hand. Donav turned to Jocab. "You hungry?"

"Starved."

Donav headed toward the street. "Me too. I know the perfect place. Let's get cleaned up first."

Jocab let out a sigh and proposed, "I'd be willing to eat first."

"Me too. Except we look and smell like the road."

Jocab gave a hearty laugh as he looked at his shirt. "I certainly fit that description."

"The inn is just two streets up," Donav motioned as they turned the corner.

Jocab opened his mouth to reply when they ran into a large crowd congregating in a small square. He could see the top of a statue in the square center along with a temporary stage erected at one end. Jocab craned his neck for a better view. Several guards were securing three bedraggled men to a large wooden beam. A temple priest in a red crimson robe took center stage and held up an official looking document. "These men have been found guilty of heresy to the temple and to our gods. Their continued blasphemous words must be silenced. So it be done."

The priest smiled as he spun around and faced the convicted. "May your cries reach the heavens. Only then can the gods grant you mercy. Only then can your lost souls receive redemption in the afterlife. So it be done."

Jocab turned away in horror as the guards tossed torches onto a pile of wood below the men's feet. "I cannot watch this."

Donav was quick on his heels. "Slow down immediately, you will draw attention to yourself."

Jocab glared at Donav. "I cannot be a part of this."

Donav placed his hand on Jocab's shoulder. "Jocab, slow down."

Jocab wrenched his shoulder free but slowed his gate. They walked in silence toward an alley a few meters away. After turning up the alley, Jocab sprinted away. He didn't care where or how far, just far enough to not hear the screams.

It was only after Jocab finished retching that Donav caught up to him. Donav leaned against the wall and sucked in air. "No man should die like that."

He spun toward Donav, the comment fueling his anger. "Then stop it!"

"They are beyond our help," Donav replied with tears in his eyes. "We can only pray they die quickly."

"Only a mercy stroke or arrow will end it soon."

Donav guided Jocab toward the inn. "I wish I could deliver it, my friend."

Two hours later, they were walking down the street, freshly bathed. Jocab finally felt well enough to eat after the previous ordeal. He pointed to a pub where some music was making its way outside. "They should have something."

Donav shook his head. "I know a place that serves good food and great ale."

Jocab's stomach complained. "Alright. But I hope it is not much further."

"Not at all."

Minutes later, they ducked into the doorway of the 'Broken Fork.' Donav steered Jocab toward an open table in the back. Several of the tables were full of patrons in different stages of partaking in their meals.

A young woman's voice yelled from the kitchen. "Donav, is that you?"

Jocab raised an eyebrow in his direction. "Been here before?"

"Once. And, like I said, they have great food."

Estellia passed through the swinging doors and gave Donav a great big smile. "What brings you back to Avalon?"

Donav gave a mock bow. "Your wonderful chicken, of course."

"HAH!" she laughed. "I knew I liked you. Now, who is this you've brought with you?"

"This is Jocab. He is the local tradesmith in my village. He can fix anything. Probably invent a better mousetrap if you need one."

She reached out and shook Jocab's hand. "Pleasure to meet you, Jocab. Now, what can I get for the two of you?"

Donav smiled and licked his chops, "Same as last time, please."

"Gotcha, and for you, master Jocab?"

"I'll have the same, please."

"Two rotisseries and ale's coming right up."

Donav and Jocab retired to a corner by the fireplace and sat back to wait for their food.

Estellia arrived within seconds, with plates full of chicken, steamed vegetables, and two glasses of ale. "OK boys, here you go. Veggies are from a neighbor's garden. Picked them myself this morning."

Jocab thanked Estellia and grabbed a drumstick. "This looks

and smells delicious."

"Why, thank you. So, what brings the two of you to my humble establishment?"

Donav took a sip of his ale and looked around, deciding if it was safe to share the purpose of their journey. "Jocab has an appointment with the High Priest."

Estellia took a small step back. Her eyes widened, and her voice went up an octave. "The High Priest? What great findings did you discover that would interest the High Priest himself?"

Donav looked down at his plate, fearing he said too much.

Estellia brandished a warm smile and leaned in. "You need not fear, your words are safe here."

Donav glanced at Jocab for permission before proceeding. "He discovered something in the heavens."

"Really? Did you find the home of the gods?"

Jocab thought of what to say as he finished his bite. "I'm not sure what it is, only that it's there."

Estellia knelt next to the table. "Oh, do tell…"

Jocab looked at Estellia, wondering if she was interested or just being kind. "It is like a huge wagon wheel slowly rotating in a circle. And…" He paused as he figured out the best way to explain. "It looks like it's made completely out of metal."

Estellia seemed mesmerized. "Metal? In the heavens?"

"It's circling above us."

"Why is it there?"

"I'm hoping the High Priest can help answer that."

She leaned into Jocab and whispered in his ear. "Be careful. This may not be good news for the temple."

Jocab looked back at her and nodded. He glanced over at the priest, but Donav showed no sign of hearing.

Jocab's mind was racing as they finished their meals in silence. The High Priest had to accept what he had found. Ayleth told him it didn't line up with scripture. Now Estellia was warning him, too. He was still in turmoil when they arrived back at the inn.

The temple was quick to schedule a meeting. Jocab figured it was because it was getting toward the evening when most other business had already been concluded. Both he and Donav were walking toward the temple after their evening meal. Donav had insisted they visit the 'Broken Fork' before going to the temple, and Jocab had agreed immediately.

Jocab enjoyed the bustling of the surrounding city. He watched in fascination as people hustled back and forth, hurrying to some important task or errand. Then the temple came into view. While Jocab had no preconceived ideas, the temple exceeded anything he could have imagined. A large rectangular stone structure stood at the top of a small incline. A metal structure, similar in size, stood behind it. Jocab stopped and admired the sun's rays reflecting off the curved metal roof. The sheer size of it gleaming in the distance seized him.

"Stunning, huh?" Donav said, breaking the spell.

"It's amazing! Both structures are amazing, but the roof…" His voice trailing off.

"Yes, it's quite intimidating. I felt like a little schoolboy when I first entered."

"I can see why!"

"The stone structure up front is the sanctuary for worshiping."

"And the back?"

"It is where the High Priests live and work. The entire building is all metal. Floors, walls, ceilings, doors, everything." I met the High Priest there in his office. His desk and chairs were metal, too.

"I find that hard to believe."

"It's an amazing gift from the gods. A must see for everybody."

"Well, only one way to do that." Jocab replied as he set off again.

Donav chuckled and caught up to Jocab, matching his stride.

Jocab continued to admire the temple as they approached. The sanctuary looked to be at least four stories tall, with twelve round Doric stone columns along the front. A large, manicured garden and promenade announced the grand staircase leading to the temple. Jocab thought the worshipers entering the temple looked so small against the grand structure.

As they got closer, he could see the stone walls surrounding the temple grounds were several feet thick, with a central curved gate in front where the street ended. Two solid wood doors stood open, inviting them to enter. Jocab marveled. Each door was eight feet wide, twelve feet tall at the ends, and fourteen feet at the apex. Jocab wished he could stop and investigate how they were held in place and wondered what they used for hinges.

When they passed through the gates onto the promenade, Jocab observed two temple guards standing at attention on opposite sides of the entrance. Jocab thought they were ceremonial, as they ignored everything around them.

It took a few minutes to cross the promenade and reach the enormous staircase. Jocab looked at the stairs before grinning at Donav. "Shall we?"

Donav, not looking forward to the climb, sighed and nodded. "We shall."

Jocab was out of breath when they reached the top of the stairs. His muscles burned from climbing all sixty steps without stopping. He took a deep breath and looked for Donav, wondering how far he had lagged behind. It pleased him to see Donav was only a few steps behind.

Donav was breathing hard. "You..., sure..., like a good..., climb, don't yah?"

"Yup. Used to race my brothers everywhere when I was younger."

"Did you win?"

"When I got older. They quit thinking it was fun after that."

"I can understand that."

They took a few minutes to enjoy the view while Donav caught his breath. Jocab, who had already recovered, turned to take in the enormous temple. Massive Doric columns lined the front, two meters wide, with smooth, perfectly formed edges reaching upward to the ceiling thirty meters above. Jocab took a few minutes and marveled at the craftsmanship. He visualized the number of hours required to polish the stone to a smooth finish. The entrance was just as grand. Four columns wide, with the overhead as tall as the columns. Two additional columns stood in the middle of the entrance, matching the locations of the main columns in front of them, adding to the majestic atmosphere.

CHAPTER 5

Jocab continued to look around as they entered the temple, eyes wide, taking it all in. Just shy of the back of the temple was a five-foot-high pedestal with the four gods standing together. A large round copper bowl for burning incense sat two meters in front of the pedestal. The designers separated the sides of the temple with a set of four Doric columns that were half as large as the main columns outside. In each corner, smaller individual statues of each god with their own small copper bowl provided the worshipers the opportunity to worship each god separately. On the right side, in the front corner, was Lip, the god of Courage and Strength. In the back right corner was Leah, the goddess of Beauty and Love. On the left front side corner was Sutter, the god of Law and Order, and in the back left corner was Amelia, the goddess of Mercy and Kindness.

Jocab walked toward the large copper offering bowl and opened a small leather pouch containing leaves and tree bark from their village mixed with incense. His wife, Ayleth, insisted Jocab burn an offering from their village. Jocab placed the contents on the corner of the bowl. He grabbed a stick from next to a small bed of warm coals under the bowl. The fire engulfed the offering as Jocab knelt and bowed his head. Donav knelt beside him, adding his own silent prayer.

It took only a minute for the flames to consume the leaves and tree bark before it burned itself out. Both Jocab and Donav respectfully waited another minute before standing.

Jocab followed Sanara and Donav into the priests' council chamber below the sanctuary. Five large chairs sat on a raised dais behind a curved table in the shape of the letter C. Several chairs sat against the wall next to the door for any guests. Donav and Jocab both took a seat as Sanara excused herself and closed the door behind her.

Just as they both sat back, a side door opened, and the priests filed in. Both Jocab and Donav took a knee as the High Priest Athels headed in their direction. He stopped in front of them and placed his hand on their heads, blessing them before stepping back to greet them. "Welcome and thank you for coming at such a late hour. Jocab, I understood you required darkness, so I thought it prudent to have this meeting in the evening."

Jocab rose with Donav. "Thank you, your Excellence, for your wisdom. The night sky is necessary."

Athels crossed the room to the dais and took his seat in the center, with the other priests sitting at his sides. Athels turned and gestured to the right, "This is Solomon and Damon." Both priests nodded. Athels then gestured to his left, "And this is Farzod and Geoffery." The other two priests nodded.

Jocab recognized Solomon as the priest that had carried out the execution earlier. His heart raced as he collected himself. This was his one chance. He must keep it together. He stepped up to the dais and knelt, briefly bowing his head. "Pleasure to meet each of you. First, I wish to express what an honor it is to stand before you today. I humbly thank you for taking the time to listen to what I have to present to you tonight." Jocab stepped forward and set his papers in the center of the table. "I placed before you my original drawings and notes of an object I have seen in our night sky. Amazingly, directly above us, there appears to be a giant metal wheel orbiting the planet."

Jocab waited while the priests observed his drawings and notes, passing them to each other. "It looks like a star to the naked eye, but when you view it through a telescope, you can see it's not a star, but a giant wheel made of metal. It is absolutely phenomenal. I believe it is man-made, or from the gods themselves."

Several of the priests had their heads together inspecting his work. They looked up in alarm at his last comment. None of them spoke but eyed him for several heartbeats before looking back at the drawings. Jocab waited in silence for them to finish, expecting a round of questions afterward. The High Priest Athels held up a large sketch of the object. "This is what you see?"

"Yes, Your Excellency."

"How did you discover it?"

"I found it when I was lining up my telescope to look at our second moon, Acrobba, several months ago. The telescope I purchased had just arrived, and I was eager to use it."

Athels smirked. "And you just found this instead?"

"You could imagine my shock, Your Excellency. It completely mesmerized me. I followed it for several nights before I had enough sense to draw it."

The priest Solomon looked up from a drawing before asking, "And who else did you show this to?"

"My wife Ayleth, sir. I had to share it with someone. Then Donav, after I had created several more drawings."

Farzod placed the copy of the drawing on the table. "Remarkable details you've drawn here. I am eager to view this metal wheel myself."

Geoffrey, sitting next to Farzod, leaned forward. "Yes, so am I."

Athels looked at the priests sitting on each side of him before smiling at Jocab. "Please set up your telescope so we can view this wonder ourselves," he commented as he extended his hand toward the balcony doors along the side of the room.

Jocab smiled back. "Certainly, your Excellence. Please allow me a few minutes."

Jocab unpacked and set the telescope on the tripod with great care. Placing the telescope against his shoulder, he addressed the High Priest. "Do you have someone that can assist with opening the door?"

Sanara jumped up from the corner of the room and headed for the door. "I'll get it…."

Jocab hadn't even known she was there, never having heard her enter. He glanced around the room to see if anyone else had entered unannounced. Seeing only Donav, he lifted the tripod and followed Sanara.

Jocab quickly aligned the telescope as the priests followed him onto the balcony. The priests took turns and gazed in fascination at the object in the night sky. Athels took his time observing before finally stepping away. "Your drawings look quite accurate," he commented.

Jocab blushed and gave a slight bow. "Thank you, Your Excellence. I tried."

Athels examined the four priests' as they gave small, imperceptive nods. Satisfied, Athels turned his smile on Jocab. "Thank you for showing us your discovery. We need time to pray to the gods and to seek their wisdom. Would you stay in Avalon for a few more days?"

Jocab, already eager to return home, looked toward Donav for guidance. Donav nodded, signaling he should agree. Jocab swallowed his thoughts. "Absolutely, Your Excellency. We can extend our trip a few more days."

CHAPTER 6

Jocab was going stir crazy. It was the third day since the meeting with the High Priests, and they had heard nothing. Jocab had promised Ayleth he would return in a few weeks, and he didn't want to break that promise. To be honest, he was just tired of waiting. Jocab knew there was plenty to do, since Avalon was the center of knowledge. He had spent all day yesterday visiting the main library, studying different things to build back in the village. He thought a water mill would help immediately, as most of the villagers back home ground their own wheat into flour daily. Jocab thought that after he built the water mill, he would have enough experience to build a larger one to generate electricity. He needed to get home first.

Donav could see Jocab was fidgeting like a two-year-old child. Donav closed the book he was reading and eyed Jocab critically. "Would you like to get some more chicken?"

"I am all chickened out," Jocab replied. "But I'd be happy to try something else. I'm hungry after a morning of just sitting here looking at these walls."

Donav placed the book on the small table and stood up. "All right then, let's go."

After a short walk, they entered the 'Broken Fork' and smiled at Estellia.

"The usual?" she called out.

"Yes, for me, but can you believe Jocab wants something different?"

Estellia played like she'd been wounded. "Oh, dear me."

Both men laughed. Estellia turned to Jocab. "I know just the thing, trust me."

Jocab matched her smile. "I trust you."

Jocab and Donav found an open table and settled in. Estellia placed two tall glasses of ale in front of them. "Please drink up while I get your food."

Donav raised his glass to Estellia. "To the best establishment in

Avalon."

Jocab followed. "To the best establishment."

Estellia curtsied. "You two are way too kind. Although, you have been good for business."

Minutes later, Estellia returned with the rotisserie chicken and a large fillet of fish with cooked vegetables. "They caught this last night."

Donav admired the fish with a little jealousy. "You have been holding out on me."

Jocab's mouth started watering as he sized up the fish. "Wow, this is one big fish. Thank you very much."

They were halfway through their meals when a messenger from the temple entered. Donav raised his hand to get the messenger's attention. The messenger, an acolyte based on his robe, scurried over. "Thank you, sir. They told me at the inn that I could find you here."

"And here we are," Donav said with a smile. "Please sit. What message do you have for us?"

The temple messenger sat tentatively while Jocab signaled to Estellia. Estellia nodded and started another plate.

"Uh, the High Priest is requesting to meet again mid-morning tomorrow."

"Thank you. I didn't get your name."

The messenger, shy and unsure how to act with being asked to join them, stammered, "Rynan, good sir."

"Thank you Rynan, I'm Donav and this is Jocab. We will certainly be there tomorrow. Now please stay and enjoy lunch with us."

Estellia appeared at the table and placed a plate of chicken and an ale in front of Rynan. "Thank you," he mumbled in appreciation.

Rynan quietly folded his hands and said a quick prayer before attacking his meal. Jocab and Donav took a swig of ale. They watched Rynan relax as he pulled off a leg and dug in.

Donav and Jocab gave him a little time to eat before starting some light conversation. "Are you new at the temple?"

"Yes sir, just over thirty days now."

"I'm guessing you're not from the city," Jocab surmised.

"I'm from a small village east of Avalon. I come from a large family. Since the farm goes to my older brother, I thought it best to leave and make my own way in the world."

"Very noble," Jocab replied with understanding. The oldest child usually received the largest inheritance, if not all of it. They sometimes left younger children with little or nothing at all. It was not uncommon for the younger children to leave the farm and make their future elsewhere.

"That was my story years ago," Donav smiled knowingly. "Although I felt called to be a priest since I was a young boy. Are you called too?"

Rynan shrugged and took a few minutes to consider his words. He seemed embarrassed as he replied. "I'm not really sure. My mother is very devout, and she convinced me to become a priest. I had nothing better, so I thought I would try it."

Donav smiled. "I remember when I first joined the temple. How are you liking it so far?"

"Honestly, it's a little difficult. I cannot read as well as the others and I take longer to complete my studies."

"Ah, yes. That does make it more difficult. Hang in there, it will get easier as your reading improves."

"That is what my instructor keeps telling me."

Donav chuckled, "As mine said to me many years back. I wish you the best in your studies. Be sure to pick your path before that decision is made for you. I cannot tell you how many people are doing what is in front of them instead of what they wish they could do."

Both Donav and Jocab drained their glasses as Estellia appeared beside them. "Another round?"

Donav shook his head. "No, thank you. But please see that Rynan is taken care of. I remember the rigors of my first year at the temple and no matter how much they fed me, I was always hungry."

She placed a hand on Rynan's shoulder. "My pleasure. I will make sure he eats enough."

Rynan blushed again as he stood with Donav and Jocab.

"Please sit and finish your meal. Estellia makes the best chicken in Avalon." Donav leaned over and hugged Estellia. "We will see you tonight for supper."

"You better! I have another dish for Jocab to try."

She watched the two leave before patting Rynan on the shoulder. "When you finish that chicken, I have some fresh pie for dessert."

Rynan's eyes opened wide at the thought of pie. "Uh, thank you ma'am, thank you."

Sanara showed Donav and Jocab into the council chambers again. The two of them sat and tried to make themselves comfortable. Jocab could not relax and found himself anxious and fidgeting again. Just when Jocab thought he couldn't take much more, the side door opened, and the priests filed in.

Jocab noticed a stiffness in their posture, avoiding his gaze as they took their seats. Jocab glanced at Donav as they knelt for the High Priest's blessing. Athels approached, placed his hands on their heads, and blessed them. "Thank you both for coming again."

Jocab could hear the impersonal, polite tone. He looked up to see Athels was smiling, but it lacked warmth. This was a much more professional smile, one practiced in the mirror. Jocab nodded and stood. "Thank you, Your Excellency," he replied. Jocab couldn't shake the feeling of foreboding surrounding him. He knew Athels would pronounce judgment shortly.

Athels turned and proceeded to his chair. Jocab exchanged worried glances with Donav as the High Priest took his seat. Once seated, Athels sat forward and folded his hands in front of him. "Jocab, I wish to thank you for coming on short notice today. We are thankful for what you have revealed to us. We also appreciate all the time and effort it took to document your discovery. We have spent many hours over the last several days praying and searching the scriptures."

Jocab tried to keep his composure as he waited for Athels to drop the hammer. The formality in the room screamed trouble. He stood tall, determined to take it like a man, regardless of the outcome.

The High Priest continued. "We have determined that there is no special significance or religious value in the object you have discovered. Nor can we confirm whether the object came from the gods. Regardless, it does not change scripture or the views of the Temple. We are requesting you to leave your telescope and your notes, so we can continue to research it. We will compensate you handsomely for your time and for your telescope. Lastly, we insist you stop researching this object. Continuing to do so is a waste of time, and if shared, will be twisted by non-believers and heretics to undermine the fabric of our world."

Jocab couldn't believe it. How could they tell him to stop? "Your Excellence, I appreciate the opportunity to be here. I also wish to thank you for taking your valuable time to pray and seek the gods. It comforts me to know that you took my findings seriously and did not dismiss them out of hand. But I do not agree with you. I believe that what circles above us is of great significance and importance. Your actions tonight confirm how right I am. Does it really matter if the object is from the gods or not? The fact this marvel exists demands we investigate it further." Jocab sensed the priests becoming agitated, especially Solomon. The High Priest, Athels, looked livid. Jocab feared he had just put his neck in a noose. Swallowing hard, he continued. "With that said, please rest assured that I will honor your request. I also ask that the Temple not curtail or diminish my study of astronomy."

The Priests sat in silence, their eyes wide in astonishment. Jocab wondered if anyone had ever spoken to them this way. He could see Athels' mind racing. Jocab knew he needed to wait him out. He took a deep breath to calm himself while being sure to look Athels in the eye.

Athels finally leaned forward. "We appreciate your candidness with this matter and are glad you will honor our request. We, in turn, will honor yours. You are free to study your astronomy as long as you cease your efforts toward the object. We will continue researching this object and will share our findings with the world when we are ready."

Jocab bowed slightly. "Thank you, Your Excellence."

Athels stood. "Thank you, Jocab. This meeting is adjourned." Both Donav and Jocab knelt for Athels to bestow a blessing before departing.

CHAPTER 7

Donav and Jocab walked in silence until they were clear of the temple. "That went well," Donav commented.

Jocab snorted in disgust. "They took my telescope, my notes, and my dignity. They threatened me into silence. If that went well, then I wonder what fabulous looks like."

"They paid you handsomely for the telescope and your research."

"It's hush coin to shut me up and nothing more," Jocab spat. "I feel violated."

Donav blanched at the words. "Please remember, I am a temple priest."

Jocab took a deep breath, letting some of his anger go. "And a good priest at that. I thought you were going to pass out when I replied to Athels."

Donav gave a low laugh, "Pass out, I was expecting him to call the guards to throw us both in a cold, dark cell so you could rethink your views."

Jocab's eyes widened. "You're joking!"

Donav shook his head. "No joke. Athels does not tolerate any threats to the temple. It was your genuine honesty that allowed you to walk out of there tonight. Had you resisted or tried to pull the wool over his eyes, this would be a different conversation."

Jocab retreated into himself as he pondered Donav's words.

They walked in silence for a few minutes before Donav spoke again. "Did you notice Solomon?"

"I did. He looked like a steam kettle ready to blow."

"Solomon has a reputation for being the most fervent of the High Priests. As you saw, he is the one that dispenses discipline to those he thinks unfaithful."

"I said nothing unfaithful."

"In the eyes of a zealot, anything that threatens their view of scripture, or the world is enough to take action."

"That is so not right."

"I didn't say it was, only that it is."

The priests remained in the council chambers long after Donav and Jocab had left.

Solomon looked at Athels. "I have a bad feeling about him."

Geoffrey smiled at Solomon. "You have that feeling about most people."

Solomon glared at Geoffrey. "My job is to protect the scriptures."

"And you find him dangerous? Unstable?"

"Now you're just trying to provoke me," Solomon snapped.

"I'm just trying to find out why. I found him to be quite articulate and intelligent."

"And that just strengthens my resolve. The man is dangerous."

Damon sat forward. "You think we should arrest him?"

"That might be going too far," Geoffrey replied.

Farzod sat back in his chair. "I suggest we watch him."

Athels looked at the others. "Good idea. We can have Donav send us weekly reports."

"Donav is too attached," Solomon countered. "We need someone not as close."

"Do we have a temple priest we can rotate?" Farzod asked.

Athels smiled. "Good idea. I'll have Sanara take care of it."

Solomon frowned. "That may take weeks or even a month."

"No worries, Jocab showed his character tonight. He'll honor his word. Few people have the courage to stand before us and say what he did."

Solomon nodded in agreement. "That's why we should arrest him. He's dangerous."

Athels shook his head. "We will rotate a new priest every few months to keep an eye on things. I'll make it a requirement of the rotation."

"I hope it's enough. We just witnessed how powerful he can be. People follow men like him to the ends of the earth."

Athels sighed, knowing Solomon was right. "I agree but arresting him might be too drastic."

Solomon was not ready to let go. "You're going to regret this decision."

Geoffrey leaned over the table. "You really think that?"

"Yes, I do! The man has charisma that is a mile wide. A man just like him lured an entire village to turn away from the scriptures."

Farzod sighed. "We all know the story of your childhood. That was almost thirty years ago."

Solomon seethed in anger. "They burned the temple down and everyone inside. He's the kind of person who could unravel everything we built here. The world is not ready for the truth yet."

Athels locked his gaze on Solomon. "He may be dangerous, but I'm not ready to lock him up. That ship overhead cannot hurt us. It's dead and will stay dead," Athels replied, ending the conversation.

CHAPTER 8

Jocab was heading home after a day of working on a few boats down at the docks. He had replaced three sets of pulleys on three different boats. He had almost reached the turnoff to his house when he noticed a traveler on horseback heading into town. Jocab slowed down to wait. It would be rude to not welcome them, especially since the traveler had already seen him.

Jocab stopped and waved. The traveler waved back and kicked the horse to go a little faster. It didn't help. Jocab could see the poor animal was worn out. Several minutes later, the traveler reached him, and Jocab held out his hand. "Welcome, sir. Welcome to Cumber."

The traveler shook the outstretched hand. "Thank you. I am Taylan."

"Nice to meet you Taylan, I'm Jocab."

Taylan froze, eying Jocab for a few seconds. "Pleased to meet you, Jocab. I'm the new priest."

Jocab tried to hide his surprise. "Is Donav leaving?"

Taylan smiled. "No, we rotate an extra priest from time to time till they find us a permanent home. I'm blessed to serve here with Donav for the time being."

"Well then. The pleasure is all mine. Welcome to Cumber."

"Thank you. Is that the temple over there?" he asked, pointing in the distance.

"It sure is. Follow the road past the general store and make a left, then up the hill. You can't miss it."

Taylan nudged his tired mount forward. "Bless you, Jocab."

Jocab watched him head down the road till he was comfortable the priest would find his way. By the time Jocab arrived home, he had all but forgotten the visitor.

Jocab had his head inside the bellows at the blacksmith's the next afternoon when he heard Donav call his name. He pulled his head out and looked up. "Hey there, Donav. What's up?" he questioned.

"Do you have a few minutes?"

"I sure do. Give me a second to let Olin know I'll be right back."

"Take your time."

Several minutes later, Donav had pulled Jocab around the side of the blacksmith's shop. Donav looked around to verify they were alone before speaking. "I'm concerned for you and felt I should warn you."

"Well, uh…, thank you. But why? What's up?"

"We have a new priest in town, but I fear he is not here to serve the village."

"Taylan?" Jocab questioned.

Donav's eyebrows shot up. "You met him?"

"Yes, He was on the main road, just coming into town when I was heading home."

"Did anything happen?"

"No. I introduced myself and he asked for directions to the temple. He said he was rotating through."

"That's just it. I fear his rotation is not just to fulfill his priestly duties."

"Go on. I'm more than curious."

"He is here to monitor you to make sure you don't cause the temple any more trouble."

"You've got to be kidding! I gave them my word."

"I know your word is iron, but others might not think so."

Jocab looked down and kicked a rock with his foot. "This is ridiculous!"

"I agree, but please be careful, Jocab. He is going to be looking over both our shoulders to make sure we behave. If he finds anything he doesn't like, it will affect everyone in the village."

Jocab put his hand on Donav's shoulder. "Don't worry. I gave my word. He simply will have nothing to report."

Donav could feel his anxiety wash away. "I believe you. But I figured I'd let you know."

Jocab gave a half smile. "Thanks, Donav."

Jocab bowed his head to allow Donav to bless him before returning to the bellows.

CHAPTER 9

Jocab was sipping his tea when Horton burst through the door. "Jocab, come quick!" he shouted. "We found a comet that is burning really bright."

Jocab stood as Horton pulled him out of the chair. "Hurry, you must see it!"

Horton was so excited, he almost fell over backwards as he turned toward the door. Jocab smiled at him as he buttoned up his coat and followed him out. Jocab knew Horton was always a bundle of energy. The boy never sat still, ever. He was always fidgeting or finding some other way to release his stored energy, like a bug bouncing on a hot stove.

Jocab stepped out into the night and walked over to the others gathered around the telescope. It took him two months to get a replacement after the temple priests "borrowed" his last one. He was thankful they had compensated him enough that he could afford to buy another one.

"So, what have you guys found?"

Horton was still buzzing with excitement. "It's amazing! Look for yourself."

Edmond backed away to give Jocab a chance to look. "I was showing Horton and Boris the rings around the planet Tureolin tonight. While lining up the telescope, I saw this star light up brighter than it was originally. It's beyond Tureolin to the right, but clearly visible."

Jocab stepped up, put his eye to the lens, and peered toward the heavens. The brightly burning object was just on the edge of his view. Jocab realigned the telescope to center it before giving it another look. "It sure is burning bright. Like it is really on fire. You can see it flickering."

"It just seemed to appear like that about three minutes ago. That was when I found it."

"That doesn't sound right. Things don't just appear out of

nowhere, and stars don't light up like that. Must have been there the whole time, and we just didn't notice it. Lot of open space out there, you know. Congrats on the find."

Edmond grinned at the idea of discovering a new object in the heavens. "Well, now that we found it, we can continue to watch it since we know where to look."

"Great idea," Jocab agreed. "Might be a comet. See if it is moving, and if so, how fast? Maybe, see where it's heading? It would be a lot of fun to determine its path."

Boris, tall for his age, spoke for the first time, "How do you do that?"

Edmond patted him on the back. "Mathematics, my boy, mathematics."

Boris moaned. "Please no. Not math. It makes my head hurt."

Jocab, still peering through the eyepiece, let out a laugh. "I'm with Boris. I'm not a mathematician, but Edmond is. He knows the math to do it."

Edmond smiled. "It is easier than you think. It's all in the Kepler equation."

"What's Kepler?" asked Horton.

"I don't know. That is what they call the math equation. They had to name it something."

"Maybe it's who, not what. They usually name things after a person."

Edmond smiled. "Who, what, where…. I don't care. I just know it as the Kepler equation."

The conversation ended abruptly when Jocab jumped back, almost knocking over the telescope. "It stopped!"

Horton, who was bouncing from foot to foot, quit fidgeting. "What stopped?"

Jocab stepped back to allow the others to look. "The star stopped burning, that's what!"

Edmond stepped up to the telescope. "That's not possible."

"Oh yeah. The star is still there, but it is not on fire like it was."

Edmond took a long look. "You are right. It's there, but the fire is hardly noticeable now."

"How is that possible?" Boris asked.

Each of them took the next minute to look through the

telescope, confirming the change.

Jocab looked at the three of them. "Well, we can confirm it's not a star."

"But what is it then?" Horton asked.

Edmond stroked his chin. "It has to be something else."

Boris' face was pale in the moonlight as he turned toward the temple and said a small prayer of protection.

Jocab stopped outside the village ale house. He was not a regular, preferring to spend his time with his wife, Ayleth instead. Tonight, though, was different. They had an object in the sky to track, and he would not pass this up.

He stepped in and stood in the doorway, letting the door close behind him. It was a small rectangular building with room for five tables arranged around a fireplace along the back wall. He spotted his friends sitting at a table near the stairs. Nodding to the bartender, he raised his finger, indicating he'd like an ale, and headed over to join his friends.

The bartender, Birx, lived in the back half of the establishment with his wife. He was a mountain of a man with thick arms and wide shoulders. Jocab thought he looked more like a woodcutter than a bartender. Birx had built a small second story above the inn with two rooms to rent. The idea was to cater to the occasional traveler, even though Cumber was at the end of the road.

Jocab grabbed the empty chair and sat down next to his friends. "So, what have you three come up with?"

Boris was the first to speak. "We want to track this thing every night."

Edmond set his half empty ale on the table. "We figured we could work in shifts. Three or four hours each night till we can track the speed and trajectory."

"That sounds good. What else?"

Horton, his foot tapping under the table, sat forward. "Birx is letting us use one of the upstairs rooms. It will make it much easier."

"Maybe he would let me keep my telescope set up there?"

Edmond sat back. "That's a great idea."

Birx arrived at the table and placed an ale in front of Jocab.

"So, Jocab. I should have known you were the mastermind of this little group."

Jocab smiled. "I wouldn't say mastermind, I'm just supplying the telescope."

Birx laughed. "And Horton is the brains of the operation."

Horton's head swiveled to Birx. "Hey!"

Everyone laughed as Edmond reached over and patted Horton on the back. "I thought he was the muscle."

Horton flexed his arms. "Yeah, I'm the muscle."

"I wish you success in whatever you are looking for," Birx replied before turning away.

"Thank you," Jocab replied, calling after him.

Jocab lined up the telescope. "I think it is dark enough now. Can one of you please kill the lights?"

Boris snuffed out the lamp and closed the door. Horton walked over to Jocab. "I'll be happy to take the first shift."

Boris laughed. "I'm sure you would. That way you can sleep all night."

Horton sat at the small table by the bed and started tapping his foot. "We can rotate the watch order every night. That way, one of us doesn't always get stuck with the mid-watch."

Jocab stepped back from the telescope. "I found it. Right where it's supposed to be."

Edmond stood and headed over. Jocab held up his hand stopping his friend. "Hold up for a second."

Edmond stopped mid step. "Uh, all right. What's up?

Jocab picked up a flat wooden box and handed it to Edmond. "I think you will want this."

Curious, Edmond opened the box and peered inside. His eyes lit up as he sucked in his breath. "A sextant," he exclaimed. "Where did you get this?"

"I bought it when I bought the telescope, I just never used it."

"This is perfect."

"Yeah, thought you might want to use for your tracking."

"Absolutely," Edmond gushed. "Now I can plot its speed and course."

"You do know how to use it?" Jocab asked with a smile.

Edmond pretended to glare at Jocab.

Jocab stepped out of the way, motioning toward the telescope. "Well then, you better get busy."

Edmond grabbed his pen and paper and hurried over. He spent no time settling in with the telescope, sextant, and a notepad. Jocab smiled at his friend as Edmond became so absorbed in his work, tuning out the others in the room. Thirty minutes later, Edmond sat back and stretched. "I have everything for now. I'll need to check things again just before dawn."

Jocab smiled and looked from one to the other. "So, who gets the first shift?"

Edmond pulled out a fresh sheet of paper to make the list. "Jocab gets the first shift every night so he can go home to Ayleth. Horton goes second, Boris third, and I'll take the last shift since I have to take another round of measurements before morning."

Jocab started to protest before Edmond interrupted. "We were talking about this earlier. You cannot stay here all night. Your wife will have our heads."

Jocab chuckled. "All right, you guys win. But I can at least switch off between the first and last shift."

"Nope, first shift. It's settled."

Jocab surrendered. "You guys drive a hard bargain."

Throughout the evening, they continued to follow the object as it crept across the sky. Jocab had headed home right after he completed his shift. Both Horton and Edmond were asleep when Boris yelled, "It's on fire again!"

Horton kept on snoring, but Edmond lifted his head. "What?"

"It's on fire again! I looked at it a minute ago and it was fine. I checked again just now and it's on fire!"

Edmond rose and shuffled over to the telescope. He pointed to his papers across the room. "Boris, can you please get me my pen and paper? I want to track this too."

Both Boris and Edmond took turns looking through the telescope at the fiery object while Edmond jotted down his findings. Ten minutes later, the brightness decreased, and they sat back, staring into the evening. Edmond motioned toward the bed. "Have you slept at all?"

Boris shook his head, "No, was too awake earlier, so I just stayed up."

"You might as well sleep now. I'll watch the rest of the night. I won't be able to sleep now, and it will be my turn shortly."

Boris nodded and headed toward the bed. "Thank you."

Edmond smiled and pulled the chair over next to the telescope. He settled in, wondering what this object could be. He took another peek through the telescope, his mind not grasping what he was witnessing.

CHAPTER 10

Edmond walked up the main street of town while keeping a keen eye out for Jocab. He had stopped by Jocab's place first and Ayleth said he was down by the waterfront working on a boat but would finish shortly. Edmond chose not to wait for him, but to go find him instead. He was too excited. The news was just too great.

He would wave or say hi to his fellow villagers as he passed. Edmond spotted Jocab just before he reached the docks. Jocab was up high on the center mast of a fishing boat, helping replace the pulleys for the mainsail. Edmond could only assume it was the captain of the vessel up there with him.

He stopped while trying to decide if he should wait for Jocab or head over to the boat and talk to him. Watching him work, Edmond waited and sat down under a nearby tree.

Edmond woke to Jocab nudging him with his foot. He smiled up at Jocab while wiping the sleep from his eyes. "I have some fascinating news for you."

"Really? Do tell." Jocab said.

"It's slowing down."

"What is?"

"The object."

"You're kidding?"

"Nope. The thing is always a little slower every time the fire goes out. We've been watching it for two weeks now and it's slowing down."

Jocab sat down next to Edmond. He took a few seconds to look around and gather his thoughts. Something was moving through space and was slowing down. "How is that possible? And what is it?"

"I don't know what it is, but I can guarantee you it is slowing down."

Edmond let Jocab process what he had just heard. The object was slowing. They didn't know what it was, why it was slowing, or where it was traveling. "Oh, my!" Edmond blurted aloud.

"What?" Jocab asked.

"I just thought of something. We know it's slowing, but we don't know why, or where it's headed."

Jocab's brain jumped ahead and landed next to Edmond's. "It's heading here!"

"My thought too."

Jocab took a deep breath to collect his thoughts. He wanted to look at this logically, but his emotions were threatening to overwhelm him. After a few more deep breaths, Jocab felt he could continue. "Think about this. If it is slowing down and coming here, that would mean it is coming here on purpose."

Edmond's eyes grew wide. "Do you think it's the gods returning?"

"I'm not that easily swayed by the priests. I'm more inclined to believe the gods have nothing to do with this. That object might turn the belief in the gods on its head."

"Don't let the priest hear you speak such heresy."

"Heresy? I don't think so. Here's how I see it. Look at it logically. One, it's coming regardless of what they think. Two, there's nothing in scripture about that thing. Lastly, the temple will scramble to align it to scripture, and I don't think they can."

Edmond frowned. He wasn't a firm believer in the temple's teachings, but he kept his thoughts to himself for fear of punishment. "I admit, I have my doubts, but I keep them to myself. You would be wise to do the same."

Jocab gave a low chuckle. "That is what Athels said to me in Avalon."

Edmond looked amazed. "Athels? The High Priest Athels? When did you see him?"

"Three months ago. Just before summer. Donav and I traveled to Avalon."

Edmond stared at Jocab like he had grown a third eye. Silence hung between them. Edmond could tell Jocab was being evasive. "You want to talk about it?"

"I can't. High Priest's orders."

Edmond huffed and sat back down. "We've been best friends ever since you got married and moved off your parents' farm. I was your best man, for goodness' sake. Now spill it!"

Jocab lowered his voice and leaned toward Edmond. "There is another object in the heavens I haven't shown you. The High Priest advised me to forget about it. For the safety of the temple, mine and my wife's health, and all those close to me."

Edmond raised an eyebrow. "He threatened you? That is outrageous!"

Jocab let out a nervous laugh. "He said it could incite the people to panic and that those close to me could come to harm."

"You're taking this seriously, then?"

"Oh yes, especially with Taylan in town."

"The new priest?"

"Yeah, Donav and I think he is a spy."

"I wondered why I didn't like him."

"You and half of Cumber."

"Forget about him. He's not important. Do you think the two objects are connected?"

"Now that you mention it, yes. I'd bet my last coin on it. Whoever put that object in orbit is coming for a visit."

"You may have found Pandora's Box, my friend, and we will have no choice but to open it!"

"Huh, I think it's been open for a while, waiting for some suckers to peek inside."

"Well, I hope it doesn't cause us to lose our heads. I find I am really attached to mine."

Both were silent for a few moments before Jocab spoke. "So, you know it is slowing down?"

"Yup, I'll be happy to show you the math and my notes."

"Nope, no need. I believe you. Do you think you could show your math to Donav?"

"Why would I do that?"

"I think they need to know so they can prepare for its arrival."

"Do you think it is friendly or dangerous?"

Jocab gave a crooked smile. "Don't know. Can you think of why the gods would be displeased with us?"

Edmond laughed aloud. "Depends on what mood they're in."

Jocab joined in the laughter. "They are not that fickle."

"If you think we should show him, I'd like to get it over with."

Jocab stood and helped Edmond to his feet. "Good, we can see if he is available."

"Sure, why not? We only live once."

"Do you need your notes?"

"We can tell him what we found and show him the math later."

"Sounds good to me."

Together they headed up the road toward the Temple in the distance. They could see it ahead, overlooking the water. Edmond felt a small chill down his spine as he wondered how Pandora would react once she was out of her box.

CHAPTER 11

Jocab woke to the sound of a rooster crowing in the distance. He rolled over and put his arm around Ayleth. "Good morning, beautiful," he said with a lopsided grin.

"Mmmm. Good morning," she replied with a sleepy voice as she snuggled closer. "I wish you didn't have to leave again."

"I wish I didn't have to either."

"Those stupid stars and wheels. Why couldn't someone else find them? Why did it have to be you?"

"I guess, I'm the lucky idiot."

"Unlucky is more like it. Idiot, only sometimes."

Jocab always had a hard time leaving Ayleth. Today was no different. He pulled her close and wrapped his arms around her. They held each other a while before Ayleth sat up, ending the moment together. "You get dressed while I get breakfast started. After all, you promised Edmond and Donav you would get an early start."

"It doesn't have to be that early."

"Oh, no! I'll not have them thinking I kept you here with my womanly ways," she said as she headed into the other room.

Jocab lay in bed for a few more minutes, staring at the ceiling while listening to Ayleth making noises in the kitchen. A few minutes later, he sat up, padded over to the dresser, pulled out a clean shirt and his travel pants. He figured he'd be wearing these during the journey to Avalon. He had already packed his travel bag, saving his best clothes for meeting with the High Priests again.

A few minutes later, he ambled out to the main room. Ayleth was finishing up with their breakfast. He was extra hungry this morning, as if his body knew he was traveling today. Ayleth had a large omelet frying in a pan and a couple of pieces of bread toasting next to it. Ayleth smiled when she saw him and asked, "That was quick. Could you grab the jam from the cupboard, please?"

Jocab headed to the cupboard. "Sure."

Jocab retrieved the jam as Ayleth cut the omelet in two and

placed them on separate plates. She grabbed the toast with the tips of her fingers, being careful not to burn herself, and tossed one on each plate. "There, that should do it."

Jocab placed the jam on the table and sat across from Ayleth. He could see the worry in her eyes. Jocab gave her a warm smile. "It will be fine, Ay. I'm not trying to turn the Temple on its head. We are just going to show the high priest what we found."

Ayleth sighed. "I know. I still worry."

"They need to know this thing is coming."

Ayleth held her tongue. She knew the pieces were already in place and that there was nothing she could do to change it. "Promise you will return as soon as you can?"

"I promise."

"No getting lost on the way there or back," she teased.

"Not if I find any new inventions between here and there," he teased back.

A calm silence settled in as they both turned their attention to breakfast. Before Jocab realized it, he had kissed Ayleth goodbye, grabbed his coat, and was heading out the door.

The sun was bright and rising in the morning sky. Jocab reached for his water bag to make sure it was full as he contemplated how warm it would get today. The village was coming to life. People were leaving their houses and entering the streets. Some were fishermen heading to their boats, while others tended to their morning errands.

He stopped at the home where Edmond stayed. Edmond rented a room from an older couple whose children had already grown and moved out. Edmond helped take care of the place. He managed the chores the couple could no longer do. Jocab wondered if Edmond would have already left town if the couple had someone else to care for them. He didn't seem too interested in courting any of the single ladies in the village. Jocab was thankful Edmond was still there. The two had quickly become friends after Jocab left his family farm and settled in the village. Five years later, their friendship had only gotten stronger.

Jocab lightly tapped on the door. He could hear Edmond holler as he was leaving, and the door opened a second later. "I was beginning to think you might be late," he said, turning to Jocab before continuing. "Waiting for the last second, huh?"

"Ayleth made a killer omelet this morning. I was extra hungry."

Edmond gave a crooked smile. "Nothing else?"

Jocab pretended to look injured. "You wound me," he replied, before attempting his best Ayleth impersonation. "I'll not have them thinking I kept you here with my womanly ways," he finished, batting his eyelashes while twirling a lock of hair around his finger.

Edmond barked a laugh. "Okay, you win. I believe you."

They met Donav at the temple stables, where four horses waited, prepped and ready. "Blessed by the gods we are," Donav said as he saw them. "We are actually getting an early start. It will be nice to get a few miles in before it gets warm."

Donav showed them to their horses, where they quickly secured their belongings to their saddles. Jocab motioned at the fourth horse, "Bringing an extra along?"

Donav smiled. "It will be nice to have a few more comforts this trip."

"Mainly cooking items and extra food. I want something better than road rations this time. Plus, I have a bag of oats for us and the horses," Donav replied as he patted a large sack balanced over the back of the horse.

Edmond appraised the size of the bag. "That looks like enough to get us there and back."

Donav smiled as he climbed into the saddle. "I certainly hope so."

Jocab and Edmond took their cue, saddled up, and followed Donav single file out of town.

CHAPTER 12

They were riding three abreast as they came up out of the riverbed. Jocab was reluctant to leave the shade of the trees. "I sure wish we could just follow this river to Avalon."

Edmond replied, "Me too. I was just thinking how nice this shade is."

"Unfortunately, we still have a few hours of riding ahead of us."

Donav smiled and tried to encourage them. "Come on you two, the weather is cooler today than yesterday."

Both Jocab and Edmond grumbled to themselves as Donav took the lead. Edmond was quick to spot something in the distance. "Looks like a work party up ahead."

Donav squinted to get a better look. "It sure does. Wonder what they are doing?"

Jocab pointed. "I bet it has something to do with the poles erected along the road."

Edmond stood up in the saddle. "Wow, look at that. Nice straight line too."

An hour later, the three arrived at the work site. Jocab spotted a dozen wagons along the side of the road with long poles and several others with large spools of copper wire. They could see groups of men digging several holes in spaced intervals along the roadside. Edmond pointed to the tops of the poles. "They are running wire along them."

Jocab looked to where Edmond was pointing. "I wonder what they are running it for. Can't be for electricity. The wire is too small."

Donav nudged his horse forward toward a tent. Three men were standing over a table, looking at a map. Edmond and Jocab followed behind. Donav dismounted and smiled at the three men as they looked up. "Good afternoon, gentlemen. Could we bother you for some water?"

The taller man in the middle with a long beard pointed to a boxy wagon next to a lone shade tree. "Sure friend. It's on the food wagon over there. Tie your horses up anywhere you like."

"Thank you, sir. We will do just that."

The three of them headed to a nearby tree and secured a picket line for the horses. Afterward, they dug out their water cups and headed for the food wagon. Just then, the cook came around from the other side. "Can I help yah there?"

Donav held his cup out and smiled. "Just a little water."

The cook patted the barrel beside him. "Help yourself." He grabbed a pair of tongs and headed back the way he had come.

Jocab, Edmond and Donav took turns filling their cups and taking a long drink. Soon, they had stored their cups and walked over to the tent where the tall man was waiting. "Was the water fresh enough?"

Donav gave a warm smile. "Yes, thank you. It was quite refreshing."

"Good. I'm Andrei."

"I'm Donav, and this is Jocab and Edmond. We are traveling from Cumber to Avalon."

"You're a little away from home. Cumber is more than a few miles from here."

Donav nodded. "That it is. We have business in Avalon with the Temple."

"The Temple? I thank the gods for the temple. We are running the wire for the voice communicators they are setting up."

Jocab raised his eyebrows in surprise. "I knew it was possible, but the nickel for the magnets is scarce."

It was Andrei's turn to be surprised. He looked at Jocab. "You know how they work?"

"A little. I studied a paper about them the last time I was in Avalon."

Andrei's eyebrows reached toward the heavens. "Maybe you could help us then? Yesterday, we accidentally dropped the communicator we used to test the connection. Now it doesn't work. No one here knows anything about how they work, so I can't test the lines we are running until I get it fixed. I'm planning on returning it to Avalon, but it will severely affect the project. I fear I will lose the contract with the delay."

"Happy to look. Not sure I can fix it, though."

Andrei looked like he could kiss them. "No harm in looking, and it might save the entire project." Andrei yelled at a man in the distance. "Conner, fetch me the voice box."

Conner, who was standing over a shovel, dropped it and ran toward one of the storage wagons lining the road. He climbed in and rummaged around before holding up a small wooden box. Andrei gave him a thumbs up and they waited while Conner hustled over with the box tucked under his arm.

Conner placed it on the table. "Anything else? Boss."

"Thank you, Conner. Get yourself a little water before getting back to your shovel."

Jocab leaned over to inspect the box. The rest of them watched, curious to see inside.

The box was thirty centimeters long, with a protective lid on top. Jocab removed the lid and noticed a loose handle to wind up or turn something. Near the bottom, a thin membrane of cloth covered a small hole. A copper tube with wires attached disappeared into the box. On the right side, there was a small latch to allow access to the interior, and a small bell centered at the top.

Jocab placed the wind-up handle aside and popped open the latch. "All right, let's see what's going on in here." He pointed with his finger while talking aloud. "Here is the transmitter, and it looks like you knocked this wire loose. And I can see this diaphragm right here is off center." Jocab looked up at Andrei. "Be glad the paper membrane didn't tear."

Looking back at the inside of the box, Jocab continued, "If we follow the wires here, we see the battery, which was dislodged when you dropped it." Jocab slid the battery into place, securing it before shifting his finger further down. "These wires go to the receiver." He paused for a few seconds before proceeding. "Everything looks good here." Jocab looked up and smiled. "You got lucky, Andrei."

Andrei grinned from ear to ear. "You can fix it then?"

"Yes, and I can show you what to do to fix it in the future. I assume you have the right tools?"

"I'm not sure. What do you need?"

Jocab examined the contents of the box again before replying, "Just a screwdriver should do it."

"A screwdriver? That's all?" Andrei asked, shocked. "I've been pulling my beard out worrying about this all day."

Andrei noticed Conner had just finished at the water barrel and hollered at him again. "Conner, please fetch us a screwdriver."

Conner jumped as if he'd been caught him doing something wrong. "Sure thing, boss, coming right up."

Conner handed Jocab the screwdriver. Jocab was leaning over the voice communicator, talking to Andrei as he worked. "There is enough length to this wire to splice this back together. I'll just loosen this screw and remove the broken piece here. Next, I'll wrap the good wire around the connector once like this." Jocab continued as he secured the wire. "Now, I'll tighten the screw back down, but not so tight that I strip it."

He looked up at Andrei to confirm he was paying attention. "There, that should do it. You can do that next time, right?"

"Absolutely!"

"Perfect. All we have to do now is unscrew these right here," Jocab said, as he loosened the next set of screws. "Then we slide the diaphragm for the transmitter back into place."

A minute later, Jocab completed everything and closed the lid. "All done and ready to test."

Andrei was beside himself, grinning and shaking Jocab's hand. "May the gods bless you. You saved me from losing money on this job!"

"It wasn't much. Just a few items got dislodged. Although it might be worth having a backup and some extra parts on hand, should it happen again."

Andrei pulled on his beard. "I think you're right Jocab, I think you're right."

Donav, Conner, and Edmond were standing on the other side of the table when Andrei noticed Conner had stuck around. "Conner, did you see what they did?"

Conner nodded with enthusiasm. "I sure did, boss. Looked

simple too. I'm surprised I didn't see that when I peeked inside earlier."

Andrei nodded toward the box. "It is now your job to make sure that blasted box stays in working order. Can you do it?"

Conner grinned. "Yes, boss."

"Good. From now on, that's your girlfriend, wife, and lover. Nothing happens to her, got it?"

Everyone laughed as Andrei addressed the three new guests. "You must join us for dinner tonight. I'll have the cook fix something extra to celebrate."

Donav, Jocab, and Edmond had joined Andrei and Conner for dinner under the tent. They had scrounged up a chair, a part of a tree stump, and a few barrels for everyone to sit on.

The cook had laid out two chickens, a rabbit, and some cooked vegetables. Andrei had told him earlier that they have been adding rabbits to their meals as they caught them. They had been extra plentiful as they got further from the city. The work crew was enjoying the extra food from the traps they set daily. Donav, Jocab, and Edmond looked forward to eating some fresh food other than their oats and dried fish. They had little time in the evening for setting traps or hunting after a long days ride.

Donav started the conversation after everyone had piled some food on their plates. "So, how far are you running the line?"

Andrei took a minute to finish his mouthful before replying. "Our contract is to run the line all the way to Liberty."

Jocab smiled at the thought. "Is there a reason not to go to Cumber?"

Andrei took a sip of ale before replying, "Not that I am aware of. The Temple has a long-term goal to connect all the towns and villages."

Donav spoke between bites, "That will take some time."

"It will, but it can be done. I'm hoping to be a part of it too. Lots of coin to be made in running the wires."

Jocab chuckled. "Going to need more infrastructure than just running the wires. The biggest obstacle is still the hard metals. Plenty of copper, but not much nickel and almost no iron. We have always had the knowledge, just not the ability to produce it."

Everyone at the table nodded their head in agreement as Jocab continued, "Just imagine where we would be if we could figure out how to produce some of what we know." Jocab pointed at the lamp. "If it weren't for the Acca tree, we wouldn't have good oil for our lamps. We'd be using animal fat and cow droppings for our candles. My biggest fear is that we are going to lose more knowledge every generation because we can't make the stuff."

Donav looked up, surprised. "You really think so?"

"Yup," Jocab said with certainty in his voice. "Look at the temple building in Avalon. Made of solid metal, so fine and strong. Their use of electricity for lighting, heating, and cooling. All the technology in the great library too. We have a wealth of knowledge and no way to use it."

Connor gave a small laugh as he spoke up. "The gods really did it to us, didn't they? Left us with the knowhow, but not the ability. Mean trick, I'd say."

Andrei looked at Donav, concerned. "Sorry for his words. No offense intended."

Donav smiled. "No offense taken. I am more a man of the soul than of science, anyway. Jocab and Edmond are the math and science guys in our village."

Andrei took a drink. "And I'm very thankful for their help today. If ever I can do anything to help repay you, please let me know. What takes you to Avalon?"

Andrei could see the three shared a look between themselves before Donav replied, "I'd say it is to have some great food at the Broken Fork just off Main Street, but in reality, the two of them are sharing some of their unique knowledge with the High Priest. It is Jocab's second visit and Edmond's first."

Andrei nodded in approval, pretending not to notice their brief discomfort. "That sounds rather noble to me. Like I said earlier, I'm glad you could help me out." He then took another drink before continuing, "The Broken Fork? Isn't that the place that makes great rotisserie chicken?"

Jocab and Donav laughed, "Yup, that's the one."

The conversation eventually lapsed into small talk for the rest of the evening. Eventually, they all went their separate ways and settled down for the night.

CHAPTER 13

It was Edmond's turn to rubber neck as he took in the sights of Avalon. The sheer size of the buildings, people moving about, and the massive temple in the distance mesmerized him. Jocab and Donav smiled at Edmond as they checked into the inn, cleaned up, and headed to the Broken Fork for dinner.

Donav entered first, with Edmond and Jocab close on his heels. The place was almost full of patrons as they'd arrived during the peak of dinner hour. Donav spotted an open table along the back wall and signaled to Edmond and Jocab his intentions. They were halfway to the table when a voice hollered, "Donav! Jocab! Is that you?"

They turned to see Estellia moving toward them. Edmond watched in amazement as she maneuvered her way like magic among the tables toward them. They all arrived at the open table together. The three grabbed a seat as Estellia asked, "What brings you back to Avalon?"

Donav gave a light-hearted smile. "It's your chicken. We make up other reasons to justify the trip."

Estellia barked a laugh. "I should have known you would say something like that. You are too kind." Estellia glanced over at Jocab and Edmond before turning back to Donav. "You keep bringing someone new. And they get better looking each time," she teased, winking at Edmond.

Edmond blushed while Jocab laughed and patted him on the back, adding to Edmond's embarrassment.

Donav held back his laugh. "I'm glad you approve. You already know Jocab, and this good-looking guy is Edmond."

Edmond continued to blush. "Pleasure to meet you."

Donav came to the rescue. "Chicken and a round of ale, by chance? We've been on the road all day and are quite famished."

"Gotcha. Three famished specials, coming right up." Estellia flashed a big grin at Edmond before heading toward the kitchen.

Jocab punched Edmond's arm. "I think she likes you," he teased. "And about the right age too."

"Ow, cut that out." Edmond complained as he rubbed his sore arm.

Estellia was quick to bring their food. "Here's your food. I wish I had time to chat," she added before heading to another table.

The three ate in silence, giving their attention to the food at hand. Edmond continued to watch in amazement, his eyes wandering the room, taking everything in. Several times, he would spot Estellia, and they would smile at each other as she took care of the customers.

They lingered after finishing their food, resting while they sipped their ale. They knew they didn't have to hurry, since they had no other plans tonight. After a while, the customers finished their meals and departed. Estellia rushed back and forth while somehow delivering a fresh glass of ale before their drinks ran dry.

At the end of the evening, Estellia brought another round of drinks and one for herself as she sat next to Donav. "I'm tuckered out. I love it when we get this much business, but we almost ran out of chickens. Pop needs to stop by the market first thing tomorrow morning to buy more. I hope they're already plucked and cleaned."

Jocab nodded his head. "That was one of the first jobs I learned while growing up. Would have loved not having to pluck them."

Estellia gave a tired laugh. "So, what brings you back to Avalon? Not that wheel again, is it?"

"Nope, they've encouraged me to leave that alone."

"I wondered. You never discussed it after your first visit. I take it the temple threaten... I mean, provided convincing encouragement?"

"I'd prefer not to go into details. The temple's been very kind."

Estellia was silent for a few seconds as she searched their faces. She knew there was more but didn't push. "Got it. I have known the Temple to provide some persuasive encouragement."

Jocab tensed, trying not to feel sick as the images of the execution returned. He sensed some anger and resentment from

Estellia and glanced at Donav. Donav sipped his ale, seeming not to notice. All was quiet until Donav broke the silence. "Business seemed extra busy tonight. Is it like this every night now?"

"We have been busier, but tonight was crazy. Things picked up after your first visit. I don't know what you did, but we've given extra tithes to the temple since."

Donav seemed embarrassed as he spoke, "I cannot claim any credit, but I am glad for your fortune."

"Be careful what you ask for, though," she laughed. "Pop will have to hire someone if it stays this busy. I hope we can hold out for a few more weeks till my brother is out of school."

"So, your family owns this place?" Edmond asked.

"Yes, my father and I do. I'm the full-time server while pop cooks."

"Your brother doesn't help?"

"He's much younger than me and almost finished with his school. Pop and I are doing everything to help him focus on his schooling. He didn't want to do this for the rest of his life. So, Pop sent him off to learn something he likes."

"This is not a bad profession."

"No, I agree. We've held our own over the years."

Jocab nodded. "I totally understand. I could have stayed and helped on the family farm. But I would not have been happy. Both my parents noticed that early on and helped me out. I moved to Cumber as the local Tradesman several years back. Both my older brothers stayed on the farm. Worked out for everyone."

Estellia got a faraway look in her eyes. "Thanks for that story, Jocab. That helps."

"Any time. I'll send you my bill," Jocab said with a smile.

Estellia laughed and took another drink. "You do that. We can always use kindling for the cook stoves."

They enjoyed a round of laughter as Estellia stood up. "I have to get these tables cleaned. For some reason, they never clean themselves."

After watching her clear the nearby table, Donav drained his ale and stood. "Let's give her a hand before we head back to the inn, shall we?"

CHAPTER 14

Jocab and Edmond strolled into the Broken Fork for an early lunch. They had agreed to meet Donav there after parting ways at breakfast. They spotted Donav chatting with Estellia at a small table near the back. Except for Donav, the place was empty.

"Jocab, Edmond!" Estellia greeted them with a big smile. "You found your way back."

Jocab laughed. "Thanks. There was a time when I would have wandered the streets, lost. Everything looked the same. Now I can tell the difference between the various shops and street corners."

"I'm glad you know your way around now. So, you boys want some more chicken or something else?"

Jocab replied, "Chicken please."

Estellia looked at Edmond and seemed to smile bigger. "And for you, handsome?"

Edmond blushed. "Uh. The same, ma'am. Chicken, please."

Estellia winked and started toward the kitchen. "Coming right up."

Jocab punched Edmond in the arm again. "Yup, she likes you. I'm sure of it… Handsome." Drawing out the last word.

Edmond gave Jocab a little shove. "Cut it out, will yah?"

"Sure thing, handsome." Jocab said, laughing as he sat down.

Edmond shook his head as he sat next to Jocab.

Donav finished sipping his ale and looked at the two. "Find anything interesting at the library?"

Jocab smiled. "Yeah, we did some research for a water wheel. I'd like to make one to generate our own electricity. I'll build a test one first. The village can use it to grind flour."

"That would be incredible. Is it doable?"

"Totally doable," Jocab exclaimed

"How was the temple?" Edmond asked.

"No problems at all. They got our initial message sent from Cumber and they were expecting us." Donav replied, taking a drink before continuing. "It won't take too long now that we're here. Especially since it will be in the evening again."

Edmond looked up. "Evening again?"

"Yeah," Donav replied. "First meeting was in the evening, too. It needs to be dark out for the telescope."

"Oh, now I get it."

Estellia appeared with three full plates and two glasses of ale. "Evening meeting, huh? I sure hope it goes better than the last one."

Jocab looked at her in surprise. "What makes you think it didn't go well?"

"You both seemed really upset and it was obvious you were trying to hide it."

Jocab sat back in his chair. "Were we that transparent?"

"Like an open book. I'm guessing they didn't like something and threatened you into silence. I mean encouraged you."

Donav smiled. "Close. It could have been worse."

"Humph, I pray it goes better this time. You guys are some of my best customers and I would hate to have the temple accidentally lose you."

"Lose us?"

"It is the nicest way I can say it."

An icy chill traveled down Edmond's spine as he glanced at Jocab. "I thought those were stories told to kids to make them mind their manners."

Estellia patted him on the shoulder. "Yeah, you keep on thinking that, all right?" She turned to Jocab. "More wheel in the sky stuff?"

Jocab shook his head. "No wheel this time and I cannot talk about that anymore."

"Can't blame a girl for trying."

Jocab looked at Donav, wondering just how much to share. Before he could answer, Edmond spoke in a low tone. "There is an object heading toward us and it's slowing down."

"From the stars?"

"Edmond!" Jocab admonished, ignoring Estellia's outburst.

"What? The temple hasn't told me to be quiet. It's not a secret for anyone who knows where to look."

"You're right. But I think the Temple will want to keep this quiet," Jocab replied, trying to keep the bitterness out of his voice.

Estellia leaned in. "OK, I get it. You won't be able to talk about this later. So, what, on Avalon, is it?"

Edmond lowered his voice to reply as Estellia took the open seat next to Donav. "We don't know what it is, but we know it's slowing down as it approaches."

"Can you prove it's slowing down?"

"Yes, we've been watching it for a while and every time we see it burning brighter, it's going slower afterward."

Estellia's eyes widened. "Burning brighter?"

"When we first saw it, we thought it was a comet. A bright object appearing in the night doesn't just happen. We found it when we were showing some friends the rings around Tureolin. It was burning bright like it was belching fire."

Estellia smiled at the two of them. "But that's not all, is it?"

"Jocab had his eye to the telescope when it abruptly stopped burning brighter. He almost knocked the telescope over."

Jocab smiled, "Yeah, I jumped out of my skin."

Estellia was enthralled. "Go on."

"We watched and tracked its trajectory. I thought Edmond might get a comet named after him."

Edmond gave a lopsided grin. "Edmond's comet does have a nice ring to it."

"So, you say it's not a comet, and it's slowing down. How is that happening?"

Edmond's eyes gleamed as he spoke. "Cause about every ten hours, it lights up real bright and when it stops ten minutes later, it's always going slower. I've done the math, and it's coming here."

Estellia was quiet for a few seconds before speaking. "Every ten hours? That's not random."

Jocab chuckled. "We came to that conclusion too."

"Something or someone is controlling it."

Estellia glanced at Donav. "Could it be the gods returning?"

Donav raised his eyebrows as he replied, "Maybe…"

Jocab glanced at Donav before continuing. "I'm not a firm believer. I'm more of a skeptic, and I don't think the gods created us."

"The heretics say the gods brought us here."

Edmond chuckled. "Created by the gods, brought here, it doesn't matter. We are here."

Estellia leaned into the group. "I'm inclined to say brought here."

Jocab nodded. "Me too. What I see and what I've read makes me believe that more every day."

Edmond snorted. "If that's the case, then why? And how long ago?"

Jocab sat back. "Those are good questions. Maybe that object coming here might provide some answers."

Estellia glanced at both of them before settling on Edmond. "Please be careful at the meeting. Choose your words carefully, both of you. Don't let them trip you up." She took another breath to continue when a small group entered, drawing her attention away.

The three sat in silence for a few minutes, watching Estellia serve the new patrons before they drained their glasses and headed out.

"See you around supper time," Donav called to Estellia as they exited.

CHAPTER 15

The three men knelt and bowed their heads as the High Priest Athels made his way toward them. He blessed each of them before stepping back. "Jocab and Donav. It is good to see you again. And you must be Edmond."

Edmond nodded. "Yes, Your Excellency."

"A pleasure to meet you. I understand you are good friends with Jocab."

"Yes, Your Excellency." Edmond replied again while bowing his head.

"Good. Jocab is a splendid example of character and integrity. I assume they cut you from the same cloth?"

Edmond's eyes showed his surprise at the question. "Why yes, Your Excellency!"

"Good. Let's get started then."

Athels joined the other priests on the dais and took his seat. Jocab sensed the same reserve from the priests he had encountered during his previous visit.

Once seated, Athels introduced the priests for Edmond's benefit. "Donav and Jocab, I know you've met the rest of the council. Edmond, this is Solomon and Damon," motioning to the right.

Solomon and Damon nodded. Athels then gestured to his left, "And this is Farzod and Geoffery." The two priests nodded as well. "So, Jocab. What new and exciting thing do you have for us?"

Jocab looked at Donav and Edmond before addressing the council. "Thank you, Your Excellency, for seeing us. It is an honor to stand before you again."

Jocab motioned to Edmond as he spoke. "Edmond is the one that made the initial discovery, and it is his hard work that led us to our conclusions."

Athels leaned forward in his chair and put his elbows on the table. "You have piqued my curiosity Jocab, please proceed."

Edmond stepped forward and explained what they had seen, how they had tracked the object, confirmed its approach, and that it was slowing down. "You have the math to prove this?" Solomon questioned.

"Yes, Your Excellency. We could show you the object too, if we had a telescope." Edmond knew full well they had taken Jocab's first telescope.

"So, if we had one, you could show it to us?" Solomon inquired as he leaned forward.

"Yes, Your Excellency. Edmond can also advise you when it will burn brighter."

Athels studied the two of them for a few seconds before glancing at Sanara. "Sanara, please have the telescope set up on the balcony."

"Yes, Your Excellence. I'll have them retrieve it now," she answered as she slipped out the door.

She returned within seconds with a temple priest carrying the telescope. Edmond was certain it was staged outside, just in case. After a brief delay, the telescope was ready for use.

Jocab approached the telescope as if he was being reunited with an old friend. Edmond gave him a pat on the back and teased. "It's a telescope, not your girlfriend."

Jocab bit back a reply as the priests crowded around them. He located the object low to the horizon a minute later. Stepping back, he surrendered the telescope to the priests, who examined the object with great enthusiasm. Edmond and Jocab took turns realigning the telescope as the object moved through the night sky. Just as they were finishing up, the High Priest Damon stepped back in surprise. Jocab laughed. "Did it just light up Your Excellency?"

"By the gods, YES!"

Edmond joined in the laughter. "Jocab had a similar reaction the first time he saw it too."

The priests took another look, marveling at the increased brightness. Jocab turned to Edmond, "How long before it dims?"

"It's always been ten minutes."

Donav took a step forward to stand next to Jocab. "May I have a look?"

Edmond and Jocab shrugged their shoulders and looked to the High Priests for confirmation. Athels waved him over. "Please take a peek."

Donav stepped up and looked into the eyepiece. "Wow, this is amazing. I can see the flames."

Jocab motioned toward the telescope. "It's close to burning out. Would one of you like to watch the transition?"

Athels stepped forward. "Yes, thank you."

Minutes later, Athels stepped back, looking like he had just won first prize at the local fair. "Just like that. It's back to a faint glow."

Jocab nodded. "Yes, Your Excellency, it stops and goes back to a glimmer. That's why we're here. We are hoping you can help shed some light on it. We are wondering who it is, and what do they want."

The priests all froze, and Athel's head snapped up. "What do you mean by that?" he replied, his voice low and menacing.

Jocab stood still, aware of his verbal blunder. He took a moment to compose himself before proceeding. "I'm sorry if I said something wrong, Your Excellency. Edmond and I have a theory. We believe it is intelligent, and not a random act of nature."

Athels seemed to calm himself and relax as Jocab continued. "Edmond can confirm this, since he's the math guy. He has timed the object and determined the brightness happens every ten hours, and that it's going slower afterward. Based on this information and current trajectory, we concluded that something or someone is coming to visit."

The silence in the room was deafening. The four priests glanced back and forth at each other while trying to maintain their composure. It was obvious to Jocab that they were struggling to keep silent. His comments troubled them, and it showed. The High Priest Athels recovered first. "Interesting hypothesis. Please leave your equations and notes with us to study so we can confirm your findings."

Edmond glanced at Jocab and Donav. "Yes, Your Excellency."

"Thank you," said Athels, "That should be all for tonight. We ask that you stay in Avalon a few more days while we pray and seek the gods."

The three bowed their heads. "Yes, your Excellence."

"We shall be in touch. Sanara shall provide you with a little extra coin to cover your extended stay."

The three of them murmured their thanks as they knelt. Athels quickly blessed them before Sanara guided them out.

Free of the temple, the three of them walked in silence. Several blocks later, Edmond finally spoke. "It is obvious they are hiding something!"

Jocab snorted. "That's an understatement. I wish I was a bug on the wall when they seek the gods."

Donav let out a deep breath, releasing the pent up tension in his shoulders. "Whatever it is, they don't want to share, and we won't get answers tonight."

Jocab laughed. "Yeah, you are right. I don't like it, but you are right."

"Good. Let's get back to the inn and get some sleep."

Athels took his seat as he watched the three follow Sanara out of the conference chamber. Leaning back in his chair, he addressed the group. "All right gentlemen, your thoughts, please."

Damon placed his elbows on the table. "Going to be tough to keep this quiet the closer that thing gets."

Geoffrey nodded his head. "I agree. Very tough indeed."

Athels snorted. "I know that. I'm more interested in what we are going to do about it."

Solomon looked at Athels. "First, we contain it. Maintain the upper hand by limiting our risk as much as possible."

Athels' gaze bore into Solomon. "What do you have in mind?"

"To start, we round up tonight's guests."

"You really think that will help?"

"Yes!" Solomon said venomously. "Those three have the knowledge to destroy us. Our current way of life, the people we care for, everything we've built."

Damon chimed in. "I don't see them as ones to burn down temples."

Solomon glared at him. "You are just trying to make this personal."

Damon shook his head. "No, I am not. You are the one who takes everything personally."

"Because the death of my parents is very personal."

"This has nothing to do with you or your parents."

"But it could cause riots and loss of lives, including our own."

Athels put up his hands. "Enough. Both of you. Arresting them won't stop that ship's approach."

Solomon sighed. "I warned you that Jocab was dangerous and look where we are now."

Athels ignored his outburst. "What will you do after you arrest them?"

"Hold them till it's safe to release them."

"No roasting them over an open fire or swinging them from a tree?" Damon teased.

Solomon grabbed his notepad and threw it at Damon. "I won't stand for this."

Athels stood. "I said, enough!" Silence filled the room as Athels glared at the two priests. "There will be order or I will find your resignations on my desk." Athels straightened his robes and sat back down. "Holding them could be awhile. What about their family members?"

"Jocab's the only one that's married," Farzod mentioned.

Solomon's smile widened. "We can collect... I mean, invite her to join her husband."

Athels frowned. "You really think it's prudent?"

"Yes, or I would not have proposed it."

Athels thought about it. "All right. You have my blessing. On one condition. I have your word you will treat them well. We may require their cooperation during this troubled time."

Solomon smiled. "Of course."

Athels sighed. "That mitigates our immediate risk, but we need a plan. This thing coming toward us requires a whole new strategy, and now."

Farzod cleared his throat. "Can we contact them before they arrive?"

"Radio waves have a hard time getting out of the atmosphere. It's the same reason we can't communicate between cities."

"Yeah, I'm aware. I'm managing the setup of the voice

communicators or telephone as they once called it. We are running lines to Liberty, Lowell and South Bay as we speak."

Solomon pointed at Farzod. "I read about that last week."

Athels grumbled loudly. "Focus people, we need to focus."

Farzod looked to Athels. "I propose we call it a night and revisit this tomorrow. My brain's half asleep and the morning will be here before we know it."

Athels pondered the idea for a few seconds. "Agreed. Clear your calendars for tomorrow. We will resume this in my office after breakfast."

They nodded in agreement and headed for the exit. Solomon caught Athels at the door. "I'm sending the guard to get them now."

"Get some sleep first. They'll be there in the morning."

Solomon pursed his lips, clearly not happy with the High Priests' decision. "I'll send them at first light."

CHAPTER 16

Dawn was just arriving when a repetitive tapping on the door woke everyone. Edmond opened his eyes. Long shadows spread across the room, giving it an eerie glow. "Why would the priests call us this early?"

The tapping continued with more urgency. Donav pushed himself out of bed. "Just a moment, please," he hollered, just loud enough to stop their incessant tapping.

Donav pulled back the bolt and cracked the door, surprised to see the temple messenger, Rynan, standing in the hall. "Come in. Come in. Rynan, isn't it?"

"Yes, sir," he said as he slipped through the door.

"Please tell me the priests are not calling us this early?"

"No sir, they are sending soldiers after you!"

Edmond bolted upright. "SOLDIERS!"

"Slow down," Donav said, taking a deep breath. "Why are they sending soldiers and why are you warning us?"

"I don't know. I was in the temple lobby. I had just finished clearing the offerings from the sanctuary when I heard the High Priests talking."

"Go on."

"They sounded angry. I couldn't hear everything. I heard both yours and Jocab's name along with sending the temple guard to arrest you."

Jocab pulled his shirt over his head, getting dressed. "What made you come tell us?"

"I don't know. It just felt right. When I heard them talking, I lingered, pretending to be busy. The guards are planning to arrest you this morning at breakfast."

Donav looked puzzled. "At breakfast?"

Jocab looked alarmed. "That means they may arrest Estellia, too."

Edmond's eyes got wide. "Why her?"

"She is our closest contact here in the city. If they are trying to squash this, it seems reasonable to assume she knows something."

Edmond glared at Jocab, not liking what he heard. "We need to warn her."

"I agree."

Donav placed a hand on Rynan's shoulder. "Thank you, Rynan. You will make a good priest if you finally decide to take the vows. Now you must leave. If they see you with us, you will share our fate."

Rynan nodded and headed for the door, unsure of himself. "What should I say?"

Donav smiled, trying to calm the boy. "That you went for a walk. Nothing more. If they press, tell them you were meditating and seeking the will of the gods."

"Really?"

"Yup, worked for me every time I snuck out," Donav said with a smile.

Rynan nodded, pondering the information as Donav let him out the door.

"OK guys. Let's pack up and make a quick stop to warn Estellia. We can stay off the main roads as we head over."

They dressed quickly and stuffed their belongings into their travel bags. "Front or back door?" Jocab asked as they exited their room.

"Out the back."

They arrived at the rear of the Broken Fork without incident. Only a few animals took notice of their passage. Donav knocked loud enough to wake anyone inside. Seconds later, an older gentleman answered, holding a solid-looking club. "What do you want?" he asked, unhappy to be disturbed this early.

Edmond stepped forward. "We need to talk to Estellia."

"She's sleeping. Come back when we open."

Edmond put his hand against the door as it swung shut. "We NEED to see her!"

A woman's voice came from within. "Who is it, Pop?"

Edmond called. "Estellia?"

Estellia pushed past her father and opened the door wider. "Edmond?"

"Can we come in? It's urgent!"

Estellia smiled. "Didn't realize you guys were that hungry."

Edmond chuckled. "I wish that was it."

"It's fine, Pop."

Pop stepped back as Estellia guided them through the kitchen and into the dining area. "What's going on?"

"Temple guards are coming to arrest us here when we come for breakfast."

"Oh, no!" Estellia said. "I take it your meeting did not go well?"

"Maybe too well. It was obvious the priests knew something and were trying really hard to hide it."

"And how does that affect me?"

"We think the soldiers might arrest you too, since you are our primary contact in the city!"

"Sounds about right. Be just like the temple to do that," Pop declared from behind them. "You need to leave, and now."

"I can't, Pop. What will you do? What will you say?"

"That's my problem. I'll manage. I'll tell them you went to visit my sister."

Estellia looked troubled and glanced around. Donav spoke in a soothing voice. "He's right. And we need to leave now."

Pop headed back into the kitchen. "I'll grab the emergency bag for you,"

"Emergency bag?" Edmond asked.

"Yeah, Pop always insisted we have an emergency bag ready, just in case."

"Nice. Wish I'd thought of that."

Estellia stood. "I better get dressed. Give me five minutes."

Pop came back with a travel pack in his arms. "You got three, little lady."

"We don't open for another hour, Pop."

"Yeah, I know. And the soldiers might be our first customers."

Estellia hurried off. They could hear her running up the stairs to their apartment above the restaurant. Jocab chuckled, "Sounds like she took them two at a time."

"Three, if I know my girl," Pop said, smiling. "Do you have a plan?"

"Nothing beyond getting out of town before the soldiers arrive."

"How are you planning on leaving the city?"

"We are closest to the main bridge heading west. I hope to get a few miles down the road before the guards realize we're gone."

"Won't work. I doubt you get a mile out of town that way."

"If you've a better option, I'm all ears."

Estellia stepped into the dining area wearing a pair of travel pants, a long loose pullover tied in the front, travel boots, and her hair tucked up under a wide brim hat. "I'm ready."

Pop turned a critical eye in her direction and examined her attire. "Excellent choice," he said, before turning back to Donav. "I think I have a solution."

"What yah thinkin', Pop?"

"Think you could get to Garret's boat before he hits the river?"

"If we hurry, it shouldn't be a problem."

Pop stood. "Good. Time's wasting and you need to catch a boat. Send word just like we talked about." Estellia and Pop hugged, wrapping their arms around each other.

"You stay safe, Pop. Get out of town if it gets crazy here."

They kissed each other on the cheek before pulling away. "I will, sweetheart. Now go, girl."

Donav, Edmond and Jocab grabbed their gear and headed for the door, giving them privacy for their goodbyes. They regrouped at the back door. After a round of hugs and handshakes, they walked single file down the alley. Pop stood on the threshold watching till they disappeared before stepping back inside.

Donav followed close behind Estellia. "Where are we going?"

"There's a small dock used by the local fishermen just south of the main bridge. Garrett docks his boat there."

"Can we trust him?"

"Oh yes. Pop and he are childhood friends. We buy most of our fish from him. We've had an exit plan for getting out of the city since I was a little girl."

Jocab's eyebrows shot up in surprise. "Wow, did you ever think you'd need it?"

"Pop said there would come a day. I remember it being an adventure when I was a girl. We would practice and Garrett would take us either up or down river. We would camp for a few days before coming home."

"Smart thinking."

They spent the next thirty minutes maneuvering southwest, along the alleyways, till they came to the main road out of town. Donav checked to see if any priests or temple guards were in view. Finding none, they hurried across the road and disappeared down an alley.

Several twists and turns later, they arrived at the docks. Estellia motioned, "It's the third boat on the right." Estellia took the lead as they emerged from the alley and casually strolled along the dock. They walked toward a gentleman loading bait boxes onto a single masted boat. "Can I help you strangers?" he said as he eyed the four of them.

Estellia spoke softly. "Garrett, we need a ride, just like old times."

Garrett stood up and looked them over one more time. "Pop, send yah?"

"Yes, he did. We need to hurry."

"Well then, grab those bait boxes and those nets over there," he said, pointing to the items on the dock.

They sprang into action and helped load before climbing on board.

"Just you today, Garrett?" Estellia asked as she looked over the boat.

"Yeah, Duncan hasn't been feeling well the last couple of days, so I've been working solo."

A concerned look fell over Estellia as she replied, "I'm so sorry. I hope he feels better soon. Stop by and have Pop give you some chicken noodle soup for him."

"I may just do that."

"Better yet, tell Pop I said chicken soup for the entire family tonight."

"I sure will. Thanks. Now get settled so I can cast off. You can help row as we have little wind for the sail right now."

Donav took a seat at the bow. Jocab and Edmond took seats in the middle and grabbed an oar. The boat was one and a half meters wide at the center, designed to allow two rowers.

Estellia joined Garrett at the stern, leaving room for him to man the rudder. Garrett stepped onto the dock and, after a few twists of his wrists with the mooring lines, he jumped aboard and pushed them away from the dock. Jocab and Edmond secured the oars and started rowing.

Garrett steered the boat out into the middle of the river. He maneuvered it with ease while keeping out of the main current. They traveled in silence until the city was at their backs before Garrett spoke. "So, what's up? You get into trouble?"

Estellia shook her head and motioned to the other three. "Temple guards were coming for them and possibly me."

"The temple? That serious, huh?"

"Seems to be. They were going to sneak out of town through the main bridge next to your docks. Pop thought this would be better."

"Yeah, much better. Not sure they'd have gone more than a mile or two. Did they break the law or spread blasphemy?"

"The priests didn't like something they showed them."

"I've never been a big believer, as you know."

"Yeah, Pop shared with me what you two believe, and I'm inclined to admit you might be correct. Especially after what I learned from them."

Garrett froze for a second. "Really?"

"Yes. Only time will tell, but it's a game changer."

The news shook Garrett. Jocab and Edmond smiled at him, but held their tongues, putting their backs into rowing.

Estellia nodded at the two of them. "I'm being rude. Please let me introduce you."

"You sure it's wise? Might be better if I stay ignorant."

"If you'd prefer."

Garrett nodded. "Might be for the better."

CHAPTER 17

The sun was high in the sky when Garrett steered the boat toward the shore. Donav and Estellia had taken turns at the oars as Garrett tried to keep out of the fast-moving current. He seemed to know just how to guide the boat upstream.

Once they got close, Edmond jumped out over the side, sloshing through the knee-high water, and pulled the boat toward the beach. Jocab and Donav followed, the three of them pulling the boat high on the sand. Estellia grabbed her pack and jumped ashore as the other three collected their belongings.

Garrett climbed over the side and gave Estellia hug. "You stay safe, young lady."

"I promise. Are you going to have time to catch anything before you get back?"

"I should. I don't have to catch much since I'll be fished alone today."

"What about all the bait?"

"It's only four small boxes. If I need to, I can dump them and get more tomorrow. The important thing is to get you to safety."

"Thanks again, Garrett."

"Anytime." Garrett climbed aboard and let Edmond and Jocab push the boat back into the water. The three of them watched as he quickly caught the current and headed downstream.

Estellia watched him go as she settled her pack on her shoulders. "I'm ready."

Jocab looked around. "So, where are we?"

"We're about twenty-five kilometers upstream. This is where we would come when we practiced leaving the city." She let her gaze wander before continuing. "We have another spot downriver too."

Donav spotted a large tree several meter away. "Let's settle under that tree and have some lunch. We'll figure out where we go from there."

Jocab smiled. "Sounds like a great idea. I missed breakfast and I'm starved."

They all dropped their packs near the tree and rummaged through them. Edmond held up the last of his food. "With having to leave so quickly, I only have a few days."

Donav pulled out some dried meat and trail mix. "I think we are all in the same boat."

Estellia smiled as she held up a loaf of bread and a brick of cheese. "I grabbed these on the way out."

All three expressed their thanks as Estellia passed them around. They quickly settled in the grass and focused on their meal, too tired to talk.

Estellia finished first and laid back next to Edmond, staring at the light as it filtered through the leaves overhead. "We made good time today."

Edmond enjoyed her presence next to him. "It helped that everyone took a turn with the oars."

Donav stretched his tired muscles. "That it did. Where do we go from here?"

Jocab leaned forward. "My family's farm. It's a day north of Cumber and we should be safe there."

Edmond looked surprised. "Why the farm? I thought you had no desire to go back."

"I don't. And that's one reason we should go there. Besides, that's where Ayleth will look for me."

Donav frowned, realizing Ayleth might be in danger, too. "You think the temple might try to arrest her?"

"I've been worrying about that all morning. Hopefully, we can send word for her to meet us there."

"That might be tough," Donav replied. "But we can certainly pray for her safety."

Estellia sat up and asked, "We good with going to the farm?"

Edmond raised his cup. "To Jocab's family farm."

The others raised their cups. "The family farm."

"What route are we taking?" Edmond asked.

Estellia perked up. "If we head northwest from here, we should hit the main road in a couple of days as it swings north."

"We could bypass Cumber and head straight to Liberty. Restock there before heading to the farm."

"That's going to add an extra week." Jocab complained.

Donav nodded in understanding. "It can't be helped. The main road to Cumber will be crawling with guards."

Jocab pursed his lips but nodded in agreement. "I suppose you're right."

Edmond finished a bite of cheese before chiming in. "We must keep to the woods as we work our way to Liberty."

Jocab moaned. "That will add even more time."

Donav patted him on the back. "Sorry, Jocab. The guards will be checking the forest, too. They know we'll be avoiding the main road."

Edmond gave Jocab his best reassuring smile. "We can hope they focus on the road to Cumber and not Liberty,"

Jocab chuckled. "We can hope."

Donav stood, ending the conversation. "We better get moving if we wish to stay ahead of the guards."

After two days of travel, they spotted the main road through the trees ahead. Jocab was tired and hungry from walking all day and not eating. They had consumed the last of their rations at breakfast. Jocab was pleased that Edmond had trapped two rabbits just before the started walking. Both were hanging from Edmond's pack to be cooked for their evening meal. All of them were looking forward to some fresh meat. As they drew closer, Jocab stopped and cocked his head to the side. "Do you guys hear that?"

The four of them paused and listened. "Nope," Donav and Estellia replied.

Edmond listened a little longer. "I hear it."

"Any idea what it is?"

"It sounds like it is coming from up ahead."

"Do we head toward it or avoid it?"

"I think we can investigate without being noticed," Donav replied.

Edmond nodded. "Sounds good to me. Any objections?" Nobody spoke up.

"OK, let's go see," he said, taking point. The three fell in behind. Edmond had become the de facto point man when they were hiking. He had a natural sense of direction and never lost his bearings.

They reached a vantage point that overlooked the road. To their surprise, they found a work party digging holes along the side of the road. Donav's eyes got wide as he recognized them. "Does that look like Andrei's team?"

Edmond worked himself forward a few more meters before returning. "It sure looks like it. I'm certain I saw Conner."

"You guys know them?" Estellia asked, surprise written across her face.

Edmond chuckled. "Jocab fixed their communicator on our way to Avalon."

"So that's good news?"

"Yup, and maybe a nice warm meal too."

Donav barked a short laugh. "I suggest we head down the road a ways till we get beyond the work party. We can exit the woods there, then head back toward the camp. That eliminates any unwanted attention from just appearing out of the woods."

"Good thinking," Jocab replied.

They worked their way through the forest, exiting the trees just beyond a small curve in the road. Insulated copper wires hung from freshly erected poles. They tried to relax as they headed up the road toward the work crew. Estellia marveled at the wire hanging from the poles. "They can speak along that wire?"

Edmond smiled as he walked next to her. "Yup, they have a box that converts our voice to electricity that travels down the wire. Jocab can explain the science better."

"Pretty amazing, don't yah think?" Donav asked.

"It sure is," Jocab replied. "I understand we've had the knowledge for a while. We just lack the metals to make it work."

"It's always been the metals," Donav quipped.

Jocab grinned. "We could fly if we had the metals,"

"Now you're pulling my leg." Edmond contested.

"It's true," Estellia exclaimed. "I saw some pictures. Pops would take us to the library when I was younger."

"Flying people?" Edmond replied in disbelief

They cut their conversation short when Andrei spotted them. He smiled and headed in their direction. "Welcome back, my friends. You look tired from your walk. Please, come to the tent and I'll get you some water."

Donav reached out and shook Andrei's hand. "Thank you, Andrei. You are so kind."

Andrei pointed out the day's progress as they walked. He looked around before commenting. "Temple guards came looking for you yesterday."

Donav nodded. "I figured they'd be canvasing the road. Thanks for the warning."

"You're welcome. You guys saved my backside. It's the least I can do."

Jocab looked around. "Do you think we'd be safe if we camped with you tonight?"

"Why not? The guards were heading to Liberty. My guess is they won't be back for a few days."

"We don't want to put you in any danger."

"My team will keep quiet. It's not like I'm harboring a murderer." Andrei smiled. "Am I?"

Donav barked out a laugh. "Hardly. The priests just didn't like what Jocab and Edmond shared with them."

"Figured it was something like that. Especially for how hard they are looking for you three." He noticed Estellia for the first time. "Not four," he said slowly. "You've added one more to your merry band."

Donav turned to Estellia and smiled. "Yes, we did. Andrei, please let me introduce Estellia to you. Estellia, this is Andrei."

"A woman? I thought, uh… hello Estellia," he said, recovering. "Couldn't tell the difference between the afternoon sun and you being dressed like a man."

Estellia giggled. "No offense taken, Andrei. And it's a pleasure to meet you."

Andrei shook her hand as he continued to compose himself. "You guys must join me for dinner, just like last time."

Estellia's smile grew wider. "We'd be honored."

Edmond handed over the two rabbits hanging from his pack. "Can the cook use these?" he offered.

Andrei smiled. "I'm sure he can."

The four of them met Andrei under the tent when the dinner bell rang and Andrei wasted no time getting down to business.

"With the temple out looking for you, what's your plan?"

Donav took a quick drink of ale. "First thing we need to do is replenish our supplies. We couldn't stock up before we left Avalon."

"You can't go to Liberty with the guards looking for you. I'll give you what you need here."

"That's very kind of you."

"Again, it's the least I can do."

Edmond spoke. "We were planning on heading west from Liberty. Since we won't need supplies, is there another route that avoids the city?"

Andrei thought for a moment. "You can head up Box Canyon. It's maybe two or three days north of here."

"Box Canyon?"

Andrei sipped his drink before continuing. "Starts out as a break between two small hills. After a few miles, it turns into a long canyon. You follow it all the way and you'll get boxed in on three sides."

Estellia tilted her head. "Then how do you get out?"

"There's a small trail up the side, but it's not an easy hike. That's the reason most people never use it."

"How do you know about this?"

"I grew up on a farm west of Liberty. My brothers and I found it one summer."

"Nice, and thanks. Do many people use it?"

"Some, but not much. Most who use it come this way cause it's all downhill."

Jocab looked relieved. "That works for us. We can catch the road west out of Liberty before heading to my family's farm."

The conversation turned to small talk as they focused on their food. Soon, they were drinking and laughing into the night.

Jocab woke early, needing to relieve himself after an evening of drinking. "Blasted bladder," he cursed to himself as he crawled out of his warm blankets. He grabbed his jacket from under the blankets, donned it, and headed toward a distant tree to relieve himself. On his way back, he saw Estellia sitting on her bedding talking quietly to Edmond. Jocab wondered if anything might develop between the two. Jocab smiled, remembering how they were both quite taken with each other when they first met. "Good morning, you two," he said, biting off adding "lovebirds" to the greeting.

They both smiled and replied, "Good morning."

Jocab was about to speak when a bell started ringing to wake the workers. They looked over to see Andrei putting his weight behind it, giving it a good swing to make sure everyone heard it. Satisfied with his results, Andrei headed in their direction.

Edmond leaned over and nudged Donav awake. "Andrei is coming."

Donav slowly sat up and rubbed the sleep from his eyes. "I'm awake."

Andrei called out, "Join me for breakfast before you hit the road?"

"Be nice to have another full meal before we hit the road," Jocab replied.

"I'll send someone over when breakfast is ready."

The four of them started rolling up their bedding and packing for the day's travel. Edmond noticed two guardsmen on horseback coming down the road from Liberty. "Uh oh, trouble!" he said, his voice low.

The three looked to see the guards approaching. Donav reached into his pack and pulled out a head covering and quickly put it on. "Estellia, put your hat on, too. Please hide your hair."

She hurriedly pulled her hair up and slapped on a large-brimmed hat, hiding her long hair. Afterward, she grabbed her jacket and put it on to hide her features. "Let's get in the chow line. Maybe we can blend in with the workers."

They headed toward the chow line. Jocab scanned the camp and eventually spotted Conner. "Let's have breakfast with Conner."

"Great idea," Donav said as they headed toward Conner while monitoring the approaching riders.

They joined Conner in the chow line and fell in behind him. "Good morning, Conner," Jocab said cheerfully.

"Jocab, it's good to see you. I thought I saw you dining with the boss last night."

"Yup, had an enjoyable meal, too. Mind if we join you for breakfast?"

"Sure. You're not joining Andrei?"

Jocab motioned in Andrei's direction. "Looks like he has company, and we'd like to avoid them if we can."

Conner's smile disappeared, replaced with a look of surprise and concern. A second later, recognition set in, and his eyes grew wide. "The guards are looking for you?"

Jocab gave a crooked smile. "Guilty."

They kept silent as they made it through the chow line. Conner led them to a place where they could talk and eat. They made eye contact with Andrei before he settled down to breakfast with the guards under the tent. Edmond noticed the workers would finish their breakfast and start working before the temple guards left. "Conner, any chance we could join the work crew this morning?"

Conner glanced at the guards. "Sure, we could use the help."

"Thank you."

Donav nodded. "Good thinking, Edmond. I was unsure of what to do."

Jocab chuckled. "Be kind of funny if we were the only ones left in camp."

They finished eating and quickly joined the team. Jocab and Edmond went straight to the back of the wagon and grabbed shovels. Conner walked to the front, opened a small trunk, and pulled out four pairs of gloves. "Y'all should wear these so you don't have blisters by lunchtime." He turned to Estellia and Donav. "Either of you good with horses?"

Estellia nodded, and Donav smiled. "Why yes, what are you thinking?"

"Help guide the horses that are hauling the poles into position."

"Sounds good," Donav agreed.

The four of them regrouped in the chow line for lunch. A fine dust covered Edmond and Jocab from all the dirt they had been shoveling. Conner caught up to them few seconds later. "So, how's your first day going?" Jocab and Edmond patted their clothes, causing a small dust cloud to emerge, making everyone laugh.

"Definitely not as messy as theirs," Donav observed.

Conner turned to Estellia. "Any trouble blending in?"

"Nope, I've had no problems. Donav has been calling me Ess, and that has helped."

Edmond gave Donav a pat on the back. "Great thinking."

They were still in the chow line when Andrei signaled for them to join him under the tent. Conner grumbled. "I hope he's feeding us. We're almost to the front of the line and I'm hungry."

They left the line and walked to the tent where Andrei was waiting. "I am glad you found something to do this morning. The guards were unexpected."

Donav nodded. "Yeah, we figured we'd better blend in."

Andrei smiled. "They certainly enjoyed your breakfast."

Donav snickered. "I bet they did."

"Please let me make it up to you at lunch."

Jocab nodded his thanks. "We should eat with the men. The last thing you need is us sitting around your table when the next batch comes riding by."

Andrei nodded his head in agreement. "I think you might be right."

Conner looked bummed. He figured he'd just missed out on a delightful meal when Andrei motioned toward the tent. "Well then, fill up your plates and grab some ale first."

Everyone gave a round of thanks as they loaded up. Donav turned to Andrei. "How long until your crew reaches Box Canyon?"

"Seven to ten days at the rate we are moving. Why?"

"I'm not sure it is safe for us to travel, even if we stuck to the woods. It would be easier for us if we could blend in as your crew."

"I'm sure we can do that. You all right with the jobs you've been doing?"

"Everyone except Ess here. I'd recommend she help with the cooking. The crew might like that too."

Andrei raised an eyebrow. "Really? Just how much help?"

Estellia flashed a big smile. "My Pop and I run the Broken Fork in Avalon."

Andrei's eyes looked like saucers. "What?"

Estellia's quiet smile removed any doubt.

Andrei squinted as he stared at her. "Now I recognize you. I always try to stop there whenever I am in Avalon. You hide well in plain sight."

She grabbed a roll and placed it on her plate. "Why thank you."

"My cook would love your help. Enjoy your lunch first and I'll introduce you."

Estellia nodded her thanks. With their plates piled high, they excused themselves and sat with the workers to eat.

CHAPTER 18

It took twelve days to reach the trailhead leading to Box Canyon. They observed the temple guards, either coming or going, at least every other day. Jocab was thankful they blended into Andrei's work crew and stayed hidden.

Andrei would join them for lunch occasionally, avoiding the tent, in case the guards showed up. "I will miss you four," he said as he passed over a small purse to Edmond sitting next to him.

Estellia beamed. "Why, thank you."

Edmond took the purse. "What is this for?"

"Twelve day's labor for four people."

Edmond stammered as he tried to hand it back. "Oh no. We can't take this."

"Oh yes, you can. I'll not be keeping a man's wages. Especially for a hard day's labor."

Edmond looked at the others, confirming it was okay to take the money. Seeing no resistance, he tossed the purse to Jocab. "You should hold this."

Jocab caught the purse and nodded. "I think I can manage that." He glanced at Donav before continuing, "It's probably best to keep it separate from the temple funds."

Donav nodded in agreement.

Andrei looked at Estellia. "The food has certainly improved during your stay with us, Ess. The crew has enjoyed the upgrade. I hope the cook can keep the crew happy after you leave."

Estellia giggled. "The stuff I showed Simon wasn't too difficult. He should be fine."

"I sure hope so."

After lunch, they said their goodbyes and slipped down the trail unnoticed. They walked in silence for the rest of the afternoon and into the evening. Edmond took point while keeping his eyes open for any temple guards. At sundown, they found a suitable place along one of the canyon walls to set up camp where they could conceal a small cooking fire.

Jocab leaned back against a rock, "They are using a lot of resources to find us."

Donav looked up. "Too much."

Edmond looked across the fire. "I've been thinking that, too. If they are having every guard across the western map looking for us, it means this is big. Really big!"

"What is it though?" Estellia said with a raised eyebrow.

Jocab pursed his lips. "They are obviously hiding something, and it has them scared."

Edmond agreed. "Yeah. They were looking like they were ready to explode. They couldn't get us out of the council chamber fast enough."

Estellia cleared her throat. "Maybe, it's because the other theories are correct?"

Edmond frowned. "What theories?"

Estellia glanced at Donav. "That the gods did not create us."

Donav smiled. "Please don't worry about offending me. I am not sold on the temple's theology. I believe the truth is somewhere in the middle."

Edmond ventured his own opinion. "I've never believed the gods created us. It just doesn't fit. But, if the gods didn't create us, how are we here?"

Estellia paused, deciding how best to explain. "The most popular theory is that the gods brought us here. Another theory is that we evolved."

Jocab snorted. "We didn't evolve. There is no evidence to support that."

Edmond poked the fire with a stick. "I agree, and that leaves us with… They brought us here."

"That also explains why we have so much knowledge we cannot use."

"But why were we brought here? For what purpose?"

Estellia gave Edmond a little shove. "That is the same as asking, why did the gods create us."

"Both theories leave us with the same question. Why?"

Donav chuckled. "Not sure we'll ever find that answer, regardless of what theory you choose."

Estellia looked at Jocab. "You've been to the library. All that knowledge had to come from somewhere."

Jocab nodded, "Absolutely."

"Pop and I believe they brought us here, because we have all this knowledge we can't use."

Edmond waved his hands in front of him. "Why would they give us knowledge we cannot use? That makes little sense."

"Unless they didn't know we couldn't use it." Jocab commented.

"That makes little sense. None of it does."

Jocab leaned forward. "So, you think that object might have the answer?"

Donav looked up and spoke in a low tone. "I think it is the answer."

Jocab's eyes bugged out. "You really think that?"

Edmond jumped up. "That's it. You're right, Donav! And the high priests know it too."

The captain of the guard knocked on the door and waited. Normally, an assistant would announce him. But not at this hour. The assistant had left some time ago.

"Enter," commanded the voice on the other side.

The captain took a deep breath and straightened his jacket before entering. He stepped smartly through the door with military precision, coming to attention in front of a metal desk, his heels clicking together.

Solomon sat back in his chair and examined the man before him. Looking him in the eyes, he studied him for a few heartbeats. "At ease, Captain. Please tell me you have apprehended our three missing guests."

The Captain relaxed from his stiff posture but was far from at ease. "No, Your Excellence, we have not."

"How is it possible, Captain?" he asked, emphasizing Captain. "How did three harmless villagers, miles from home, evade the entire western regiment of the Temple Guard?"

The Captain stood ramrod straight under the withering glare and sharp criticism. "We are doing everything we can to find them, Your Excellence. Guards are patrolling the main roads out of town, from Liberty to Cumber, checking all the inns, the library, and watching the eating establishment they frequented."

"Have you found anything?"

"No, Your Excellency. I just expanded the order to search one kilometer on both sides of the roads. If they have left the city, we will pick up their trail."

"Have you searched the river?"

"Yes, Your Excellency. Ten kilometers in each direction."

"So, you are telling me you do not know where they are?" His voice rising in pitch.

"Correct, Your Excellency. But I assure you, we will find them."

"I appreciate your confidence, Captain," Solomon replied, emphasizing Captain again. "But I believe it's time to escalate things."

"What do you have in mind, Your Excellency?"

"Jocab has a wife in Cumber. Apprehend her! Jocab will come out of whatever hole he is hiding in to guarantee his wife's safety."

"Is that wise, Your Excellency?"

Solomon jumped up, venom dripping from his words. "Are you questioning me, Captain?"

The Captain kept all expression from his face. "Of course not, Your Excellency."

"Good! Now get that wretched woman and drag her back here."

The Captain took his leave, quickly closing the door behind him. Never had he seen Solomon like this. He was like a man possessed, not the calm and mild-mannered priest he saw leading worship.

It was midday. The sun was high in the sky, and Jocab was exhausted. His legs burned with each step he took. The sweat dripped down his forehead and into his eyes. He breathed in another breath of hot stale air as he forced himself onward. His pack became heavier with each step as he worked his way up the canyon wall. Overall, he was miserable. The climb seemed to go on forever. The high canyon walls dashed every attempt to glimpse the top overhead. "You were right, Andrei," he mumbled to himself, remembering why Andrei said no one used this as a shortcut.

Jocab leaned against the rock face, hoping to find some shade. Glancing back, he watched the others work their way up the narrow path. They were spread out, caught up in their own personal misery, their discomfort clearly visible as they trudged along. Jocab smiled, knowing he wasn't the only one suffering. He started up the trail again mumbling, "Misery loves company."

The sun had passed its zenith and was well on its way toward sunset when Jocab crested the ridge and exited the canyon. He looked around while he waited for the others. In front of him, a large valley opened. Multiple farms lay like a patchwork quilt, covering the valley from one end to the other, with a road working it's way through the middle.

Jocab was still enjoying the view when Estellia stepped up next to him. "So, which way from here?"

Jocab motioned into the distance. "I suggest we work our way down these rocks. Then we can follow the edge of the farms till we hit the road on the far end."

"Will we be safe taking the road now?"

"I'd be willing to chance it. It'll take us days to get past the farms if we must stay off the road. We've been gone a lot longer than I like, and we still need to send word to Ayleth to meet us at the farm."

Donav surveyed the valley and nodded. "Sounds like a plan. Keep your eye out for someplace secluded to camp tonight."

They worked their way west along the edge of the valley, doing their best to keep out of sight till the sun started setting in the distance. Jocab figured this was the last populated area west of the city. Once they were past the farms and into the hills, they stood a much greater chance of success.

CHAPTER 19

The four temple guards spurred their horses into a trot when the village came into view. "Not much to look at, is it?" One guard said as the horses picked up the pace. "We get sent to some backwards fishing village, just to apprehend a woman?"

The Sergeant glared at him. "Shut it, Tanner. We do what we're told. The priests have their reasons."

The other two riders glanced at each other but held their tongues. Half an hour later, they reached a grouping of buildings surrounding a well. They reined in as the sergeant commanded. "Tanner, water the horses."

Tanner dismounted, pulled a water bag from his saddle as Boris strode around the side of the tavern and called out a greeting. "Good day, gentlemen. Welcome to Cumber."

The four guards eyed Boris as he approached. The sergeant asked, "Can you direct us to the temple?"

Boris motioned over his shoulder. "Just follow this road behind me. It's up there on the hillside."

The sergeant grunted at Boris before turning to Tanner. "Tanner, let's go. You can water them at the temple."

Tanner bit his lip as he tucked the water bag into his belt. The sergeant headed up the road, forcing the others to follow.

Boris shook his head. "They weren't real friendly."

"What's that all about?" Birx asked when he saw Boris enter.

"Four temple guards came into town asking for directions to the temple."

"What!" Birx exclaimed. "You sure?"

"They're armed and wearing the temple colors."

"That's not good. Jocab and Edmond are late. Now, temple guards show up out of the blue."

"Is that unusual?"

"Very. We have to warn her."

Boris looked confused. "Who?"

"Ayleth, that's who, you knucklehead." Birx looked around the tavern and spotted Horton. "Horton, can you come here, please? I got a job for you."

"Sure. What yah thinking?"

"I need you and Boris to run out to Jocab's and warn Ayleth."

"OK, what for?"

"Jocab is already three weeks late and suddenly, temple guards arrive in town. I'm guessing they're after his telescope and stuff."

Boris frowned. "That sounds bad."

"Yeah, it is. Now get going and help her." Both of them stood there, dumbfounded. "Now, you two!" Birx demanded.

They bolted for the door and ran up the road toward Jocab's place.

Ayleth held the laundry basket against her hip with one hand while pulling clothes off the line with the other. She set the basket down when she noticed a winded Horton and Boris running up the road. "You two see a ghost?" she hollered.

"Temple guards," Boris called out, gasping for breath.

"Temple Guards. What about them?"

"Birx said to warn you that temple guards arrived," Horton blurted out. "He thinks they're coming here next!"

"Oh, my!" she gasped, covering her mouth with a trembling hand. "Jocab!"

"Birx said they may come to get Jocab's telescope and stuff. Said we should help you out."

"By the gods, no!" she replied, fighting to control herself. "We better hurry then. Horton, please saddle the horse and turn the cow loose."

Horton nodded and made a beeline for the barn. "Boris, I need your help to gather a few things in the house."

Boris nodded. "Are you going to leave?"

"Yes, I think it is safer that I do."

"Where will you go in case Jocab comes back?"

"It's best you don't know. Besides, Jocab knows where to find me." Ayleth ran toward the house, Boris right behind her. She flung the door open and headed toward the bedroom. "Boris, please grab a bag under the kitchen counter and fill it with bread, cheese, and anything else I should take. I have to get some clothes together."

It seemed only seconds later that Ayleth exited the bedroom dressed in a pair of Jocab's pants and a long wool shirt, dragging a travel bag behind her. Abandoning it by the door, she scampered up the ladder to the loft. She glanced at Boris to see he was tying off a bag of food.

She looked back as she reached the top. "Can you catch what I toss down?"

"I'll try," he said nervously.

"All I can ask for," she said before disappearing from view.

Seconds later, she was at the edge with the telescope in her hands. "Ready?"

Boris nodded; a look of terror crossed his face. "What if I drop it?"

She smiled. "You won't. I trust you." And tossed it down.

Boris caught it, placed it on the table, and turned to see Ayleth toss the tripod before disappearing again. He caught it and placed it next to the telescope. By then, Ayleth was climbing down the ladder with a small wooden box and several books in her hand.

After they packed the telescope and things, they grabbed her travel bags and headed outside. Horton stood waiting with the horse, saddled and ready. "I'll take the cow to my Pa's place and keep her safe there till you get back."

She tied the bags behind the saddle. "Great idea, Horton."

Horton beamed with pride. Ayleth hugged and kissed them both on the cheek. "Thank you both for everything."

Both men hugged her back. "It was Birx's idea," Horton replied.

Ayleth smiled as she swung into the saddle. "Tell him thanks too. Stay safe."

They both nodded.

"Now get going. You don't want to be near here when the guards arrive."

She spurred the horse and headed toward the tree line behind the house, while Boris and Horton guided the cow down the road. Ayleth quickly disappeared among the trees, swallowed up by the shadows. She continued moving through the trees for several minutes before turning north, using the soft grass and leaves to hide her trail.

Horton and Boris walked side by side with the cow in tow. They dove into the tall grass beside the road when they heard hoof beats rumbling toward them. The temple guards came into view ahead, pushing their mounts hard. "Stay calm." Boris whispered, speaking more to himself than to Horton. They lay still and watched the guardsmen thunder by. Neither moved until the riders disappeared toward Jocab's place. "Looks like Birx was right," Boris commented as they climbed to their feet and hurried away.

The guards reined in their horses outside the now empty house. They looked around, taking stock of their surroundings. Clothes were hanging on the line, the basket resting beneath them, and the front door stood ajar.

"She must have heard us coming, Jon," one guard said.

"Or the villagers warned her," the other replied.

"Shut it, Carlos," the guard commanded as he dismounted. "You two check the barn. Mitch and I will check the house."

Carlos and Tanner nudged their horses toward the barn while Mitch and Jon stepped into the house. Once inside, the evidence showed that Ayleth had left in a hurry. Mitchell searched the living quarters while Jon entered the bedroom, calling out what he saw. "Clothing's been tossed around and some bedding's missing."

Mitchell hollered from the living quarters, "Coals in the fireplace are still hot and banked and the cupboard's been cleaned out."

Jon exited the bedroom and headed for the ladder. "Wonder what we'll find up here?"

Mitch followed Jon up the ladder and stood on the top rungs while Jon looked around. The loft was full of supplies for the upcoming winter on one side. A table, chair, and small desk occupied the other side. Several building plans covered the table. "Nothing here," commented Jon. "Let's see if Carlos and Tanner found anything."

They exited the house to see Tanner and Carlos keeping the horses from wandering off.

"What did you find?" Jon asked.

"Couple of empty stalls and a workshop. Lots of tools and stuff." Tanner said. "Didn't find any hidden hideouts or root cellars in there."

"She's gone then." Jon replied. "Mitch, you and Carlos see if you can find a trail. I want to look in the barn."

Jon wandered into the barn, stopping just inside to let his eyes adjust to the reduced light. The two stall doors stood open, evidence that they kept animals inside. He took his time exploring the workshop. It had an extensive selection of tools made of wood, stone, and copper. A small smelting pot and a workbench occupied the back wall. Satisfied he had seen everything, he walked out into the afternoon sun.

Carlos and Mitch were just coming out of the trees.

"Sorry, Jon. Looks like one horse, but we lost the trail in the creek. I think she headed east toward the mountains. Perhaps we can pick up a trail there in the morning."

Jon nodded, then turned to Tanner. "Get a few torches going."

Tanner's eyes got wide. "What for?"

"Simple. Someone tipped her off. We need to set an example by torching the place."

The villagers huddled inside their homes, watching the fire burn in the distance as the guardsmen returned to the temple. No one would venture out and investigate until it was dark. Until then, they hid in fear wondering if they would find a burned corpse later tonight.

Ayleth kept a steady pace northward while keeping eyes and ears open. The sun was working its way down when she noticed smoke rising in the distance. She stopped her horse to verify her bearings. Ayleth realized immediately that her farm was on fire. She sat in shock for a several minutes and watched the smoke climb into the sky. Tears streamed down her cheeks as her home went up in flames. Everything she and Jocab had worked for drifted skyward.

For the first time, Ayleth tasted fear. She feared for herself. She feared for Jocab. But worst of all, she feared she would never see him again. Her thoughts overwhelmed her as she nudged her horse forward. They continued to torment her as the tears flowed. Soon, large sobs racked her body as despair devoured her resistance. Overcome by her emotions, she cried herself out. After a while, Ayleth slowly regained control. She knew she couldn't give up. She needed to stay strong for Jocab. Clenching her jaw, she sat taller in the saddle, wiping away the tears. Yes, for Jocab, she would stay strong.

CHAPTER 20

Ayleth kept riding long into the night to keep ahead of any pursuers. She finally stopped under a sparse tree after almost falling off her horse while dozing off. Exhausted, she tied the reins to a low branch before pulling her bedding out. No sooner had she wrapped herself in her blanket than she was fast asleep.

Ayleth woke at dawn from a dreamless sleep. She could see the morning through a thin blanket of leaves overhead. "Not much of a covering," she muttered. She slowly climbed to her feet, her body complaining from yesterday's riding and the rock she had slept on. She stood and pulled her bedroll aside and nudged the rock with her foot. "You were a pain in my side."

Ayleth found a place to relieve herself before shuffling over to her food sack. Rummaging through, she pulled out a small piece of wax covered cheese, a small roll of bread, and two small apples. She tossed the cheese and bread on her bedroll and held the apples out for the horse. "Here you go. You deserve these." She stood there, stroking his neck as he munched on the apples. Once he finished, Ayleth plopped onto her bedroll and took a bite of bread. She knew she needed to get moving in case the temple guard came looking this way. She ate quickly, packed up, and forced her tired and sore body to climb in the saddle and keep moving.

It was just past noon when Ayleth crested a small hill that overlooked a large valley below. She saw five small farms with fields full of crops. A creek that meandered its way north and south through the valley. Ayleth remembered Jocab telling her that this creek merged with another creek further downstream before making its way through the village of Cumber. Her eyes followed the road. It made its way through the valley before disappearing into the hills on the other side. Ayleth focused her attention on the creek until it ran through a farm on the north side of the valley. She could see a farmhouse, a barn, and two other small buildings clustered together. Ayleth smiled, knowing that she was almost there. She hoped beyond hope Jocab was there or had sent word.

Ayleth nudged the tired horse forward, letting it pick its way down the road. She gazed at the fields, mentally picking out the different crops that grew there. She recognized the wheat, potatoes, and strawberries, but couldn't identify the others. Ayleth could clearly see the rows of rocks that help separate the crops and give it a patchwork pattern all its own.

Once she was down among the fields, she enjoyed the peace and serenity of the valley. The fields spread out around her. As Ayleth made her way along the road, she could hear an occasional dog bark or cow moo in the distance. Ayleth tried to picture Jocab growing up here, finding things to tinker with or fixing a broken farming tool. She wondered. "Did he always try to take things apart?" and smiled at the thought.

A young boy suddenly appeared in the middle of the road, spooking Ayleth. She fought to keep from falling out of the saddle as she gathered her wits about her. It seemed he had materialized right out of thin air. Ayleth guessed he was about seven or eight years old, freckle faced with a mop of light brown hair. His shirt hung over a pair of trousers that stopped at the ankles, showing a pair of sandals tied to his feet.

She took a deep breath to compose herself. "You gave me a fright there, little man."

"Sorry mum. I saw yah coming down the road earlier. We don't see many travelers from your way."

Ayleth felt her heartbeat returning to normal. "It's fine. You appeared like magic. What's your name?"

"Benjamin, but me pa calls me Benni," he replied, standing tall.

"What a glorious name, Benjamin. I'm Ayleth. I'm here to visit some of my family."

He bounced back and forth on his toes. "Yah are? I'll help yah find them if you'd like."

She smiled down at him. She knew where she was going but played along. "Why thank you, young Benni. I'm looking for Ethan's farm."

Benni leaped with joy. "That's my farm!"

"Well now, Benni. You must be Ethan's boy."

Benni puffed out his chest. "Yes mum, that's my Pa!"

Ayleth dismounted to walk with him. "Well then, Benni. Please, show me the way."

Benni looked like he would explode with excitement. "It's this way."

Ayleth gave a small tug on the reins and fell into step next to Benni. "How do you know my Pa?" Benni asked.

Ayleth looked down and smiled. "I'm married to his brother, Jocab."

"You are?" he said, amazed. "Pa always says he has brothers, but I've never seen 'em."

Ayleth felt a pull on her heartstrings. "That's because you were just a baby the last time we visited."

Benni was a bundle of energy. He pointed out what was growing in the fields. He talked about how the cow got loose last week and how he had learned his letters recently. Ayleth listened, enjoying the boundless energy of the young man beside her. Nothing like the joy of a young child to help drive away your troubles.

Once they turned off the main road, Benni ran ahead toward the farmhouse yelling, "Ma! Pa! Ayleth's here!"

Ayleth watched Benni run to the house as she led the tired horse up the small road. Soon, everyone emerged from the house, looks of surprise written across their faces.

Ethan's wife and mom, Miriam and Wyndee, came down the steps to greet her. "Ayleth! It's good to see you," Wyndee said with concern in her eyes.

"Is everything all right?" Miriam asked. "Where's Jocab?"

Ayleth tried to stay strong. Her resolve quickly crumbled as her jaw quivered and tears streamed down her cheeks. Wyndee pulled Ayleth into a hug and let her sob into her shoulder. Ayleth had no memory of the family guiding her into the house. Nor how she ended up sitting in a chair with a warm cup of tea in her hands. Once the sobs receded, Ayleth managed a few small sips of tea. She sucked in a deep breath as everyone waited. Looks of fear and worry stared back at her.

She looked down at her tea, gathered her strength, and announced. "Jocab never came home. He went to Avalon to show the High Priests something he saw in the heavens."

Over the next hour, she brought them up to speed. What Jocab had found, that he was late coming home, her fear for his safety, her escape, and watching the smoke as their house burned. As she finished, she saw little Benni sitting on the floor, mesmerized by her story.

Ethan stood and started pacing. He was a few years older than Jocab, with similar wavy light brown hair and green eyes. His large set shoulders and strong back a product of years of farming. He looked over at his father and murmured, "This doesn't bode well."

Ethan's father, Gabriel, looked back at him. "Let's not get ahead of ourselves. Borrowing trouble will get us nowhere."

Gabriel was a few inches shorter than his son. The same light brown hair covered his head, although Ayleth could see the gray slowly taking over. Smile lines at his temples blended into the suntanned skin. She thought about how handsome he looked. She imagined how handsome Jocab would be when he reached the same age. Ayleth forced herself to take another sip of tea as she smiled at Benni, still sitting on the floor. He flashed a big smile back at her. Ayleth wished she could lose herself in the innocence of youth.

She looked at Ethan and his father Gabriel, "I take it you have not heard from Jocab?"

Both of them shook their heads. "No," Gabriel murmured.

Ayleth took another deep breath and let it out slowly. Tears threatened to overwhelm her again. "I don't know what else to do."

Miriam placed her hand on Ayleth's shoulder. "Well, the first thing is to get you settled. I'll get some food rustled up and Benni can show you where you'll sleep."

Benni jumped up. "She can have my room, Ma."

"Really?"

"Yeah, I can stay in the loft real easy."

Miriam turned to Ayleth. "He loves climbing that ladder. Made himself quite a little hideout up there."

Ayleth smiled and offered Benni her hand. "It would be an honor to use your room, Benni. Thank you. Please show me the way."

Benni took her hand and led her to a door across the living quarters. "I know you will like it. I got a new bed last winter and the morning sunlight comes right in my window."

"I'm sure I will, Benni."

CHAPTER 21

Edmond hustled next to Jocab. "Slow down, buddy."

Jocab smiled and slowed his pace. "Sorry about that, we're getting close."

"Yeah, but you're going to wear us out if you keep going like this."

Jocab laughed. "You're right. You should take the lead."

"Alright," Edmond replied as he turned to see the others several paces behind. They stopped to allow Donav and Estellia to catch up.

"Speedy here, promised to go slower."

Both Donav and Estellia gave a little laugh. "He's going faster the closer we get. I'm wondering how close we get before he's sprinting home."

Ayleth, Miriam, and Wyndee were sitting on the front porch, having tea. They had finished the breakfast cleanup and were enjoying a few minutes to themselves before starting on the morning chores. A cool breeze blew as the sun made its way higher in the cloudless sky. "It's beautiful out here," Ayleth commented.

"It sure is," Miriam replied. "Peaceful too."

"How did you end up settling the farm here?" Ayleth asked.

Wyndee smiled and got a faraway look in her eyes. "Similar story why Jocab left us. Gabriel's the youngest of three boys. There wasn't enough farmland for the three of them. Gabriel recognized this early on. He left and found a place he could farm himself."

"Where did he come from?"

"His parents had a farm out two days east of Liberty. He gathered a few friends in the same situation and they started looking. Once they saw the valley and the rich soil here, they were hooked."

"First few years must have been hard."

"I heard it was. Gabriel and his friends spent the first summer building houses for each of them. They spent the next year clearing fields and making them ready for planting."

"How soon before you moved here?"

"He asked for my hand right after he had the fields cleared. I moved out with him after winter broke. He used every bit of his inheritance to buy a wagon and seeds."

"Wow, that's quite a story. You must be proud of what you built here."

"The gods have blessed us, that is for sure."

They sat for a few more minutes before Miriam stood. "We better get the chores done before the dust bunnies start multiplying."

Jocab was eager to arrive. They had been on the road seven days since leaving the valley west of Liberty. He was worried sick about Ayleth. All he could think about was getting a message to her, but he needed to get to the farm first. They would arrive today, but they still had a long walk ahead of them. Jocab could see the road heading down into the valley in front of him. It followed the creek into the valley till it turned sharply to the right after reaching the fields. Jocab had always wondered, since he was a kid, why the road turned instead of following the creek. He laughed to himself, knowing he'd never get the answer to that childhood question.

The sun had set when they finally entered the far end of the valley. The clouds were turning different shades of pink as the sun shone through them. Jocab hardly paid any attention to the spectacular view, his focus on arriving. Edmond and Estellia talked quietly with each other as they walked a few feet behind him. Donav, caught up in his own thoughts, took up the rear. It thrilled Jocab that they pressed on to the farm instead of stopping for the night. It was dusk when they turned off the road toward the farm. Jocab could see the farmhouse ahead, with its light streaming through the windows. As they got closer, Jocab could see several people sitting on the front porch.

"Hello!" he hollered out to announce their arrival.

A tall figure jumped up and looked in their direction. "Jocab? Is that you?"

"Yeah, Ethan. It's me."

"Jocab!" a frantic voice screamed from within the house. Seconds later, Ayleth flew out the door and flung her arms around him.

Jocab wrapped his arms around his wife and hugged her back as she cried into his shoulder.

Edmond, Donav, and Estellia stood back, giving the two some privacy for their homecoming. Ayleth eventually pulled back a little and started hitting his chest between sobs. "You had me so scared!" she cried while beating on him. "I didn't know if they got you." She collapsed back onto his shoulder, crying louder. "Oh Jocab, I was so scared!"

Jocab held her tight, relieved she was already there. "It's all right, Ay. I was worried about you too." He looked up and saw the rest of the family smiling from the porch. He nodded to them as he cleared his throat. Ayleth finally unwrapped herself from him and grabbed his hand, gripping it hard. Jocab turned and motioned to his traveling companions. They stepped forward, stopping at the bottom of the steps so Jocab could make introductions. "Ma, Pa, you remember Edmond and Donav."

Edmond smiled and gave a small wave, while Donav gave a slight bow. Next, he motioned to Estellia. "And this fine lady is Estellia. She helped us escape from Avalon."

Estellia gave an awkward curtsy. "Hello."

"Estellia, that big lout there's my older brother Ethan and his wife Miriam. Behind them are my Pa and Ma, Gabriel and Wyndee."

Estellia stepped forward to shake hands when Jocab noticed he had missed one. "And you must be Benjamin." he said as he knelt down to Benni's height.

Benni smiled, "Uh, yes, um," he replied, trying to sound confident.

Jocab stood and announced. "This young lad is Benjamin. Benjamin, this is my best friend, Edmond. This is our temple priest from Cumber, Donav. And that is Estellia from Avalon. She makes the best chicken in the world. Aside from my wife's, of course."

After a few rounds of handshakes and hugs, Miriam spoke up. "Let's everyone get inside and get something to eat. I'm sure you must be hungry."

Ayleth's eyes widened. "Oh my. The bread! I had just put it in the oven." She dashed back through the door.

Everyone laughed as they followed her into the house, the smells of dinner filling their senses. Inside, Ayleth smiled at Jocab as she placed a platter of bread on the table. Jocab smiled back before joking. "Well, it looks like it is safe to eat the bread."

Several hours later, they all gathered in the living room, eager to swap stories. Jocab found a spot on the floor near the fire, Ayleth glued to his side. Edmond and Estellia settled close together on the other side of the fireplace. He smiled to himself, thinking Edmond and Estellia made a great couple. Both he and Donav had watched the two become closer during their travels. Jocab had watched as Edmond lost his shyness and started flirting back. Witnessing the romance bud had made the troubles they endured less difficult.

Ayleth noticed Jocab watching the two and leaned into him. "Am I seeing what I think I am?"

Jocab smiled and nodded. "Yup," he whispered. "Edmond was tongue tied at first. Couldn't keep his eyes off her."

"What about her?"

"She started flirting with him the moment we walked through the door."

Ayleth laughed. "Oh, my! I bet Mister Shy didn't know what to do with himself, huh?"

"You nailed it."

Everyone finished getting settled as Ethan tossed another log on the fire. Jocab looked around the room at the expectant faces and captive audience. "Well," he paused before continuing in a serious tone. "Once upon a time, a fool looked into his telescope."

The room erupted in laughter. Ayleth gave Jocab a little shove. "Stop it," she said, drawing out the words.

Jocab waited for the laughter to die down before continuing. "Edmond found an object in the night sky…"

Jocab gave a brief account, the others adding missing details as he went along. Afterward, he listened in amazement as Ayleth told of her narrow escape and looking back to see the smoke from their farm rising in the air. Donav and Edmond seemed equally troubled by the news.

Donav broke the silence. "It's getting late, and we cannot do anything tonight."

Gabriel nodded. "That is true. We can finish discussing things in the morning. The roosters will crow, regardless of how tired I am."

They all stood and said goodnight before bedding down for the night. Jocab and Ayleth headed up the ladder to the loft. With nine people in the house, they had played musical sleeping arrangements. Benni now slept on the floor in the living area, with Donav and Edmond, while Estellia took Benjamin's room.

Jocab felt he had just closed his eyes when he heard the roosters announcing the dawn. He tried to close out the noise a little longer, but eventually sat up. Ayleth wrapped her arms around him and hung on. "You going somewhere?" she said with a sleepy smile.

Jocab leaned over and gave her a kiss. "Not without you, I'm not."

Ayleth grabbed him again and pulled him back, releasing him only after he'd been thoroughly kissed. "Well, I'm wide awake now."

They climbed down the ladder and saw that Donav and Edmond were up and folding the last of their bedding. Benni was watching the two men as he sat with his blankets over his knees. "Good morning, Benni," Ayleth said as she smiled at him.

Benni beamed as he replied, "Morning, Aunt Ay."

"Would you be willing to fetch some eggs for everyone this morning?" she asked him as she crossed to the kitchen to join Miriam.

Benni jumped out of bed. "Sure, Aunt Ay,"

Miriam looked up, surprised. "He'd find a reason to complain if I asked him to do that."

Ayleth smiled. "It's always more fun when your Ma ain't asking."

Miriam laughed as she grabbed the bag of flour out of the pantry. "I guess you are right."

After breakfast, the men gathered in the living room. The ladies continued working in the kitchen but could hear the conversation. They had just finished cleaning up after breakfast and were making preparations for lunch. Gabriel settled into his seat and looked at Edmond. "So, you found this thing coming toward us?"

Edmond nodded, surprised. "Yes, sir."

"Would you be willing to show me your math?"

"I can't. The temple priests kept everything we took to Avalon. The originals were at Jocab's place." He turned toward Ayleth. "I'm guessing the fire destroyed them?"

Ayleth shook her head. "I have them. Boris helped me grab your telescope, the sextant, and the two notebooks and the pile of papers off your desk."

Edmond lit up. "You did?"

"Yes, they're in my bag."

"That's wonderful. Bless you, Ayleth."

Ayleth smiled. "Thank Boris and Horton. I wouldn't be here without them."

"We certainly will," Jocab replied.

"So, if she has the notes, then yes, I can show you the math."

Gabriel nodded, satisfied. "And what do you think is approaching?"

Jocab nodded to Edmond. "Go ahead. You can tell him."

Edmond took a deep breath and continued. "Not a what, but who."

"Who? Why do you think that?"

"Things in the heavens don't slow down on their own. After that thing finishes its bright glow, it's going slower. In addition, we've discovered that it does this every ten hours."

Gabriel sat back in his chair. "So, it's intelligent?"

"Yes. We think that."

Gabriel looked over at Jocab. "You agree?"

"Yes, Pa. It seems logical and fits with the other thing I found."

Gabriel raised an eyebrow in his direction. "There's more?"

"I found what looks like a giant metal wheel orbiting overhead."

Benni couldn't contain himself. "A wheel?"

"Yes, a big shiny metal wheel. It's rotating around like it's traveling down an invisible road."

Gabriel glanced over at Wyndee. She had stopped working and was listening intently. Jocab saw her give the slightest nod before going back to mixing flour.

Jocab looked at Gabriel. "What is it, Pa? What are you not saying?"

Gabriel sat back, looked at the ceiling, and pondered what to say. "We have some old writings. Given to me by my father. I always wondered why I got them instead of one of my older brothers, but he insisted they were part of my inheritance. Your ma and I have kept them hidden, waiting for the right time. I think that time is now."

Ethan frowned. "Writings? First I've heard about them."

"Because it wasn't time to share them."

Jocab could see Ethan did not appreciate this. How could his father hide this from him all this time? Jocab tried to give Ethan a consoling look as he asked, "Where did Grandpa get them?"

"My pa said they've been in the family since the beginning. Could never get anything more out of him."

"If you think they might help us figure things out, I'd love to see them."

Gabriel stood from his chair and headed to his bedroom. "One second, I'll get them."

Solomon pounded his desk as he raged. "You did WHAT! You stupid imbecile. How could you burn the place down?"

The guard stood ramrod straight and silent. He knew nothing he said would save him.

"Not ONLY did you let her escape, but you also torched the damn place! Do you realize that has turned the town against us?"

Solomon stomped over to the door and yanked it open, almost tearing it from its hinges. "Get out of my sight before I beat you senseless!" he roared. "You're a disgrace!"

The guard pivoted on his heels and made a quick retreat.

"I want your resignation on my desk immediately!" Solomon bellowed as he slammed the door.

He returned to his desk and sat, visibly shaking, wondering what was happening. Why was this bothering him so much? Was it those childhood memories?

He pushed back the vision of flames engulfing the temple and hearing the screams of those trapped inside.

CHAPTER 22

Gabriel returned to the room with a small metal box. "Where did you get that?" Ethan demanded.

"Family heirloom," Gabriel said with a wicked grin.

Estellia's eyes almost leaped out of their sockets. "That's priceless, you know."

Gabriel's grin only got larger as he sat back in his chair, opened the box, and handed Jocab a small book.

Jocab took it gingerly, as if it were made of glass. He ran his hand down the cover, his fingers stopping at the small, stitched letters "Leah's Journal" embroidered across the front.

"Leah, huh?" Jocab said. "Named after the god?"

Gabriel's eyes twinkled. "Something like that."

Jocab cracked open the cover to see a small handwritten note penned across the page. He cleared his throat once before beginning. His voice was almost a whisper as he read.

Leah,
Happy mating day.
I made this journal
for you and I hope
you like it.
Yours forever,
Lipinski

Jocab struggled to comprehend what he held. He looked up at Gabriel while trying to keep his hands from trembling. Gabriel nodded. "Keep reading." Jocab slowed his breathing and turned the page to read the first entry.

I absolutely love my new journal.
This was so very sweet of Lip.
He knows how I like to write. This
is such a perfect gift. How he

made it without me seeing him do
it is beyond me. Fabricating
something isn't easy to hide.

Lipinski will be a wonderful mate.
He already takes such good care of me.
I can see the love in his eyes, in how
he holds my hand, and in his kisses.
I look forward to spending the
rest of my life with him. Now
and when we reach Avalon.

Jocab looked up from his reading to the stunned faces staring back at him. Donav, who looked white as a ghost, walked over and knelt next to Jocab. "May I?" he asked reverently.

Jocab hesitated, getting a nod of approval from Gabriel before handing it to Donav. Donav wiped the sweat from his palms before taking it. He held it as one would hold a sacred object, closed his eyes, and said a small prayer. His lips barely moving. Finished, he opened the journal and read the caption again before looking at Gabriel. "This is a family heirloom?"

Gabriel stared into Donav's eyes. "Handed down from the beginning." Gabriel's firm answer left no doubt in Donav's mind. This was the real deal. The fact they kept it in the metal box helped prove its authenticity.

Estellia was grinning from ear to ear. "Does that make you guys direct descendants of the gods?"

Edmond picked his jaw off the floor, glanced at Estellia, then back at Jocab. "This is incredible."

Ethan was outraged. "You knew this, Pa? You've been aware of this all these years?"

Gabriel let out an enormous sigh as he sat back in his chair. "Yes," he said firmly. "Changes your views of the gods and the temple, doesn't it?"

Estellia laughed, "Confirms mine, that's for sure."

Ethan, not quite ready to let go, continued. "Why didn't you tell us?"

"The temple priests have been getting stronger every year. My

Pa warned me that being related has its risks."

"I'm not sure I agree," Ethan stated. The anger clear in his voice.

Donav tore his eyes from the journal. "He's right, Ethan. The fact we are sitting here having this discussion proves it."

Ethan stopped arguing and glanced at Donav. "I disagree," he replied with less force than before.

Donav glanced at Benni before looking back at Ethan.

Jocab watched his brother as the impact of the truth hit Ethan full force. Ethan finally deflated and glanced nervously at Miriam and Benni. Miriam, reading his mind, walked over and placed her hand on Ethan's. "It'll be fine, dear," she said, reassuring her husband. "No harm will come to him."

Edmond cleared his throat. "This blows a kilometer wide hole in the temple's teaching."

Donav chuckled. "That it does, Edmond. That it does."

Estellia took Edmond's hand. "You really didn't believe gods with superpowers created this world and brought us here?"

Edmond shook his head. "No, I didn't. It never added up. But how did we get here?"

"That thing coming toward us might have the answers," Estellia replied.

Ethan turned to Estellia. "What makes you think that?"

"Because. They let Jocab go the first time, because he promised to keep his mouth shut. It wasn't until the High Priests saw the object approaching that they wanted to arrest you."

Donav handed the journal back to Jocab before speaking. "I believe the High Priests are working on damage control at this point. The story that the temple created is about to come crashing down."

"Oh, yeah!" Estellia exclaimed. "They need a new narrative to sell to the masses, and fast."

"And having us running around knowing the truth makes us dangerous," Edmond stated.

Gabriel looked at Ethan. "Now do you understand?"

Ethan looked at Miriam and Benni again before nodding. "I'll take this secret to the grave before I let my family suffer," his voice steadfast.

Jocab ran his hand across the journal one last time before giving it back to Gabriel. Gabriel placed it inside the metal box, then held it out to Jocab with outstretched hands. "This belongs to you now."

Jocab hesitated before reaching out and taking possession of it. As he stared into his father's eyes, a proud and relieved Gabriel stared back at him, happy to pass the torch to the next generation. Jocab turned to Ethan, concerned his brother might be angry, but Ethan surprised him with a hug. "I agree. That belongs to you."

Jocab felt the weight of the responsibility hit him full force. It was as if Ethan had just abdicated the throne. He fought back tears and with a lump in his throat, replied, "I will take good care of it. I won't let any of you down."

Gabriel laughed, breaking the solemn mood. "I've a strong feeling you're going to do more than keep it safe."

Everyone joined in the laughter. Miriam stood up and spoke above the noise. "We better get a move on, it's getting to afternoon and the chores don't do themselves."

Jocab leaned over and gave Ayleth a kiss. "Thank you, again, for saving the notes and telescope. That was good thinking."

Ayleth kissed him back and smiled. "You're welcome. You better put that away now," she replied, motioning to the box.

Jocab nodded and headed to the loft, metal box in hand, when Gabriel intercepted him. "Do you think we could see that object with your telescope tonight?"

"Oh yeah," Jocab replied. "It's a great opportunity to see how much closer it is."

"Great," Gabriel said as they ended the conversation.

The men worked all afternoon putting a new roof on the barn. Ethan was grateful for the extra hands since it made things easier and much faster. Jocab put his back into it, but his mind kept going to the metal box. He was eager to investigate its contents and read more of Leah's journal. He was still coming to terms with being a direct descendant. That changed everything. It meant they weren't gods after all. Jocab wondered what else the Temple was hiding. How did they get it wrong, or had they spun the story like Estellia said? Jocab knew you just needed to change the truth a little to make it believable. He made a mental note to talk with Estellia and Donav about it.

"Hey, daydreamer," Edmond said, hitting his arm.

"Ow, what?" Jocab replied while he rubbed his bicep.

"You're back. Hand us a few more boards, will yah?"

"Yeah, sorry about that." He put his thoughts aside and handed a couple of boards to Edmond.

Jocab finished setting up the telescope. The skies were clear and there was no moon, making it a perfect evening. He turned to Edmond and asked, "Where do you think it is now?"

Edmond opened the notebook to review his findings before scribbling a few more calculations on the page. "Over there," he replied, pointing slightly overhead. "If my math is correct, we'll be able to see it light up in about two hours."

Jocab smiled as he spun the telescope in the right direction. He was still trying to locate it when Edmond spoke. "There it is. I can see it with the naked eye. It's just left of the cross constellation."

Jocab removed his eye from the eyepiece and looked where Edmond was pointing. Benni hollered, "I see it too, just above the bottom star." His excitement overflowing.

Edmond nodded, "Yup, that's it."

Benni ran in the house yelling, "I see it! I see it!"

The rest of the family followed a very proud Benni out the door. He was pleased with himself and took delight in showing the others exactly where to look. The cross constellation had seven stars along a center line with five running perpendicular across the night sky.

Benni asked, "Why is it called the cross constellation? It looks like a lowercase T to me."

"Cause that's what the gods named it," Edmond replied.

Benni sighed to himself. There had to be a better reason but knew he would never get one.

Jocab finished aligning the telescope and motioned to Gabriel. "Come have a look, Pa."

Gabriel came forward and took his time peering through the eyepiece. "It sure doesn't look like a star," he said as he stepped back. Edmond was next and started jotting down more numbers as he switched between the sextant and the telescope.

Benni asked, "What are you writing?"

Edmond replied, "I'm tracking its size, location, and speed." He knelt down and held the book open for Benni to see. "This page is the math for its location and speed," he said, pointing to the page. "And this page is where I'm recording the size."

Benni just saw math equations, nothing more.

Gabriel wandered over and looked over Edmond's shoulder. His eyes bouncing around the page. "Based on those numbers, it will be here before we know it."

"That's if I did the math correct."

Gabriel motioned to the notebook. "May I?"

Edmond handed him the book. "Sure thing. I'd love a second pair of eyes."

Gabriel took the book and wandered over to a lamp hanging from the porch. He leaned against a post as he flipped through the pages. Gabriel returned the book several minutes later. "Math looks good to me, I'm impressed."

"Thank you, Gabriel. That means a lot."

Gabriel gave Edmond a pat on the back. "You're welcome, and good job."

They took turns monitoring the object as the night grew darker. Jocab could sense everyone getting anxious. They all wanted to see it light up, and Edmond promised it would happen soon. Jocab eventually settled near the lamp to read more entries in Leah's journal. He opened the cover and turned to the next entry.

We're mated for a year now
and finally can apply to have a child.
Lip and I are so excited at the
possibility. Lip feels we should
get approved and sees no reason why
they would deny us. We are going
to submit an official request form
tonight after mealtime. Lip tells me
the board meets in 15 days. I can't wait.

Jocab could feel the joy in her writing and how excited she felt. There was no divinity in her words. Nothing that indicated that she was a god. It also puzzled him why they had to seek permission to have a child. Why would anyone need to do that? He turned the page again, eager to read the next entry.

One fabricator quit working today.
Took me two hours to diagnose the issue before
I could even think about fixing it. The little
motor for the servo that controls a filament
nozzle shorted out. I had to pull the
plans for the motor from the central database.
Tomorrow morning, I will pull the list of raw
materials. After that, I can see how to program
the other fabricator to build it. I sent the
instructions to Lip to verify I got everything.
It's been a while since I had to make
something this small.

Jocab smiled at the thought of her making things. He did not know what a fabricator was, or a servo, and made a mental note to find out the next time he was in Avalon. The great library will have the answer. He turned the book to catch the light better and read the next entry.

We are devastated. The board denied
our request. Lip and I have to wait till
we arrive before we can have a child.
That's at least six or more years.
They said it would be best to wait till
we were settled on our new home.
They think a young child now would be a
greater risk at this point, but I disagree.
Our child would be six by the time we
arrive, and could help contribute to our
success. Lip thinks it will be harder on
us if we wait. Caring for a newborn in

the early stages of the settlement versus
when they are six or seven doesn't
make sense. Lip tried to explain this
to the council, but they have already
made up their minds. They don't understand
that Lip and I will be less available for
the colony if we have to focus our energies
on an infant. At least a six-year-old is
somewhat self-sufficient.

Lip held me while I cried myself to
sleep last night. I don't know what I'd
do without him. He is such a wonderful
and caring man. I cannot believe I
lucked out by being mated to him.
I cannot write any more. I have to get
to work now.

Jocab swallowed hard as he fought back the tears. Ayleth saw and sat down next to him. "What's the matter?"

Jocab handed Ayleth the journal and pointed to the page. "Better you read it than me explain it."

Ayleth read the entry to herself before closing the book. She put her arm around his shoulder. Jocab returned the embrace. "That doesn't sound like a God, huh?"

Ayleth didn't answer. Jocab looked up at her before she replied, "Not the Temple's version."

Jocab opened the journal and turned the page to the next entry. They both read the next entry together.

Lip covered for me at work today.
He could tell how depressed I was feeling.
I couldn't focus. I'm so baby crazy
right now and it is difficult to
accept waiting. I thank the
stars for Lip and I'm glad there was not
much work listed today. We completed

*fabricating the pumps for the water
filtration systems yesterday. Today is
just cleaning the fabricator. It's messy,
but totally a one-person job.*

"They become people when you read this," Ayleth said.

"We definitely get an up close look, that's for sure."

Ayleth closed the book and pulled him into a hug. They held each other as they processed what they had just read.

Both Jocab and Ayleth jumped when Estellia yelped, "It's brighter!"

Edmond, who was standing beside Estellia, took a quick look before calling to Gabriel. "Now's your chance, Gabriel."

Gabriel hurried over, put his eye to the lens, and stared in amazement. The flames were clearly visible, burning bright through the telescope's lens. "How long does it last?" he asked.

"Ten minutes," Edmond replied.

Gabriel nodded and stood back to allow others to have a turn. While they gathered around, Gabriel called Jocab aside. "The closer that gets, the more danger you're in."

Jocab could see the genuine fear in his father's eyes. "I agree. We can leave in the morning. Any chance we can get horses?"

Gabriel furrowed his brow as he thought for a moment. "There is the one Ayleth rode."

"She's too old and we need more than one."

"Can't spare them. All the farms share the horses already."

Jocab nodded in understanding. "Keep the old mare. We will go on foot."

"I can use the wagon to take you a few miles out before letting you off somewhere."

"I don't know where to go. The temple will catch us, eventually."

"I have an idea."

CHAPTER 23

Gabriel turned to Ethan. "Can you ask Edmond to show Benni and you the planets and moons while we talk?"

Ethan gave Jocab and his Pa a concerned look. "Sure. Call me if you need me."

Gabriel led Jocab into the house. "Do you have the box?"

"It's in the loft with my stuff."

"Can you fetch it?"

Confused, Jocab followed along without question. "Sure, one second while I get it," he replied as he scampered up the ladder. Pa had cleared off the table by the time he had returned. "Here it is, Pa."

"There are some papers under the journal."

"I saw those, anything special?"

"Very," he replied with a lopsided grin.

Jocab placed the box on the table, opened it, and retrieved a handful of papers underneath the journal.

"That one, Jocab," Gabriel said as he pointed to one.

Jocab separated it and handed it to his father before returning the rest. He could see other treasures in there for him to explore later. Gabriel unfolded and spread the paper out on the table. Jocab recognized it as a map. He leaned over, astounded by the level of detail. The terrain and colors were amazing.

"The farm is here," Gabriel said, pointing to the map. "And Cumber is right here. Both didn't exist when they printed this. You can see where they listed Liberty and Avalon."

Jocab followed the terrain and the marked roads with a finger. "The roads and cities look like someone added them with a pen later."

"It sure looks that way. Although the penmanship is exquisite."

"What is this down here?" Jocab pointed to some lines and numbers in the bottom corner.

"That is how you measure the distance."

"What does 'Satellite Image' mean?"

Gabriel shrugged. "Not sure."

Jocab took a few minutes to study the map. "So where do you think we should go?"

Gabriel pointed to a spot further north. "Here. I was thinking right here."

Jocab followed his finger to where he pointed. He read the following text, 'Settlement number two' written below a dark ink spot. "What's that mean?"

"Locate Avalon for me. Tell me what you see."

Jocab leaned over the table and ran his finger over Avalon. He read 'Settlement number one' in faded print. "So, the gods built cities in multiple locations?" he asked.

"Exactly! And I believe this one is independent of the Temple."

"How so?" Jocab asked.

"We've always been told that stretch of woods is dangerous. They teach kids not to venture there."

"Why wouldn't it be safe? Why wouldn't the temple have influence there?"

"It's isolated. The forest is thick there. I believe the temple is hiding its existence."

"That is quite a stretch, Pa. You don't even know if they really settled there."

"You're right, but you don't have many options either."

Jocab pondered his words before nodding in agreement. He leaned over the table and studied the map some more. "Any other settlements?" he asked.

Gabriel nodded and motioned to the box. "One far to the east, and several more on another map. But there's a lot of water in between."

"Settlement number two seems like the only choice. Although, I won't go unless the others agree."

"Sounds reasonable."

After a quick breakfast and long goodbyes, Jocab was eager to get on the road. He placed his pack in the wagon, taking extra care to not damage the telescope. The morning was still early as he climbed over the edge and sat in the back corner. He stretched his arms along the sides as Ayleth settled next to him. Edmond and Estellia occupied the opposite corner while Donav joined Gabriel and Benjamin up front. They all spent the morning enjoying the ride as the horses plodded up the road.

"You saved us a day's walk today," Donav said when they stopped about midday.

"Least I could do with how far you have to go."

They unloaded their belongings and slung their packs over their shoulders before giving hugs and saying their goodbyes. "Stay off the road," Gabriel said. "You should be able to follow the ridge line north instead."

"We will," Jocab replied as he released himself from his father's hug. "Tell everyone I love them."

"I sure will. Now get moving," Gabriel replied as he climbed back on the wagon. The five travelers waved and headed single file into the tree line, setting a quick pace as they headed deeper into the forest. Gabriel watched them disappear before turning the wagon around and heading home.

The first night after leaving, they settled along an open meadow. Edmond had snared a rabbit and was cleaning it while Ayleth added twigs and small branches to a cooking fire. Estellia and Donav had volunteered to collect firewood, while Jocab set up the telescope in the middle of the meadow.

Ayleth called out to Edmond. "How soon till that is ready?"

"It's ready now," he replied as he walked over to the fire. Together, the two of them created a spit over the growing flame.

Ayleth sat on a small rock. "This is going to take a little getting used to."

Edmond chuckled, "Miss the cooking pot already?"

Ayleth huffed. "Oh yes. Very much."

After dinner, they gathered around the telescope while Edmond took his measurements. Donav came over and stood beside Jocab. "You mentioned back in Avalon that you had more than one brother. I only met Ethan at the farm."

"Yeah, Ethan is the oldest and inherited the farm. Clancy left about a year after I came to Cumber."

"Where did he go?" Donav asked.

"Clancy was always a hunter growing up. He would disappear into the woods for days, just to appear with wild game for dinner. He helped sustain us one winter when we had a crop failure."

"I can imagine."

"Yeah, there was little rain that year. I'm certain we would not have made it, if not for him."

"What happened?"

"One summer day, he gave Ma a kiss and said goodbye. Said it was time."

"That must have been hard on her."

"It was. There was no warning or heads up. Just goodbye. She cries whenever something reminds her of him."

"Has he ever sent word? Maybe a letter or something?"

"Nothing. Going on four years now."

"How awful," Estellia murmured.

"Yeah, Pa thinks he passed. He never speaks of it with Ma."

"How was she when you left?" Estellia asked.

"She was sad, with her baby leaving the nest, but was relieved when I settled in Cumber."

Ayleth leaned over and kissed Jocab. "So was I."

Estellia burst out laughing. "I bet you were!" She reached over and grabbed Edmond's hand. "I'm not sure where we will end up, but I'm not letting him go."

Edmond blushed. "It will be someplace nice, I'm sure."

The morning sun was just coming over the trees when Jocab opened the metal box. The humid air promised another hot day as they made their way north. He pulled the map out and laid it out in front of him. He glanced over to see Ayleth and Estellia stirring breakfast while Donav and Edmond finished packing their belongings. Turning his attention back to the map, he identified the ridge line would follow and figured it would be several weeks before they reached a mountain range that blocked their path. Somehow, they would need to navigate through it to reach the second settlement site.

He eyes drifted to the northern horizon and he wondered if anyone had really "settled" there. "We shall find out," he murmured to himself as placed the map back in the box. His eyes fell on some of the other contents and he figured now was as good a time as any to investigate. He'd been too busy to think about them earlier. Wondering what other great treasures the box held, he set the map and journal next to him, and gingerly unfolded a piece of paper. "Certificate of Mating" was printed across the top in large official lettering.

"This certifies that Leah and Lipinski (Lip) were officially united and mated on the 8th day of September in the one hundred and eighty-ninth year of our voyage. This mating shall stand for a term of ten years and may be annulled or extended every ten years as agreed upon by both parties."

His mind exploded with questions. A mating certificate? The Gods, Leah, and Lip, were mated? One hundred- and eighty-nine-year voyage? From where? The questions kept coming. Could someone walk away from their spouse after ten years? Why would they do that? What did they travel in? "Donav, you need to see this!"

Donav walked over, noticing his friend looked a little pale. "What is it? Did you see a ghost?"

He handed Donav the certificate. "Not a ghost, but close."

Donav took the paper from Jocab and studied it. "Fascinating. This is truly fascinating."

"Were they married?"

Donav smiled as he handed the certificate back to Jocab. "Looks like married with a term limit."

"But what about the date? one hundred and eighty-ninth year of the voyage. What's that all about?"

Donav pondered his words. "I'm not really sure. I've seen nothing about it in the scriptures. It aligns with Estellia's theory though."

"Exactly! And what do we do about it?"

"I suggest nothing at the moment. Unless you wish to lose your head."

Jocab frowned as he placed the contents back in the box and closed the lid. "That's not right."

"I couldn't agree more."

"How can you still follow your priestly vows knowing the scriptures aren't truthful?" he asked without thinking.

"I became a priest to help people."

"But the scriptures?"

Donav reached out his hand to help Jocab up. "I've taken a vow to serve. There's a lot more truth to come out before we're done. I can reevaluate things after that. Until then, I will still follow my vows."

Jocab accepted Donav's help. "That sounds reasonable."

Donav patted him on the back. "Atta, boy," Donav replied as the two men went to grab some breakfast.

CHAPTER 24

Solomon stepped into the room and glanced around. Two young temple priests sat at a desk studying the scriptures. "Who's in charge?"

One of them replied as they both knelt in reverence. "Uh, I am Your Excellence."

"And... you are?"

"Oslo, Your Excellence."

"Alright Oslo, is that communicator working yet?"

"Yes, Your Excellency. The connection to Liberty is live."

"Good. Now get your excuse of a priest off that floor and help me talk to them."

The two priests bolted for the communicator, with Solomon trailing behind. A small box sat secured to the center of the table. A hand crank on one side and a microphone connected by a wire on the other. Oslo grabbed the hand crank and spun it for several seconds before picking up the microphone and speaking. "Jaylee, you there?"

Within seconds, a voice answered from the box. "I'm here. Is this Oslo?"

"Yeah Jaylee, it's me."

"Did you need anything? Or just to talk some more?"

"I have his Excellency, the High Priest Solomon here, and he wants to talk to someone."

A few seconds of delay filled the room before Jaylee replied cautiously. "Be happy to help, Your Excellence."

Solomon grabbed the microphone from Oslo. "This is the High Priest Solomon. Get me the captain of the guard now."

"Yes, Your Excellency, sending for him now."

Solomon put the microphone down and paced back and forth. Oslo and the other priest sat rigid in their seats, pretending to read the scriptures. After what Solomon thought was an eternity, Jaylee's voice rang out. "Here he is, Your Excellency."

Solomon walked over to the communicator and grabbed the microphone when a voice spoke over the speaker. "Hello Your Excellence. This is the Captain of the Guard, Kenneth speaking."

"Kenneth, we need this conversation to be private."

"One moment, Your Excellency."

The two priests took the hint and bolted from the room. Solomon closed and secured the door behind them.

"They have left, Your Excellence. I am alone."

"Good. I need your help to apprehend some fugitives."

Jocab followed the ridge line, paralleling the road, for five days before it turned east toward Liberty. He had everyone take a short break while Edmond scouted ahead, knowing they would be exposed when they crossed the road. Jocab tried to relax as they waited, anxious to be safe among the trees on the other side. Only then, could they travel without fear of being seen.

Jocab had drifted off when Edmond nudged his shoulder. "Hey, wake up. We got company."

Jocab jolted himself awake. "Where?"

"Seems the temple guards are watching the road."

Ayleth looked startled. "Think they are looking for us?"

Edmond shrugged. "Doesn't matter. We should treat them like they are."

Jocab sat up. "What should we do?"

"I've been thinking about it for a while."

"And what did your big brain come up with?" Jocab teased.

"Hand you over and take the reward," Edmond replied.

"Hah," he laughed. "They want you just as bad."

Donav spoke in a low tone. "We should wait and cross tonight."

Edmond nodded. "I agree. Maybe just before the changing of the guard."

"Any idea when that is?"

Donav nodded. "Usually it's every four hours, but that depends on how many guards they have."

Jocab shook his head in frustration. "That really helps."

Edmond placed his hand on Jocab's shoulder. "Relax, Jocab. We can cross further back where the road dips as it passes through a small ravine."

They spent the next hour quietly backtracking through the trees. It was mid-afternoon when they settled in to wait. "We should all try and get some sleep," Donav suggested.

Jocab was still wide awake as he leaned against his pack to rest. He felt the metal box dig into his side and reached in and pulled it out. Eager to explore more of its contents, he pulled out the journal and cracked it open.

Lip's birthday is tomorrow. I talked
with the cook and he said he would make
Lip a small birthday cake. I'm hoping
he likes it. The cook said he does this
for other people and for special occasions, too.
Although I've been doing much better
the last couple of months, I am still having
difficulty with being denied a child. Lip
tried talking to the board again. They were
steadfast in their decision. I know it lies
heavy on his heart, too. I don't understand
how he keeps it all together. I'm glad he
is not keeping his feelings from me, although
I know he hides it from the others. He's in
line for chief engineer and he's afraid it
could disqualify him. I told him it doesn't
matter to me if he becomes chief or even
the director. I love him regardless.

Jocab smiled as he turned the page.

We had the birthday party for Lip today.
Everyone in our section showed up. Frank gave
him two days off for his birthday. I'm so
jealous cause I still have to cover my shifts.
Afterward, Lip and I had a small dinner. The cook

gave us an extra piece of meat from the synthesizer.
The cake made the night extra special.
He deserves it.

Jocab closed the journal and placed it beside him. Now was the time to see what else was in the box. His hand settled on a small smooth object a millimeter thick and about three centimeters square with the word 'STORAGE' written on it. He flipped it over in his hand a few times before setting it on top of the journal. Reaching in again, he pulled out a small, round silver object the length and circumference of his index finger. One end was clear glass, and the other was black, soft and squishy. He turned it in his hands and read the words 'Atomic Diamond Torchlite' in faded lettering along the side. Again, not knowing what it was, he placed it on top of the journal.

Next, he pulled out a small pouch pulled tight by a string. After loosening the string, he could see two coins inside, approximately five centimeters in diameter. Jocab removed one to examine it. One side showed a woman in a flowing dress, holding a torch high in one hand with the words 'LIBERTY' along the top. He flipped the coin over and admired the picture of a bird in flight. The words 'United States of America' written across the top and 'One Dollar' along the bottom. The detail was amazing. Examining the coin some more, he noticed some lettering 'E Pluribus Unum' and 'In God We Trust' along with some numbers repeated along the edge.

Jocab reached into the cloth bag and pulled out the second coin. It had an arrow appearing from behind a planet that got bigger as it moved across the front of the coin. The words 'Avalon I' written along the top with 'United States of America' in smaller letters along the bottom. Jocab turned the coin over, sucked in his breath, and stared at the coin in disbelief. It was the same wheel he had seen through his telescope. The wheel had some additional details along the edges, but Jocab was certain it was the same object. He ran his fingers over the picture as he read the words 'Gateway Voyager' along the top.

He was still examining the coin when Ayleth spoke up, surprising him. "What you got there?"

"More contents from the box," he replied as he gathered the items he had removed and slid over to sit beside her. "Prepare to be amazed."

Ayleth sat up, eager to see what had so captured his attention. Donav opened his eyes to watch but did not join them. Jocab handed her the small card with 'STORAGE' on it. "I'm not sure what it is. It's made of some material I've never seen before."

Donav reached out his hand. "May I?"

Ayleth looked at Jocab with a raised eyebrow. Jocab nodded. "Sure."

Ayleth leaned forward and handed it to Donav. Donav took it and flipped it around in his hands. "It's made of plastic."

"Plastic?" Ayleth asked.

Donav reached out and handed it back to Jocab. "Something from the gods. The temple has a few plastic artifacts."

Jocab placed it in the box and picked up the round silver object and passed it to Ayleth. Ayleth turned it in her hand and read 'Atomic Diamond Torchlite' inscription along the side. Next, she examined the clear glass end before flipping it over to inspect the other side. She ran her finger over the soft material and felt a hard point sticking up in the center. She pressed down gently on the soft squishy material, trying to feel the point underneath. "Ahh!" she screamed when it gave way, making a clicking sound.

Jocab looked at her, alarmed. "What?"

Ayleth handed it back to him. "It clicked when I pressed this."

Donav shot up from where he was resting. "There is light coming from it!"

Light shone at his feet as he took the torchlite from Ayleth. Jocab moved his hand back and forth, the bright spot moving on the ground at their feet. "What did you do?" Jocab asked, shocked by what he saw.

"I was pushing on it, right there." she said, pointing to the other end. "I thought I broke it when it clicked."

Jocab put his thumb on it and pushed. It gave another click, and the light stopped. Pushing it again, the light reappeared. He pushed the button several times, the light flickering on and off with each click.

Donav gave a crooked smile. "That will come in handy later."

Jocab smiled back as he continued to play with it a little longer, clicking it on and off.

Donav sat up. "What else you got?"

Jocab handed the coins to Ayleth and Donav. "A few coins."

Donav turned his coin over in his hand as he examined both sides. "One Dollar?"

"Yeah, what caught my eye was the writing on the edge."

Donav turned the coin and read the small print along the edge. "What part?" he asked. "Pluribus Unum or In God We Trust?"

"I do not know what Pluribus Unum means."

"Me neither."

"It's the 'In God We Trust' I was talking about. Did they believe in only one god?"

Donav handed the coin back. "I don't know."

"Did our gods believe in a god? Is there a god of gods?"

Donav chuckled. "Both are interesting questions. I'd love to know what Athels has to say."

Ayleth frowned at Donav's comment. "What about this coin?" she asked, changing the subject.

Jocab became excited. "It has the wheel on it! It proves the wheel is from the gods."

His excitement woke Edmond from his light sleep. "What's all this god stuff you guys are talking about?"

Ayleth handed the coin to Edmond. "Look at what Jocab found. It was in his box!"

Edmond reached out and took it before leaning back again. Estellia leaned into Edmond's shoulder and admired the coin with him while he flipped it over in his hands.

Jocab could see Edmond tense up before handing the coin back to Ayleth. "I have some hard questions for the temple." His voice stern.

Donav spoke, breaking the tension. "That's a topic for another time. It will be dark soon. I suggest we all eat something and get ready for tonight."

Edmond took the lead and helped everyone hide under a large overgrown tree next to the road. They lay on the ground as they tried to stay invisible to any watching eyes. Edmond signaled to Jocab to search the road heading east as he searched west. They needed to see how far apart the guards were.

Jocab nodded, rolled out from under the branches, and headed back into the forest. He made his way up the road, keeping an eye out for the guard. The one moon, Acrobba, was low on the horizon. This made it easier for him to hide in the darkness. Unfortunately, it also helped the guard.

It was too dark to see, and Jocab would have missed him, except the movement against the trees giving him away. The guard stood in the road, trying to stay alert while in the middle of nowhere. Jocab smiled, pleased to have spotted him as he headed back to their hiding spot. Back at the overgrown tree, he made a mental note to tell Edmond that he had picked the perfect hiding place. Even standing next to the tree and knowing his friends were there, it concealed them thoroughly.

He was working his way back under the tree when Edmond returned. "This should work perfectly," he announced in a hushed voice.

Edmond had warned the group to murmur and that a whisper traveled on the air better.

Jocab nodded, "My guard is down the road about fifty meters."

"Yeah, we are almost in the middle of the two," Edmond replied.

"So, any change in the plans?" Jocab asked.

"Just like we talked about. Go in teams of two. Jocab and Ayleth first, Donav and Estellia next. I'll follow behind once you cross. Keep going for at least 100 meters and then find some cover. Once there, lay down and wait. We can regroup in the morning if needed."

Everyone nodded. Jocab and Ayleth rolled out from under the tree and held hands as they made their way to the road. After a brief pause, they dashed across and disappeared back into the trees. The two were still holding hands as they continued their pace deeper into the forest, putting distance between them and the road. Ayleth thought they had gone on forever when Jocab finally stopped to look around for some suitable cover. Ayleth motioned toward a few fallen trees.

Jocab smiled. "That's perfect. I knew I loved you."

Ayleth shoved him forward. "Then move it, you big lug."

They found a comfortable spot between the logs and settled down to wait.

After what seemed like an eternity, Edmond motioned to Donav and Estellia. They crossed without incident and quickly disappeared into the trees. Edmond sat back and started counting to give them ample time to hide before it was his turn.

Jocab could see Donav and Estellia approach their position. He watched to verify they were not being followed before calling out in a hushed voice. "Donav! Estellia! Over here!"

Estellia noticed Jocab first, and grabbed Donav's arm, pulling him in the right direction. Jocab led them to their hiding place, where they settled down to wait for Edmond.

Edmond finished counting to a hundred before making his way to the road. He checked both directions for any sign of the guards before sprinting across the open ground. He had cleared the road and was almost to the trees when he twisted his ankle on a large rock. His momentum carried him forward where he crashed heavily to the ground.

CHAPTER 25

Edmond could feel the air get knocked out of him as he landed. He lay face first in the dirt, stunned and unable to breathe. It seemed an eternity before he relaxed his diaphragm and filled his lungs with air. Fearing the guards had heard him, he scrambled to get out of sight. He was crawling into the trees on his hands and knees when he heard someone yell out. "Warren, is that you making all the noise?"

Edmond dropped behind a bush and tried to slow his breathing. Further down, he heard the another solder answer, "I thought that was you. Sounded like you fell in a hole or something."

"Not me. Besides, you're the clumsy fool anyhow."

"Stuff it, Dierck."

Edmond heard the voices getting closer as they approached from opposite sides. Fearing they would find him if he stayed, he struggled to his feet and made his way further from the road. He gritted his teeth at the stabbing pain as he inched his way forward, leaning on trees and hopping on one foot as fast as he could.

Estellia looked at Jocab with growing concern. "He's taking too long."

Ayleth placed a hand on her shoulder. "Give him a few more minutes."

"No, something happened," Estellia replied when she heard the guards yelling."

"I'll go check on him," Jocab said as placed his pack next to him.

Ayleth pulled him close and kissed him. "Stay safe."

Jocab made his way back toward the road while staying hidden. He stopped and knelt in place when he heard some noise several meters in front of him. Seconds later, he could see Edmond limping toward him.

Jocab stood and headed in his direction. "Edmond!" he called out in a low voice.

Edmond stopped and leaned against a nearby tree. Relief written all over his face.

Jocab hurried over and put his arm around Edmond. "Here, let me help you."

Edmond leaned against Jocab and grunted. "Thank you."

"What happened?"

"Turned my ankle on a rock crossing the road."

"Ouch."

Edmond gave a small laugh between gritted teeth. "Just a little."

"You didn't make that noise?" Dierck asked.

Warren shook his head. "I promise, it wasn't me."

"OK, you want to search the road or tell the lieutenant we heard something?"

Warren gave it a few seconds' thought before replying, "I'll let the lieutenant know. He'll most likely want to investigate."

Dierck groaned, "You know that means we're not getting any sleep tonight."

"Yeah, I know," Warren replied before trotting off into the darkness.

Once they had joined the group, Jocab helped Edmond sit. "Looks like graceful here sprained his ankle."

Edmond gave Jocab the stink eye. "Yeah, feels like I rolled it bad."

Estellia came over, pulled his pant leg up, and probed his swollen ankle. "We need to wrap it." She reached for her pack, rummaged through it, and pulled out a shirt and a small knife, quickly cutting the shirt into strips before wrapping Edmond's ankle.

"Thank you," he murmured.

Estellia smiled and batted her eyelashes. "Anytime, clumsy."

Edmond stood and tested his ankle, still unable to put any weight on it. "We have to keep moving. I landed hard, and the guards heard me, so we need to be long gone when they come to investigate."

Warren returned with the lieutenant and four additional soldiers. Two were holding torches in the air, providing some light to search by. The lieutenant turned to Dierck. "What have you found?"

Dierck saluted. "It is too dark to see much, sir."

The lieutenant returned the salute before turning to the rest of the soldiers. "Search both sides of the road in both directions," he hollered. "Find me what made the sound." He turned back to Dierck and Warren. "This better not be one of your stunts." The venom clear in his voice.

"No, Sir!" they answered in unison.

"Good. Now go help the others."

Edmond placed his arms over Donav and Jocab, allowing them to half carry him as they put some distance between them and the road. It was imperative they made good time. Edmond continued to grind through the pain, taking Estellia's advice that it would heal quicker the more he used it.

They were skirting the edge of a small valley, sticking to the tree line when the sun came up. This proved to be faster than staying in the trees. The undergrowth was getting thicker the further they traveled. The constant ducking under branches and stepping over rocks made it impossible to help Edmond.

"What do you have?" the lieutenant asked.

Warren pointed to his right. "They hid under that tree there. If you kneel here, you can see their tracks. They crossed the road here before heading into the trees over there."

The lieutenant knelt and examined the tracks on the road, following them until they disappeared into the trees.

Warren knelt nearby and picked up a rock. "You can see scrape marks on the ground and on this rock here. I'd say he tripped and fell, maybe twisted an ankle."

"That would account for the noise."

"He also didn't hide his tracks after he fell."

The lieutenant looked at the churned-up dirt and leaves. "How far does it go?"

"He went about twenty meters on his hands and knees before standing and heading deeper into the woods."

The lieutenant nodded. "It should be easy to catch up to them."

"Not really, sir."

The lieutenant raised an eyebrow. "And why is that soldier?"

"It gets pretty thick in there and we won't be able to use horses."

"You're positive?"

"Yes, sir. Grew up on this side of Liberty. You're not getting through that on horseback."

The lieutenant stood looking into the woods. Warren waited, the silence unnerving. Warren was about to ask him for his next orders when the lieutenant replied. "I want twelve volunteers. Find them and be ready to move out in fifteen minutes."

"Yes, sir."

"The rest of us will head back to Liberty and alert the captain that we've found them."

The sun was setting when Jocab found a nice place to camp between a large boulder and a fallen tree. Edmond was doing his best, but still couldn't put any pressure on his ankle. The walking stick Estellia gave him didn't seem to help, either. He had thought about tossing it many times but had kept it because Estellia had given it to him. Edmond was in love, and he knew it. Jocab watched Edmond lean against a large boulder as Estellia and Ayleth started digging a hole for the fire. Ayleth said it would help hide the fire when it got dark. They could bury it in the morning. Jocab looked back down the mountain. "Did anyone see them today?"

Estellia, who had taken up the rear, shook her head. "Nothing. Didn't see or hear anything."

"They will follow our tracks. We did nothing to hide them."

Edmond nodded. "It will take them a few days to catch up. They will gain on us every day."

Donav gave a half smile. "I hope they're as tired and hungry as we are."

Jocab woke everyone at first light and had them eat a warm breakfast. He had Ayleth leave a pot of oats on the coals, cooking overnight. Jocab knew they needed a warm meal in them before they tried to outdistance their pursuers. He had also lightened Edmond's pack. Edmond gave a token challenge about carrying his own weight, but Estellia silenced him with a stern look. After that, he grudgingly allowed Jocab and Donav to distribute some of his belongings between them. It didn't take long before they hit the trail again.

Edmond, with a lighter pack and his walking stick, fell in line behind Jocab and Ayleth as they continued to journey north. The woods thinned as they gained elevation. Edmond grimaced as the ground grew rockier the higher they climbed. He had to take extra care to keep from stepping wrong. They had been walking uphill for most of the day, the ground steadily rising. After stopping for a quick break, Jocab glanced at the mountains in front of him. "Let's stop here for the night."

Edmond shook his head. "We have another hour of sunlight. I can keep going."

Jocab studied Edmond. "You sure?"

"Yeah, it isn't throbbing as much as it did yesterday."

Jocab tried to guage the strength of Edmond's words. Seconds later, he nodded. "All right, let's keep going."

The shadows were getting long when Donav pulled to a stop. "I'm falling asleep on my feet. And we don't need another one of us twisting an ankle."

"Set up camp behind those boulders then," Jocab said, pointing just off the trail. Each of them nodded and headed in that direction. Jocab watched them go, noticing how they slumped over and dragged their feet. A frown of concern crossed his face as he forced himself to follow.

It thrilled Jocab to see the area was perfect, secluding them from the wind and giving them plenty of room for their bedding. Estellia had dropped her pack and was reaching for the cooking pot when Jocab placed a hand on her arm. "I think it's best if we cold camp tonight. I'd prefer to not give the soldiers any help."

Estellia let out an enormous sigh. "I was hoping for a nice cup of tea."

Ayleth chuckled. "So was I."

"I'm sorry, ladies."

Ayleth gave him a tired smile. "It's alright, sweetheart."

Edmond remembered nothing after they stopped. He didn't even remember crawling into his bedding, being totally disoriented, when Estellia nudged his arm. "Time to hit the trail, sleeping beauty."

Jocab barked out a laugh. "Sleeping what?"

Estellia stuck her tongue at him. "You be quiet," she said as she threw her boot at him.

Jocab continued to laugh, easily dodging her boot, only for Ayleth to whack him on the arm.

"Hey!" he exclaimed.

"Leave them alone, will ya?"

Jocab continued to laugh as he finished rolling up his bedroll.

It took them just a few minutes to finish packing and sling their packs on their backs. Donav handed out a few apples and jerky as they broke camp. No sooner had they started out than Donav pointed to the forest below. "Look, I think I spotted the soldiers." They stopped and turned to where Donav had pointed. They could see a faint bit of smoke making its way through the trees below.

Edmond tested the weight on his ankle. "It's going to get harder to lose them once they leave the trees. This rocky terrain is already slowing me down."

Jocab settled his pack and adjusted the straps. "Let's get moving then."

Jocab led them along a small gully up the side of the mountain. It took several hours to reach the top, where they took a quick break. Jocab pulled out his map to get his bearings and plot their next moves. The others enjoyed the view while they rested. Jocab ran his finger along the map until he identified where they were. He looked at the small valley below where it sloped downward before leveling off. Following the contour on the map, Jocab avoided the valley and worked their way along the top of the ridge instead. He felt they would make better time staying at their current elevation. Jocab put his map away and shouldered his pack again. The others climbed to their feet and followed.

They made better time. Edmond was grateful, as the hard packed ground making it easier to travel. He could walk on his ankle now, but not without favoring it. A rich black and blue color ran down his ankle, but it no longer looked like a balloon. The swelling had decreased to where you could see his ankle bones.

They had stopped for a quick lunch, comprising of another apple and some smoked meat. Estellia lifted her canteen and shook it, the water sloshing inside. "We're going to need water soon."

Jocab grimaced. "I know. How are we doing on food? I'm afraid the higher we go, the less likely we'll be able to replenish either of them."

They were still working across the top of the mountain when they stopped for the evening, leaving them exposed to the elements. They had tucked themselves into little crevices and behind rocks to avoid the icy wind that whipped across the mountain. It had picked up earlier in the afternoon, sapping the heat from their bodies. Jocab, clearly aware they lacked cold weather gear, feared things would get worse before they reached the other side. He ran his finger along the map looking for a water source, figuring they had two days of water if they rationed it. Food was not much better. They had hoped to hunt game to supplement their food, but it would be another day or two before they descended below the tree line where they could hunt.

His biggest concern right now was the water supply. The map showed a small river that ran through a valley east of them. The issue was that it was in the wrong direction. Jocab also feared the river might be dry this time of year. While it was getting colder, there was no rain in sight. He looked at the map, frustrated and reluctant to decide. It didn't help to know the soldiers were only a day behind them. Ayleth came over and sat next to him while he agonized over their situation. "You find what you're looking for?"

"I see options, but nothing without risks."

"Why don't you show the others? Let them help decide."

Jocab took a deep breath and held it for a few seconds before exhaling. "You're right. We should do it while it's still light out to see the map."

She smiled at him. "Of course, I'm right." She leaned over and kissed him, putting some passion behind it. "I'm always right."

Jocab grinned at her while he recovered from the kiss. Once he had regained his senses, he gathered the others around the map. "OK, here is what I can see. We are here. This is the mountain we are climbing. I expect we should reach the peak by late afternoon tomorrow." He made sure everyone was following before he continued. "We have two days of water and three days of food if we start rationing now. The only known water source is behind us and we'd have to contend with the soldiers."

Donav leaned in. "So going back is not an option?"

"Correct. If we keep going, there's a river about a day's travel east of this pass." Jocab looked at them as they nodded their understanding. "Except, it might be dry this time of year."

Nobody said anything as they digested the information. Edmond finally broke the silence. "What are your thoughts?"

"I'm thinking we go east. I am concerned that if there's no water, we'll be in worse trouble."

"Is there anything if we go west?"

"Nothing," Jocab replied.

"If we take the most direct route and ration the water, how long will it take?"

"Possibly two days without water."

"So, we're guaranteed to die if we go west," Estellia commented.

"And guaranteed to be captured if we go back," Donav added.

"Sounds like the creek to the east is the best option." Edmond stated.

"The other option is to turn ourselves in," Jocab mumbled.

"You're kidding?" Edmond snapped. "We didn't make it this far too just turn in. Besides, we don't know what they will do when they capture us."

"East," Ayleth announced.

"East," Estellia followed.

"East," Edmond said.

Jocab looked at Donav. Donav smiled. "East."

"Then it's settled. We go East. Now let's see how we can stay warm tonight."

"Easy," Edmond said. "We gather some rocks and make a windbreak around us."

"That will take a while."

"Yeah, but I would rather not freeze to death."

The wind picked up as they gathered rocks and started piling them up. An hour later, they had constructed a meter high wall around an area big enough for them to sleep in. "This works great," Donav said as they laid out their bedrolls.

They could hardly feel the wind blowing over them as long as they were lying down.

Estellia smiled at Edmond. "Going to be close quarters tonight, but at least we will be warm."

"Works great for Jocab and I," Ayleth said with a crooked smile. "But maybe Donav should sleep between the two of you."

Edmond blushed a deep red. "Just what are you insinuating?" Estellia said as she feigned innocence.

Ayleth laughed as she wiggled her eyebrows. Donav came to the rescue. "They promised me they would be good. Besides, we're right next to each other."

CHAPTER 26

It promised to be another chilly night when they stopped to set up camp. They found the small river still flowing and had followed it deeper into the valley since then. Ayleth and Donav were busy gathering large piles of leaves and pine needles for their bedding. They added about a half a meter of leaves under them, with another meter piled on top. While it was difficult to crawl into, it provided the necessary insulation to keep out the cold. Jocab couldn't believe how well it worked.

Ayleth had a pot of water warming next to a small cooking fire. They were all hungry and tired as they sought to stay ahead of the soldiers. Jocab had occasionally spotted them in the distance, noticing they were gaining on them daily.

Edmond plopped down next to Jocab, pulling him from his thoughts. He placed a few small squirrel-like creatures he had trapped earlier over the fire. "I'm curious how that meat is going to taste."

"Just like chicken," Estellia said, laughing.

"Hah," Jocab replied, joining in the laughter. He sat off to the side, studying the map again. "My parents used that line when they wanted me to try something new."

"Mine too."

Ayleth smiled. "I think every parent did."

Edmond leaned over the map. "Did you find a path down this monster?" he asked as he motioned to the mountain next to them.

Jocab placed his finger on the map. "Looks like a spot right here. Unfortunately, we will be exposed as we descend."

"So, the soldiers might spot us?"

"I'm afraid so."

"Think we can descend safely in the early morning light?"

"Maybe. It would be worth a try."

"How far is it from here?"

"Not too far. Just around that ridge over there."

"That looks like it's about an hour away."

"I guessed that, too."

"We wake up early and have a cold breakfast first."

After dinner, they headed for the bedrolls, thankful for the hot meal. Jocab threw a few handfuls of dirt on the fire before he joined the others. He watched them as they climbed into their bedrolls while trying not to disturb the leaves piled on top of them. They had taken to sleeping next to each other to help conserve heat and allow them to make only one pile of insulation over their bedding. They took turns sleeping on the edges as it was usually colder there, and you didn't have to worry about an elbow or knee in your back. It was Jocab's and Donav's turn tonight. Jocab finally got settled and quickly dropped into a dreamless sleep.

Jocab snapped awake when he felt something hit his foot. He laid still as he opened his eyes to look around. Not seeing anything moving in the darkness, he slowed his breathing and listened, expecting to hear an animal rummaging through the camp. Several seconds later, he felt it again. Thinking Edmond must have gotten up and was kicking his foot, he pushed himself up on his elbows to see what he wanted. He opened his mouth to speak when he noticed a tall, hooded figure pointing a bow in his direction.

He drew the bow back further. "No sudden moves."

Jocab nodded in understanding.

The dark figure motioned toward the others. "Wake everyone and keep it quiet."

Jocab sat all the way up and raised his hands shoulder high. "I'm unarmed."

The hooded figure acknowledged him with a nod. "Wake the others."

Jocab reached into his bedroll and pulled out his outer coat and boots, holding them up for the stranger to see. "It's cold, I'd like to put these on first."

Again, the stranger nodded. Jocab pulled the coat over his shoulders and quickly laced his boots. The commotion caused Ayleth to wake. "Let me guess, you got to pee?" she asked.

"No sweetie, we have company."

Ayleth jolted awake. "Company? What kind of company?" she whispered.

"This nice gentleman for one, but I suspect there are plenty more we haven't seen yet."

Ayleth looked to where Jocab was gesturing and sucked in a deep breath when she noticed the bow strung and arrow drawn.

"Wake the others and keep it quiet," the hooded figure said again.

Jocab rolled out of his bedding and gently woke the other three. Once they were all awake, the stranger commanded, "Now get dressed and pack up."

As Jocab rolled up his bedding, he spotted several hooded figures surrounding the campsite, with bows strung and arrows ready. They weren't trying to hide, but it was hard to see them in the darkness. Jocab was unsure of their motives, but felt they were not bandits or thieves. He admired their patience as they waited in the darkness.

It took only a few minutes for everyone to finish dressing and pack their bedding. The hooded figure had lowered his bow, but still had an arrow secured between two fingers as he held the bow. There was a relaxed confidence about him as he waited. He stood sideways to Jocab and the rest of the group, with his feet shoulder width apart. Jocab could see he was a skilled archer. He wondered how fast the archer could draw an arrow if needed. Hopefully, he would never know.

Jocab finished packing and shouldered his pack and watched as Donav and Estellia shouldered theirs a few seconds later. Jocab looked at Edmond and Ayleth. They already had their packs on and were waiting for the rest. Jocab turned to the hooded figure and nodded. "We are ready."

The hooded figure motioned to a comrade in the distance, who quivered his arrow and unstrung his bow in a quick and fluid motion. As he approached, he uncoiled a rope at his side and held it out. "Please put your hand in this."

Jocab noticed several leather straps intertwined in the rope. Knowing there was no other option, he placed his hand through the loop. The stranger pulled on the strap and the loop tightened against his wrist. A few more tugs here and there, and Jocab's right hand was bound to the rope.

The stranger went down the length, adding Ayleth, Donav, Estellia, and finally Edmond.

They stood a meter apart from one another with their right hands secured to the rope. The loop was binding but not enough cut off their circulation. Satisfied with their capture, the hooded figure approached. "I'm trusting you to behave yourselves. Please don't dishonor that trust or someone will get hurt."

Jocab looked at his friends before replying, "We will not give you any problems."

The hooded figure nodded in acknowledgment. "Good, now let's move."

The stranger led them along what appeared to be a small game trail toward the mountain north of them. Jocab was curious, as the path they were going to take was further east. The map showed they needed to go around the mountain to reach the settlement. Confused, he settled in for the long walk. As he walked, he spotted three more hooded figures in the distance, making him wonder just how many there were. His mind wandered back to their capture. What did they want and why had they apprehended them? Jocab was positive they had been observing them for a couple of days.

They marched for several hours, gaining altitude along the way. No one said anything as they plodded along. The sky was just welcoming the dawn when the hooded figure spoke. "See that rise there? We need to get to the other side of that before it gets light out. I don't want the soldiers to see where we went."

They raced the dawn for another half hour before successfully crossing over the rise. Afterward, they relaxed their pace as they dropped into a ravine on the other side. They followed the ravine as it traveled horizontally to the mountain, with an enormous cliff rising a half a kilometer on one side. Large crevices worked back into the side of the cliff and large rocks lay scattered nearby, where they had fallen from above. Jocab was deep in thought and had to stop immediately to avoid running into the stranger leading them. Looking around, he noticed they stood in front of a large crevice about forty meters in height and five meters deep. The hooded figure approached again. "I'm going to untie you now. Take your packs off and carry them for the next part," he said. "Do not misjudge my trust as weakness."

Minutes later, they were free of the rope and had unslung their packs. Jocab found it cumbersome to hold it and slung it over one shoulder. The others took their cue from him and followed suit. Satisfied, the hooded figure walked into the crevice and disappeared. Jocab shared a glance with his fellow captives before following. Solid walls rose on both sides and narrowed quickly. He had to turn sideways for the last two meters and drag his pack beside him. Just as he reached the end, there was a meter tall opening at his feet. Jocab dropped his pack down in front of him and pushed it through the hole. He worked himself down on his hands and knees and started forward. He had to push his pack in front of him while he crawled in the darkness. Jocab struggled for about two meters before he pushed past a thick leather curtain. Working his way through, he saw he had entered a small cavern about four meters wide. Torchlight created shadows around the cavern and disappeared into the darkness above. The hooded stranger stood next to four other woodsmen, one of them holding the burning torch aloft.

Jocab shoved his pack against the wall and grabbed the next one being pushed through at his feet. He placed it next to his and helped Ayleth to her feet. She took a moment to get her bearings before moving out of the way. Jocab smiled at her before grabbing the next pack at their feet. He continued helping Estellia, Donav, and Edmond as they entered the cave.

After Edmond was safely through, the hooded stranger signaled to a crew member. Two broke ranks and headed deeper into the cave, returning with a large water jar and two cloth sacks. They opened the sacks, revealing dried meat and dried fruit. The hooded stranger stepped forward. "Please help yourselves," he said as he grabbed a piece of dried fruit." We have a lot more walking ahead."

Jocab grabbed his cup before helping himself. Ayleth followed, and soon all of them were sitting in their packs, enjoying a bite to eat. While they ate, two more hooded figures made their way into the cavern, pushing the leather curtain aside as they entered. "Clever," Edmond commented quietly.

"It sure is," Donav replied. "Simple and effective."

"Everyone doing alright?" Jocab asked.

They all nodded with a "yes" and "doing well" sprinkled in between bites.

"Good. Let's try to rest while we can." He leaned back against the wall to close his eyes when another figure appeared through the opening. He watched as they stood and brushed themselves off and walked over to the leader.

Jocab could hear them talking. "We've finished covering our tracks. Bert and Gus will stay behind and monitor the soldiers."

"Thanks, Jerry. Good job. Get some food and rest."

Jocab watched Jerry grab a handful of dried fruit, a cup of water, before he disappeared deeper into the cave.

Jocab didn't realize he had dozed off until Ayleth shook him awake. "You're needed."

Jocab sat up and rubbed the sleep from his eyes. The hooded figure knelt beside him and pulled his hood back. He had shoulder length black wavy hair and a crooked nose, obviously broken at some point. "My name is Garron. I am the captain of this merry band," he said as he waved his hand toward those behind him. "The soldiers chasing you are no longer a threat. They will track you to your campsite, but no further. My men have hidden our trail here."

Jocab nodded. "Thank you. We've been losing ground to them daily."

"We noticed that too. I'm sorry we had to take you by force. But it was necessary to evade the soldiers."

"What happens now?"

Garron smiled. "We keep going. We have a day's walk through the mountain."

"And then?"

"I believe you will reach your destination."

"My destination?" Jocab asked. "And you just happen to know my destination?"

Garron gave a deep chuckle, ignoring Jocab's sarcasm. "I believe I do," he said as he stood up, motioning to his men. "All right, time to move everyone."

Garron's men climbed to their feet and gathered their belongings. Jocab stood and swung his pack up onto his shoulders. He was settling the straps into place when Garron spoke. "You must leave those here."

Jocab didn't hide his anger. "You're kidding me?" His tone harsh.

"There are places where your packs will not fit through."

Jocab glared at Garron as he dropped his pack in front of him. "I have stuff that I will not leave behind," he replied, daring Garron to deny him.

Garron locked eyes with an icy stare, his men shifting their feet back and forth in discomfort. Jocab could see a few slowly reach for what he assumed were weapons. Garron conceded and broke eye contact. "Get our friend here, an empty sack he can use." He looked at Jocab again. "Grab your food and water and take only what you must. Leave the rest against that wall."

Jocab, not realizing he was holding his breath, let out a long sigh. "Thank you, but we will need two sacks please."

Garron nodded and spoke to the room at large. "Two sacks for our friends, please. And gloves if we have them."

Jocab and Edmond started rummaging through their packs. They wrapped the telescope, notebooks, and metal box some of their bedding before placing them into the sack. Donav and Ayleth busied themselves by gathering their meager food supplies and placing them in the second sack.

Garron handed out gloves to them. "Please put these on. They will protect your hands as you follow the guidelines."

"Guidelines?" Edmond asked.

"Yes," Garron replied as he reached down and grabbed a rope lying on the ground. "We will all hold on to this. It is your lifeline to the world outside. As long as you're holding it, you can find your way out."

Jocab hadn't paid attention to the rope when they entered. The rope, secured to the wall next to the small entrance they used, disappeared down the tunnel. Edmond leaned over to Jocab. "Rather clever idea. Always have a way out. Even in total darkness."

"Exactly!" Garron replied, overhearing the conversation. "You lose the rope, and we might find you months later by the smell of your decaying body." He paused for effect before continuing. "It is impossible to find your way out in the dark. Even with a torch, it is easy to get lost."

Turning to his men, Garron announced. "Let's move."

Garron lit a second torch before giving it to the man in the back. He instructed one torch up front and another in the rear. The lead man grabbed the rope and headed down the tunnel, holding the torch high overhead. The rest grabbed the rope and followed leaving about a meter between them. Jocab found himself behind two men carrying the sacks of extra torches. He was thankful for their foresight. The thought of stumbling through the darkness with only a rope as a guide terrified him.

CHAPTER 27

Several hours and a few torches later, Garron called for a brief rest. Jocab set his sack down and immediately checked on his friends. Ayleth smiled as he handed her his canteen, and Jocab smiled back. He lived for that smile and would take it any day, anytime, anywhere. While Ayleth took a drink, Jocab helped Donav hand out some dried fruit. "We need to keep our strength for whatever is ahead."

"You're not thinking there will be trouble, are you?" Ayleth asked, concern in her voice.

"No. There's still a long walk ahead of us."

Ayleth nodded as she stuffed a few bites into her mouth.

Jocab continued to check on the others. Edmond had taken up the rear and had unloaded his food and water for the others. Estellia smiled her thanks to Jocab as she held up a handful of dried. Jocab smiled back. "How is it back here?"

Edmond sat against the cave wall. "As good as can be expected."

Jocab patted his friend on the shoulder. "I figured. How are the others doing?"

Edmond shrugged. "They're fine. We're just holding on to the rope while we walk."

Jocab looked back down the tunnel. He spotted several of Garron's men resting with the last man holding the torch aloft.

"They giving you any trouble?" he asked

"They've been keeping a safe distance and leaving us alone."

Jocab nodded, relieved. "That's good."

"How are things up there?" Edmond asked, nodding toward the front.

"No different."

"Any idea how much further?"

"Garron said a day's walk. But who knows what time it is."

"Yeah, it's hard to tell how much time has passed."

"I know the feeling. I'll be happy when this part is over."

Garron hollered to the group, ending Jocab's and Edmond's conversation. "All right, the next part is along the edge of a pool of water. Watch your step so you don't fall in."

Everyone stood up and prepared for the next leg. Jocab gave Edmond a hand up before making it back next to Ayleth. He secured the food and canteen inside his sack and lifted it to his shoulder.

They each grabbed the rope again and set off down the passage. A hundred meters later, they entered a huge cavern that disappeared into the darkness. Jocab could see the torches reflecting off the water to his left. They made their way along a narrow ledge, a half meter wide, against the cavern wall. The ledge ended abruptly where it sloped down toward the water several meters below. Jocab wondered how big the cavern was when the rope suddenly jerked left, shoving him over the side. He scrambled to keep his grip on the rope as he slid down the incline. He said a quick prayer for Ayleth as she had followed him off the ledge. Jocab manage to wrap his arm around the rope just before he slammed into the ground. At the same time, he heard three splashes as several men fell into the water. Hoping Ayleth held on, Jocab twisted his body to see who fell in. He was relieved to see Ayleth grasping the rope with one hand while she struggled to get her feet under her. Behind her, Estellia was sitting on her bottom, half off the ledge. Edmond, behind Estellia, pulled hard on the rope to keep it as taut as possible. Jocab shifted to get a better look below him where he saw Donav and two guards struggling to exit the water. They attempted to climb the rocky edge, only to slide back in. Jocab knew that everyone, including himself, would need help to get back to the ledge. He kept a firm hold on the rope and laid flat against the incline to keep from sliding any further. "Just hang on till they get to us."

Ayleth looked at the water below. "Don't worry your little head. I'm not going anywhere. I kind of like it right here."

Jocab couldn't help but laugh. He loved that she always kept her sense of humor. Jocab watched Garron's men throw a line and rescue the three from the water. His respect for Garron increased when they rescued those in the water first instead of those closest to the ledge. Only after everyone was safe and away from the water did Garron call another stop. "Let's take an inventory. Who slipped and what got wet? Did anyone get seriously injured?" he called out.

Jocab looked at Donav. "You holding up?"

"I'm soaked from head to toe," he said with a half-smile. "I have a couple of scrapes and a few bruises. Nothing serious."

"Estellia, how about you?"

Estellia rubbed her side. "A few scrapes and bruises."

"Nothing serious then?" Both shook their heads no. "That's good news. Ayleth and I both got banged up, but not bad. I'll see if they have any dry clothes for Donav and some salve for all our scrapes." Jocab searched out Garron in the dim light of the torches. He found him standing alone as his men took stock of their situation. "Garron, we need dry clothes for Donav and some salve for some cuts and scrapes."

Garron reached into the bag he was carrying, pulled out a small container, and handed it to Jocab. "Here. Take this. Hold on to it in case you need to apply more later."

Jocab took the salve. "Thank you. Do you have something dry for Donav? He will catch a fever if he stays in his wet clothes."

Garron thought for a few seconds before removing his long, hooded coat. "This is the best I can offer."

Jocab took the coat and nodded. "Thanks. We can make it work." He returned to the group and handed Ayleth the salve. "Would you and Estellia please help each other with your cuts and scrapes?"

Ayleth smiled at Jocab. "Of course."

Jocab leaned in and kissed her. "Thanks, Sweetheart."

He turned to Donav. "This is the best they have," he said, holding the coat up.

Donav pursed his lips. Jocab could tell he was unhappy but acknowledged there was no alternative. "Thanks, it will have to do."

Donav struggled out of his wet coat and shirt before donning the long coat. Once it was over his shoulders, he turned his back on the group and stripped his pants off. A few more seconds and he had fastened the buttons and tied the straps around his waist. He turned around and held his hands out from his sides.

Edmond commented to Estellia. "That looks a little big on

him, don't you think?"

Estellia gave a wicked smile. "Just a little. He might grow into it though."

Donav sighed. "I'm so glad my predicament is providing you some entertainment."

Edmond gave a small laugh. "Sorry, Donav."

Ayleth interrupted any further chiding when she held the salve out to Donav and Jocab. "Your turn, guys."

They both reached their hands out, took a liberal helping of salve, and started applying it where needed.

Once they were all done, Jocab placed the salve in his bag and checked on the telescope. He pulled it out, unwrapped it, and ran his hands over the exterior and the lenses for any damage. He was wrapping it back up when Edmond knelt beside him. "Did it survive?"

"Yeah, it looks good so far. I have no way to check the optics until we set it up again."

"Did you shake it?"

Jocab gave a quick laugh. "No."

Edmond smiled. "Maybe you should."

Jocab gave it a small shake, being extra careful not to drop it. He smiled when nothing rattling inside.

"I need all eyes and ears on me," Garron shouted, loud enough to get everyone's attention. "First, thank you to those that gave up their coats. Second, while our food survived, the extra torches did not. Both sacks of torches got wet when Willie and Justin took a bath."

A few of the men groaned.

"I don't need to tell you what that means. It is vital to keep hold of the rope once the torches burn out." Garron waited for the mumbling to cease before continuing. "With limited time, we'll be picking up the pace. I'd like to get as far as possible before we lose our light. Any questions?"

All of Garron's men shook their heads.

"Then grab the rope and let's get moving."

They made it another hour before the lead torch sputtered and died. Garron had the torch from the rear brought up to the front immediately. As the torch passed him, Jocab figured it wouldn't last much longer.

Garron pushed the men forward for another fifteen minutes when the second torch started sputtering. At that point, he called a halt to eat and rest. "Last chance to eat or drink before we lose the torch. I suggest you sit on the rope so you can find it easily in the dark."

Jocab pulled the sack open and was reaching for the food when he felt the metal box with his hand. He sucked in his breath and froze. Ayleth leaned into him and whispered in his ear. "What is it?"

He put his mouth up next to her ear. "Atomic Torchlite!" he whispered so only she could hear.

Ayleth's eyes got wide as she realized what he was saying. "Do you think it would be safe?"

"No, I'm not sure. But I sure don't want to stumble through the dark holding a rope."

Ayleth stood still, thinking things through. "Do it!" she urged.

Without further delay, Jocab pulled the metal box out and opened it. The shadows from the cave walls were closing in quickly as the distant torch struggled to stay alive. Jocab could hardly see anything as he reached inside the box, his fingers fumbling for the device.

"Garron!" he called out. "I have something that can help."

Garron took the dying torch and made his way toward Jocab. "What is it?"

"First, I need you to guarantee our safety."

"You've always had that guarantee. My men and I will not hurt you," he spoke as the torch burned itself out.

Jocab couldn't see anything. It felt as if the cave walls around him fell away. He squeezed his eyes closed for a few seconds before waving his hand in front of his face. Jocab couldn't see it. The darkness was complete, threatening to overcome him. He heard Garron somewhere in the darkness. "Whatever you got, now would be a good time."

"All right," Jocab said as he felt inside the box. "Have your men look away from me and close their eyes."

"Are you serious?" Garron replied, his voice higher with each word.

"Yes, but only for a second."

"Alright everyone, look away from him and close your eyes."

Jocab fumbled in the box with his fingers. Grasping the torchlite, he placed his fingers over the front lens to dampen the brightness and pushed the button on the back. The light exploded between Jocab's fingers. Even with his fingers over the lens, it was brighter than the torches. Garron and several of his men gasped in disbelief.

Jocab slowly removed his fingers from the front of the lens to allow their eyes to adjust to the brightness while he smiled at Garron. "Will this work?"

Garron, eyes wide, stared at Jocab. He could not find his voice. He finally worked his jaw closed and nodded.

Jocab leaned over to Ayleth. "Can you hold this? I want to put the box back."

She smiled another radiant smile that took his breath away. "Why sure, I'd be happy to."

Jocab closed the metal box and quickly placed it in the bag. Garron's men crowded around to see how the bright light worked.

Jocab looked at Garron. "How do you want to do this?"

Garron continued to stare at the light with eyes as big as saucers. He finally gained control over his senses and asked, "What are you suggesting?"

"I'm holding the torchlite."

"Agreed. That it? Nothing more?"

"Once we get out of here, you will answer all my questions."

Garron nodded, "You have my word."

CHAPTER 28

They were all exhausted when they exited the tunnel. Garron told Jocab that the cave structure originally started out as a mine. Over the years, they had tunneled throughout the mountain in search of precious metals and found it riddled with natural caves. Eventually, they found a way that allowed them to navigate through the mountain. Jocab admired the strategic advantage it provided. Besides eliminating the long trips around, it afforded them a base of operations on that side.

Jocab stepped away from the entrance and breathed in the fresh air. It was chilly with the sun setting in the distance. He took a few minutes to enjoy the breeze on his face as he scanned the valley below. A tiny village sat a kilometer away, the rooftops mingling with the trees. He could smell the smoke from the chimneys, and it drifted upward in their direction.

Garron stepped up next to Jocab. "I'm looking forward to eating something other than road rations."

Jocab barked a laugh. "Yeah, me too."

They stood together, enjoying the sunset as they waited for everyone to exit the cave before heading toward the village. That was when Jocab realized Garron was no longer treating them like captives. It had happened sometime after the torches had burned out. Jocab smiled to himself as he patted the torchlite in his pocket as he followed Garron down the trail.

Garron reached the village first and waited for Jocab and his companions. His men smiled as they continued on. "When we get inside, please let me do the talking," Garron said. "Folks here are leery of strangers."

"Had some trouble in the past?" Jocab inquired.

"Once or twice. It only takes once though."

"Ain't that the truth. We had our share in Cumber."

"You're from Cumber? That's quite a trip north."

"Most of us are. Estellia is from Avalon."

Garron's eyebrows shot up. "Seat of power. I cannot wait to

hear your story. Maybe I'll be there when you share it with the elders."

Jocab smiled but said nothing as the caught up. "Thanks for waiting," Edmond said as he adjusted the sack on his shoulder.

"No problem. Garron advised us to mind our manners and let him take the lead."

Edmond raised an eyebrow. "Had a few rotten apples before?"

Garron nodded. "A few."

Donav, who was standing behind Edmond, spoke up. "We'll follow your lead."

Garron nodded. "Thank you. This way, please."

Garron led them between two buildings and into a central courtyard before turning right. Jocab and his companions had their heads on a swivel as they looked around. The square was about hundred meters wide, with the buildings along the edges. Additional buildings made their way into the trees, with their rooftops blending into the scenery. Jocab heard a hammer striking an anvil and quickly spotted the blacksmith's shop across the courtyard. Next to the blacksmith's shop looked to be the tanner. Large pieces of leather were stretched and drying. Jocab watched Garron's men scatter to the different buildings or homes up behind the courtyard.

Several pairs of eyes in the shadows followed them from different doorways and windows. A few young children ventured out to stare wide eyed at the strangers.

After passing two buildings, Garron climbed the steps and pushed open the door with Jocab following behind him.

Upon entering, Jocab could see it doubled as an inn and the local pub. Garron was already at the counter. "Ian. Can we get a few rooms for our guests?"

Ian's eyebrows crawled up his forehead as he looked Jocab's way. "Guests?"

Garron brow furrowed. "I wouldn't be asking if they weren't. They'd be locked in the cellar."

Ian gave Garron a long look before relenting. "How many do you need?"

"Give me three please."

"I only have two. Leaky roof in the other."

Garron nodded. "Two will have to do."

"Upstairs on the right," he announced to the group.

Garron turned to Jocab. "Get settled and catch some sleep. Ian will bring some food shortly. I'll be back in the morning."

Jocab woke to the sound of the roosters in the distance. He opened his eyes, feeling very refreshed. He had almost forgotten how nice a bed was. Ayleth, sleeping soundly, had her arm over his shoulder. He slowly turned to lie on his back while being careful not to disturb her. Jocab smiled when he heard Ayleth quietly snoring in his ear. He tried unsuccessfully to turn his head far enough to see if she was drooling on the pillow. The thought alone caused him to laugh to himself. There was nothing more personal than seeing your significant other sound asleep, snoring, and drooling.

Jocab lay there for a few minutes before deciding it was best to get up. Sliding out from underneath her arm, he sat up and padded over to a small washroom. He took his time splashing water across his face and taking care of his morning business. He was thankful for the washroom. Some places still required the trip to the outhouse or placed a chamber pot in a corner of the room.

Ayleth was sitting up and smiling when Jocab returned. He smiled back. "We have to get one of these in our next house."

Ayleth's smile disappeared at the thought of their house reduced to ashes. "You think so?" she said absentmindedly.

Jocab saw the change in her face and wrapped her in a hug. "I'm so sorry. That must have been traumatic for you."

Ayleth nodded as she buried her head in his shoulder. "I was so scared," she mumbled, fighting back tears. "I thought I lost you…"

Jocab let go and knelt beside the bed. Their eyes level. "Well, they couldn't get rid of me that easily. Remember, I'm the offspring of the gods."

Ayleth laughed aloud. "Don't let that go to your head. Cause I'll be happy to beat that ego right out of you."

A knock on the door interrupted their laughter. Jocab opened the door to find Garron standing in the hallway. "Good morning. I hope you slept well?"

Jocab stood back and motioned him to enter. "Very well, thank you."

Garron stepped inside and nodded to Ayleth before replying, "That's good. We'll be traveling again today."

"Oh?" Jocab answered, his voice rising in question as he closed the door.

Garron grinned. "We have a half a day's travel before we arrive at our destination."

Jocab met his grin with one of his own. "And where might that be?"

Garron gave a short laugh. "You know exactly where we are going, and they are expecting you."

"Sent a runner already?" Ayleth asked from across the room.

Garron nodded. "Last night. They returned just before dawn."

Jocab looked at Ayleth to guage her reaction. She gave a small smile and shrugged. He turned back to Garron. "So, when do we leave?"

"We can leave after breakfast."

"Few hours walk?"

"No, we'll be on horseback."

Ayleth stood, grabbed Jocab's arm, and smiled. "That's a delightful change."

Garron opened the door to leave. "I'll be downstairs getting breakfast."

Jocab nodded. "Sounds good. I'll let the others know."

Solomon leaned over the table as he spoke. "We need to go after them," he said fervently. "We cannot let them get away. They know too much already."

"I agree, and they are smart enough to fill in the blanks," Damon replied.

"Fill in the blanks!" Solomon almost shouted. "Those wretched heretics will fill everyone's minds with more poison," his arms getting more animated by the second. "We must go there and demand their return now!"

Farzod sat back in his chair and smiled to the room at large. "Solomon, you've always had a flair for dramatics. I think we ignore them and start thinking about how we can get ahead of what's coming."

Geoffery nodded his head in agreement. He looked at Solomon

as he placed elbows on the table. "We already have to make adjustments. Let's make a plan before that thing arrives."

"Agreed. Better to mold the story. We will keep our credibility that way."

Geoffery joined in. "Tell everyone we found a new discovery someplace. Then we can adjust our teaching to fit the new narrative."

"But we know where they are going," Solomon countered, trying to refocus on Jocab. "We have to stop them. They will destroy everything we've built here."

Farzod frowned. "Forget them. If we don't get out in front of what's coming, this house of cards will fall. Regardless of whether we have them in custody."

"Exactly," Geoffrey replied. "We've got an uphill battle. And only a few more months to figure things out."

"We have," Damon replied.

"What?" Solomon asked, perplexed.

"It's 'We have', not 'We've got'."

"Whatever..." Solomon said dismissively, while waving his hand in the air. "I cannot believe you pick now to give us grammar lessons."

Damon chuckled, but said nothing more.

Athels sat forward in his chair. "That's enough, all of you. We've been going around in circles for the last hour."

The room quieted as all eyes focused on Athels.

"Here's what we are going to do. Solomon, you can take the guard in Liberty and head north. See if you can persuade our lost souls to return. And by the gods, you will not engage in armed conflict." He paused, looking directly at Solomon. "Am I clear?"

Solomon fought for control as he spoke between gritted teeth. "Crystal."

"Good. May the gods bless you with success."

Solomon stood and glared at the faces around the table before turning and exiting the room.

"Now," Athels said after Solomon left the room. "How do we get out in front of this?"

CHAPTER 29

They had been riding all morning, passing several wagons along the way. The road cut through the woods, running parallel to a small river. Tree branches stretched forth fighting for the sunlight and leaving the travelers to ride in the cool shade.

Garron, Jocab and Ayleth rode three abreast with the others taking up the rear. Garron leaned toward Jocab and Ayleth before speaking. "We'll be exiting the trees in a few minutes. Once we do, you'll see the town off to your left."

"How much further after that?" Ayleth asked.

"About two hours."

"That'll be nice. I'm done traveling."

Jocab smiled. "Me too. I was done weeks ago."

As they neared the forest's edge, Jocab could see the sun shining in the distance. It reminded him of when they exited the cave the previous day. The small opening grew bigger and brighter as they got closer. Jocab squinted both eyes, almost shutting them to keep out the afternoon sun. The horse continued as his eyes adjusted to the brightness. Glancing over, he noticed Garron had pulled his hood up over his head. "That really comes in handy against the sun."

"Yeah, it sure does," Garron replied from within his hood.

Jocab looked down the road after his eyes adjusted to the light. They widened like saucers at the same time he heard Ayleth gasp beside him. He was attempting to regain control of his lower jaw when Edmond exclaimed, "By the gods, there are two of them."

Garron pulled his hood back, a grin plastered across his face.

Estellia burst out. "I knew it. The High Priests are such lying sacks of horse dung."

Edmond laughed at her outburst. "That's putting it mildly. I'd say, chicken poop. It stinks more."

Two metal structures gleamed in the distance, the afternoon sun reflecting off their smooth surface. Multiple two and three-story buildings grew up around the structures, with wide streets and a central courtyard.

Garron looked at Donav. "You don't look too surprised."

Donav gave a weak smile before admitting. "We've known you were here for quite some time. Most people who want to avoid the temple disappear north."

Jocab turned to Donav in surprise. Garron nodded in agreement. "Very few will return. If they do, it's usually to collect their loved ones."

Donav sighed. "The temple does not tolerate heretics. If they don't burn them at the stake, they will send them to the mines east of here."

"Others come for different reasons," Garron added. "Some are fortunate to travel freely between the two."

"That is true. There is some trade between us. We used to get most of our heavy metals from here before we set up our own mining operations."

Edmond frowned in disgust. "The temple has its own mining operations?"

"Yes. It's an ugly side of the temple that I've never been fond of it myself. It's one reason I am happy to be assigned to Cumber."

"Really? If you're lucky enough to not be executed, you're blessed with a long life of hard labor," Edmond replied, the sarcasm dripped from his voice.

Donav was silent for a few seconds before replying. "I understand your feelings, Edmond, and I feel the same disdain. I joined the temple to help people. The temple happens to be the best avenue for me to do that. You can agree or disagree with the Temple, its scriptures, or its methods, but it is what we have, and by the gods, I will use it."

Edmond locked eyes with Donav and saw nothing but honesty. He lowered his gaze and relented. "I'm sorry, Donav."

Donav nodded. "No apology needed. Your passion is just."

The team sat there as the uncomfortable silence hung around them before Garron broke the spell. "Shall we continue our journey?"

Everyone nodded, nudging their horses forward. They were wrapped up in their own thoughts when Jocab asked, "So how big is the settlement here?"

Garron thought about it. "Settoo has a population of almost five thousand."

"Settoo?" Ayleth asked.

"Settlement Two. But we call it 'Settoo'. Easier on the tongue."

Ayleth gave a small laugh. "Sounds logical. Is it just Settoo and the mining town we left?"

"No. We have a few small towns or villages scattered around. There's several along the mountains to the north and west. We try to leave a buffer zone."

"Buffer zone?"

"Liberty controls the farming lands to the north and south of the city, and the temple has their mines northeast of here. The woods provide a good buffer."

"Why a buffer zone?"

"The temple holds sway over everything from Liberty south. They know we exist but leave us alone. Works out for both of us."

"They don't divulge your existence either," Donav added. "That's why we're able to coexist."

"Sad, but true. Otherwise, we would have to maintain a standing army."

Jocab, who was listening to the exchange, replied, "This truce cannot last forever."

Garron nodded his head in agreement. "Very true. And I dread that day."

Garron led them through the city streets to a stable at one end of the central courtyard. They dismounted and led the tired horses inside. A few stable hands were sitting on hay bales, playing cards. Upon seeing the group enter, they jumped up to assist.

Garron smiled at them, "Good afternoon, gentlemen."

The tallest boy smiled back. "Hello Garron."

"Why hello, Leon. I've not seen you in a while."

"I've been working with the blacksmith for the last couple of months. I'd be there today, but the bellows broke. Thought I'd stop by and say hi."

"I can see it in your arms. Swinging a hammer?"

Leon stood taller at the compliment. "That, and a lot of lifting and carrying things."

"Can you guys handle these tired mounts? We've been on the road since morning."

Leon smiled. "Sure, we can. We'll get them rubbed down, watered, and fed."

"Thanks. Much appreciated."

After leaving the stables, Garron led them to a small eatery for an early dinner. Once seated, Edmond leaned into Jocab and asked in a low tone, "Any chance we can set up the telescope today? It's been a while since we tracked that thing."

Jocab glanced at Garron, who was sitting at the other end, before replying. "I'm certain we can."

Edmond nodded and went back to focusing on his food. Both glanced at Garron, relieved to see he showed no interest in their conversation. As the food disappeared from their plates, Leon approached the table. Garron looked up and smiled. "You want to join us?"

"It smells good, but I promised the guys I'd hang out with them. I came to notify you the elders want to see you."

Garron shook his head. "Figures. Can't even wait for me to get a hot meal," he replied, his laughter forced.

Leon shrugged his shoulders and smiled. Garron took a last drink of his ale and stood. "Sorry guys. Please enjoy the rest of your food. I'll be back shortly."

The group nodded as Garron turned and followed Leon out the door.

Leon assisted them with getting settled in a small house several streets back from the central courtyard before heading off with his friends. It was big enough to accommodate the entire group, with a large central room and several small bedrooms along the sides. Donav and Edmond were relaxing at the table as Estellia and Ayleth rummaged through the kitchen. "Found it!" Estellia hollered as she held up a teapot. Jocab, who was kneeling over the fireplace, looked over his shoulder and replied. "Good, the fire is ready."

Estellia walked over to the kitchen sink and turned on the faucet. Cold water flowed from the spout. "It sure beats pumping water from a well."

Jocab nodded as he came over to the sink. "It's because they have that big water tank out there. Put it high enough and gravity does the rest."

Ayleth had just placed the kettle next to the fire when Garron entered. All eyes turned in his direction. Garron plopped into an empty chair. "The chief elder would like to see you tonight rather than in the morning," Garron said to the room at large. "I tried to postpone it, but he's quite stubborn."

Donav chuckled lightly. "That seems to be the way of things. Good thing we didn't have any plans for tonight."

Jocab smiled as he leaned against the kitchen sink. "How soon?"

"Noon yesterday," Garron replied sarcastically.

Donav stood and offered Garron his hand. "Well then. Shall we get this over with?"

Garron grabbed his hand, letting Donav help him up. Estellia moved the kettle away from the flames, while Ayleth grabbed the poker next to the chimney and banked the fire.

CHAPTER 30

They followed Garron through the streets to one of the metal buildings. There was a giant staircase with broad steps that led to an entrance several floors up. "These are the original settlement pods," he said as they started climbing.

Donav nodded. "They built the temple next to the one in Avalon. They are on the same level."

Garron nodded in understanding. "They considered constructing a building next to the pods and connecting them."

"Why didn't you?"

"You still have to climb the stairs. You'd just do it inside a building rather than outside."

Jocab laughed. "Very true."

"And there are plenty of stairs to climb outside the temple too," Donav added.

Upon entering the pod, Jocab noticed that the hallway walls and ceilings looked to be a duplicate of the one in Avalon. He couldn't help but think about the entire structure being hard metal. Walls, floors, ceiling, and even doors. It felt different from the temple. The temple seemed to flaunt the wealth. Here, it was just part of the city.

Garron saw the wonder on their faces and said, "We have residents that live above and below the main floor here. We have designated this floor for governing the city."

Ayleth looked back at the stairs. "I'm not sure I would want to climb those stairs, only to descend again to reach my home."

Garron gave a quick laugh. "I think that is why so many choose to live outside the pods."

"Yeah. I bet. Those stairs got old really quick."

"It has its trade-offs. The pods do offer amenities that don't exist outside." Garron paused outside a door. "When we go in, please take a seat in one of the open chairs." He made sure everyone understood before he opened the door and entered. They followed him into a large rectangular conference room with a long oval table in the center. A well-dressed individual seated on the other side stood and welcomed them. "Please take a seat," he said. "I'm Harlen, the chief elder. I wish to thank you for coming at such a late hour."

Jocab and his companions introduced themselves as they grabbed a chair. "Thank you for seeing us." Jocab gave the room a quick glance before continuing. "I have a lot of questions."

Harlen leaned back and smiled. "I'm sure you do. I'll try to answer what I can. First, though, I need to hear your story."

Jocab took a deep breath and started with the wheel he had found in the sky. He talked about Edmond spotting the object arriving, the temple's attempt to arrest them, ending with the metal box and their flight north. Several of the team added bits and pieces to the story as he went along. Harlen paid rapt attention while keeping his questions to a minimum. "That's quite an adventure," Harlen commented. "I'm sure we'll have a long list of questions to ask in the coming days. But I'm guessing you also have questions of your own."

Jocab nodded and took a breath to reply. Harlen smiled and politely held up his hand, forestalling him. "I figure it would be best for us to give you a quick history of ourselves first."

Jocab nodded his agreement. "Yes, thank you."

Harlen sat back and examined his guests. "Please understand, what I have to say goes against the temple's teaching." Harlen locked his gaze with Donav before continuing, "I hope it will not be an issue."

Donav gave a comforting smile. "I took some of my training in Liberty. I learned about Settoo and understand the differences you speak of."

"That makes things much easier. First, we call ourselves Settlement Two, or Settoo for short. Settlement one has always been the city of Avalon."

"Settlement?" Edmond asked.

"The wheel in the heavens that Jocab speaks of. It's what's left over of the spaceship that brought us here. Once we arrived, the pods, like this one, separated from the ship and landed on Avalon.

Over the years, the pods have been dismantled for their metal. The original settlers were unaware of two things. One, that hard metals were difficult to come by, and two, the thicker atmosphere limited communications. They found that out after they landed. Since neither settlement had an ample source of iron, they were unable to fabricate most of the technology they brought with them."

Jocab nodded. "I've seen bits and pieces of that technology in the great library in Avalon, including communications devices. I think they called them radios."

"So you understand. After years of little to no communication, we grew apart. They created their religion and built their temple, while Settoo did not. Once they started pushing their belief, Settoo withdrew even further." Harlen turned to Donav. "Do you want to correct anything?"

Donav shook his head. "You're good so far."

"Today, the High Priests pretend we don't exist. They have removed Settoo from their maps and try to cover up our existence. They spread stories about murderers and thugs that live in the woods to the north. This helps keep the population from venturing into our territory and expanding in our direction."

"Eventually, this will change," Jocab said.

"I agree. There will come a time when we cannot coexist. By then, generations will have believed in the gods. I'm afraid that is when the real conflict will start. The further we go in time, the more firmly the temple's teachings become truth. These conflicting truths will clash at some point. I'm hoping the object you mentioned will be the catalyst that draws us together."

Donav gave a small laugh. "Or it will be what divides us further."

Jocab's eyes grew wide. "You know what it is?"

Harlen nodded. "From what you've said, I think it is another ship coming toward us."

Edmond leaned into the conversation. "Like the wheel?"

"I have not seen it, so I cannot be sure. You might tell me. What does the object look like through your telescope?"

"All we can determine from this distance is the brightness of the object, and that it gets brighter every ten hours. Once the brightness stops, it is slower than before."

"That sounds like the engine is slowing it down. You should be able to determine the shape of the ship as it gets closer. Have you figured out how much longer till it reaches us?"

Edmond shook his head. "I can't be certain because we haven't been able to track it since we left Jocab's family farm. We are hoping to set up the telescope tonight and get an update."

"Will it be difficult to make a determination once you view it again?"

"Not really. Just work out a few math equations."

"Based on your current data, what is the estimated time of arrival?"

"In three or four months."

Harlen grimaced. "That doesn't give us much time."

"Time for what?" Jocab inquired.

"To contact them and figure out what they want."

Donav gave a sideways smile. "It might be nice to give them a heads up on the politics and religion before they arrive."

Harlen nodded. "Something for us to think about. Jocab, you mentioned the metal box. Would you share more about it?"

"My father gave it to me before we headed north. It contains a map showing settlement two. We used that to come here."

"What else did it contain?"

Jocab was silent for a few moments, deciding just how much he should share. Harlen patiently waited. Ayleth leaned over and whispered, "I think we can trust him."

Jocab looked at her before turning back to Harlen. "A journal from my ancestor, Leah."

Harlen's eyebrows bounced off the ceiling before he gathered himself. "You're a descendant of Leah? Did you know history tells us she married the god Lip?"

"Yes, I read that. His full name was Lipinski."

"What else does it say?" Harlen asked.

"That they denied her having children until after they arrived. I've read just a few pages so far."

"I would love to see what it contains, if you are willing."

Jocab smiled before replying, "I'm sure we can arrange that."

Harlen leaned forward to ask another question when the door opened. Harlen's eyes shot up, fixing on a cloaked figure entering the room. "What's the meaning of this?"

All eyes turned to the stranger. "Sorry for the interruption," he said as he pulled his hood down. "But I think I can help."

Jocab gasped and jumped out of the chair. "Clancy!" he exclaimed, as he wrapped his arms around his brother. "What are you doing here?"

"I've been here for three years now," he replied, returning Jocab's hug. "Heard there was a Jocab here, and I knew it had to be you."

Harlen looked at the two standing together. "I see the resemblance now. You must be brothers. Please join us, Clancy. Jocab has told us quite a tale."

Clancy grabbed a chair. "Thank you," he replied as he squeezed in next to Jocab. "I can't wait to hear it for myself."

The two of them sat next to each other with huge smiles painted across their faces. Jocab had trouble staying focused, seeing his brother after all these years. "So where did this ship, that's heading toward us, come from?" he asked, finally getting his thoughts together.

"Our history records say we came from another world. One similar to ours, called Earth. We were the first generation ship sent to colonize the stars."

Edmond leaned forward. "Generation Ship?"

"Yes, it took almost two-hundred years for it to arrive. Multiple generations lived and died on it during their long voyage. Their only hope was believing their descendants would eventually set up home here on Avalon."

"So why is a ship still there?" Ayleth asked.

"They constructed the ship with seventy-two pods like this. All around the base of the ship. Once we arrived, the pods, by design, separated and became the landing craft."

"What happened to all the pods?" Edmond asked.

"Our records show a few didn't survive the descent and burned up in the atmosphere. They recycled most that survived for their metal content. I suspect others landed elsewhere and are thriving like we are."

"There are others we don't know about?" Ayleth asked, surprised.

"I assume there are several across the ocean. Maybe an additional one or two further east. We estimate four or five additional settlements, depending on how many pods survived entry."

"How did your two pods arrive here?"

"Avalon was the primary landing site, and this was an alternate. The original settlers here were expected to land at Avalon, but they had a steeper entry and when they realized they wouldn't make it, they detoured and landed here. It took several years to establish contact. By then, we'd already settled."

"Any contact with the other settlements?" Jocab asked, intrigued.

"Nothing. We sent a few expeditions east but found nothing. I don't think anyone has built any sailing ships big enough to cross the oceans."

Clancy laughed. "That's because the temple won't let them. If the people knew there was land beyond the horizon, they would have left yesterday."

Harlen nodded in agreement. "You may be right."

The conversation turned to small talk. Harlen listened for a while before calling an end to the meeting. "Thank you for coming."

With the meeting over, everyone headed for the door. Clancy put his arm around Jocab. "Join you?" he asked.

"Absolutely!" Ayleth exclaimed before Jocab could find his voice.

They were descending the stairs when Edmond announced. "Jocab is going to set up the telescope tonight. I need to get an update on the object approaching."

Clancy looked at Jocab. "Object?"

"We are tracking what Harlen says is a ship coming toward us."

Clancy stopped dead in his tracks. "A ship?"

"Oh yeah," Jocab said, smiling. "You missed that part of the meeting."

Clancy ruffled Jocab's hair. "And I knew you when."

Several of them laughed as Jocab attempted smooth his hair.

CHAPTER 31

Clancy was in awe as he looked through the telescope. Jocab showed Clancy some of the other astronomical sites in the night sky, while Edmond verified his finding of the incoming ship. Based on how much the ship had slowed, Edmond confirmed it would arrive in just under three months' time.

Ayleth and Jocab were cleaning up after lunch when Clancy entered. "Good afternoon, Clancy," Ayleth said, greeting him with a smile.

"Afternoon, everyone." Clancy said to the room at large. He hung his jacket on a peg beside the door, then turned to Edmond. "Hey Edmond, Harlen wants to see your findings if you're done."

"Sure, I finished them last night."

Estellia frowned and shook her head. "What happened to our quiet afternoon together? You promised a walk around the town this afternoon."

The pout in her voice tore at Edmond's heart. "Could we push it into the evening?"

Clancy shook his head. "Harlen is expecting you. Better to get it over with."

Estellia shot them a hard look, excused herself to the other room, and slammed the door.

Edmond sighed and stood. "Let's get this over with so I can try to salvage the evening with her."

Ayleth chuckled. "I'll talk to her, you get going."

The men gathered their jackets and headed out the door.

Harlen invited them to sit. "Thank you for seeing me again this afternoon. What did you find out?"

"It will arrive in just under three months."

"That doesn't give us much time."

Jocab asked, "Can we really send them a message?"

"It is possible we can communicate by laser. We'd need to set it up on a mountaintop and broadcast from there. That's the only way the signal can penetrate the atmosphere."

Edmond turned to Jocab. "You understand any of this?"

"No. Although, we can look it up in the library afterward."

Edmond stood and headed for the door. "You go ahead. I need to deliver on my date with Estellia."

They watched as Edmond exited before Clancy spoke. "What is a laser?"

Harlen closed his eyes while trying to figure out how best to explain things. "What types of communication are you familiar with?"

Jocab smiled. "I helped repair a voice communicator. They were running wires from Avalon to Liberty."

"Perfect," Harlen said. "Instead of sending the signal down a wire, we use a high-powered light to transmit it."

Jocab nodded, "That makes sense, but I'd like to read about it if possible."

"I'm sure there's an open terminal at the library you can use."

Clancy leaned forward. "What's required to send this message?"

"I need a few technicians to disassemble the laser, transport it, and set it up on a mountaintop."

"We can't do it from here?"

Harlen shook his head. "I'm not sure the signal can penetrate the atmosphere. We have to get to a higher elevation."

Jocab motioned to the sky. "Closer to up there?" he asked, smiling.

"Exactly." Harlen replied, standing up. "Thank you all for coming. I'll check with the technicians about moving the laser."

The morning arrived sooner than Jocab wanted. He was still half asleep as he tried to focus on breakfast. Clancy was due in a few minutes, and Jocab wanted to be more awake when he arrived. He looked at Donav, checking to see if he fared any better. Donav looked fine and smiled at Jocab while he finished chewing.

Clancy banged through the door with a severe case of morning person. Jocab groaned, thinking they needed a law against so much cheeriness first thing in the morning. Clancy, seeing Jocab's distress, smiled even bigger. "What's the matter, Jocab? Did my little brother get attacked by the grumpies?" he said with an emphasis on little.

Jocab harrumphed at Clancy. He had a fleeting image of Clancy's big dumb smile with a few missing teeth. It brought a small smile to his lips before Clancy turned to Ayleth. "He must not have gotten enough beauty sleep last night. Although, I'm not sure it would make him any prettier."

Jocab pursed his lips, remembering growing up with Clancy's unending banter. He took a deep breath and counted to three before letting it out slowly, forcing himself to relax. He tried to focus on what he might learn at the town library. Clancy had arranged access to a terminal, whatever that was. He told Jocab he would reveal everything when they reached Pod B. A letter differentiated each pod. Pod A contained the seat of government and several residences. Pod B contained more residences, the library, and other things Jocab didn't understand. Jocab continued to shake off the morning as he finished breakfast. A short time later, Jocab, Donav, and Clancy were heading down the street toward Pod B.

Jocab followed Clancy and Donav into the library. It was one floor below the main entrance. It surprised Jocab with how small it was. The library in Avalon was huge compared to here. This room was about ten meters wide and thirty meters long. While there were several bookshelves along the walls, it paled in comparison.

Clancy caught his look of disappointment and smiled. "Patience, brother, patience. There's more than meets the eye." He led them over to a meter wide table with a glass top and a single chair where he pushed a button on the side of the table. Jocab jumped back when the entire table lit up with a pale blue light. Clancy laughed. "This is a terminal. You can access everything about anything from here."

Jocab sat as Clancy guided him through the search menus, showing him how to access the materials from the console. Jocab was in awe as he flipped through the different tables and subjects available. "How is this possible?" he asked.

"There's a mainframe computer in the pod that has a copy of everything. A mainframe is a device that stores data electronically. This terminal connects to that mainframe."

"But how?" Jocab asked.

"You can read about it from here. You'll probably understand it better than me. I'm content to know that it works."

Jocab knew it was the best answer he would get. He turned toward the marvelous device and started flipping screens like Clancy had shown him. Jocab realized it was like turning pages in a book, but he only had to touch the glass to make it happen. He was so consumed by what he was reading and didn't notice when Clancy led Donav to another terminal.

Jocab surfaced when his stomach made a loud noise. He did not know how long he'd been reading. He just knew he was quite hungry. When he looked up, he saw Donav smiling at him. Jocab smiled back, stood and arched his back, stiff from sitting so long.

Donav stood and walked over to him. "Find anything interesting?"

"Yeah. I was reading about the torch we used in the caves. There's a little diamond battery. It has a radioactive core, whatever that is, that provides the power. Best I can understand is there is a very tiny piece of the sun inside the diamond. I don't understand most of it, but it's a start."

"Sounds very interesting," Donav replied. "Beyond my comprehension, but interesting."

"What did you read about?" Jocab asked.

"I was reading about the distant home we came from. Earth, they call it. Seems there were lots of different beliefs. Some believed in different gods. Several religions had only one god."

"Really? That explains it. One coin in the metal box has an inscription 'In God We Trust' on it."

"I remember. I would love to see it again sometime."

Jocab's stomach rumbled again. "Certainly. But we'd better get moving before my stomach shakes the entire pod. I'm starved."

Donav laughed as they both headed for the door. Jocab looked around to find Clancy, but it was obvious he had left a while ago.

Jocab and Donav returned from the library. Jocab reclined in his chair and kicked off his boots. He could hear Estellia and Edmond arguing in the other room. Luckily, he was far enough away that he could not hear the conversation. He sat back and closed his eyes and did his best to give them their privacy. A minute later, Jocab heard Edmond enter, grab his coat, and slam the door behind him on his way out.

Ayleth came out of the kitchen and sat next to Jocab. "Why don't you ask Donav to marry those two? They're going to fight like this until they tie the knot."

"You're kidding! You think that's why they are fighting?"

Ayleth nodded. "Trust a woman's intuition here. They'll be insufferable until then. Can't you see the pent-up frustration?" She leaned over and kissed him. "I know what I'm talking about. Now please, talk to Donav."

Solomon entered the central courtyard and advanced toward the Captain of the Guard. "Good morning, Kenneth. Are your men ready?"

Kenneth, a tall, broad-shouldered man with a narrow face and dark eyes, gave a quick salute before replying, "Yes, Your Excellence. Would you like to inspect the guard before we leave?"

Solomon glanced at the men standing at parade rest. "No," he said dismissively. "Not really. I'd prefer to get moving. We are losing daylight standing here."

Kenneth was aghast but kept his face neutral. He despised men that didn't respect those under them. "Yes, Your Excellence," he replied, before turning to the men behind him. "Mount up," he commanded.

They broke ranks and headed to their horses. It looked like organized chaos as the guards climbed into their saddles and formed two lines.

Two acolytes provided horses for both Solomon and Kenneth. Both men quickly climbed into their saddles.

Kenneth immediately turned his horse and rode down the lines, making a quick inspection before returning to Solomon at the front. "We are ready."

Solomon nodded and sat straighter in the saddle. "Let's go then."

Kenneth lifted his right hand in the air and brought it down quickly while he yelled, "Forward!"

Solomon dug his heels into the side of his horse as he matched the pace Kenneth had set. One hundred and fifty riders followed closely behind, their hooves clattering across the cobblestone as they exited the temple grounds.

CHAPTER 32

Jocab sat under a tree and enjoyed his lunch. He was watching the hustle and bustle as the town of Settoo started preparing for the wedding with childhood abandonment. The entire town came alive. Everyone tried to be a part of the ceremony. They hung decorations and banners in the central courtyard and strung an amazing string of lights across a small stage. A dance floor occupied one corner with a long pole in the center. They hung streamers from the pole to the edges of the dance floor. Tables and chairs were set up to prepare for a feast in honor of the bride and groom. Several men dug a large pit and were adding wood to a roaring fire. Jocab was told they would roast some animals called pigs in the pit. The men assured him he would love the taste.

On the other side of the courtyard, they erected the competition fields. Archery, ax throwing, log splitting and rock smashing were set up in one corner with wrestling, running, and jumping in the other.

The chief elder had advised Jocab that the newlywed couple would stay one week in the honeymoon suite on the top floor of Pod B overlooking the city. Several married couples were making arrangements to deliver meals during their blissful stay.

Estellia, Ayleth, and the town seamstress, Birgit, set about making the wedding dress. Since Estellia had arrived with only the clothes on her back, the town rescued her by providing a bolt of cloth so soft that Estellia felt guilty using it to make a dress. Birgit was a small, graceful woman. She floated from one place to another as she walked. Her dark brown eyes held a warmth that matched her beautiful smile. Auburn hair cascaded down her shoulders, framing her face and accenting her high cheekbones. Ayleth and Estellia noticed how infatuated the single men in town were with her. Both ladies spotted a few bold suiters openly vying for her hand.

Estellia leaned on Birgit and Ayleth to help her keep her sanity as the wedding day drew near. With the dress chosen, the three ladies were deep in pins, needles, and strips of cloth. Birgit seemed to thread them into an astonishing dress as if by magic. Estellia and Ayleth had the rudimentary skills necessary to make a standard outfit. Birgit, on the other hand, understood how to sculpt cloth to the human body, creating a masterpiece for the wearer. They watched as Birgit merged the best of both fashions from Avalon and Settoo. The dress was full around the hips with a meter long tail behind her. It was form fitting and narrowed into straps that ran over her shoulders to the back of her neck. While open in the front, it was high enough that it didn't reveal any cleavage. Something Estellia insisted on. "They are for my husband's eyes only. I'll not have every guy in attendance leering over them."

Several of the young ladies had gathered flowers and were making a wreath for Estellia's hair, keeping in contact with Birgit to make sure they matched the dress.

Harlen had given Edmond a pair of the same smooth cloth pants and a long double-breasted jacket. Both were midnight black with creases down the arms and legs. Someone else had donated a white pullover shirt with three black buttons up the front instead of the usual laces, making for a stunningly handsome groom.

The afternoon was bright as everyone gathered for the ceremony. The townsfolk were excited to see the outsiders get married. Donav stood on a raised pedestal in the middle of the stage. He smiled as he waited for the music to start. Several flutes and stringed instruments started a spirited little jig. Once the music started, both the bride and groom entered from opposite sides of the stage. Upon seeing them, the audience took their cue and stood. Edmond and Estellia strolling across the stage. Ayleth followed Estellia, while Jocab trailed behind Edmond. They timed their arrival together and stopped next to Donav, facing each other with Alyeth and Jocab standing a step behind.

Donav nodded to the musicians, and they wrapped up their tune. "Thank you, everyone, for coming to be part of this union between Edmond and Estellia," Donav said to the crowd. "It seems like only yesterday when Edmond walked into a small eatery and shared his first smile with Estellia. Over the next several months, it became apparent the two were in love and destined to be together. It is with great pleasure that I officiate this ceremony that unites them forever."

Donav nodded to Ayleth, who stepped forward and handed Donav a soft, braided white rope. Donav accepted the rope and said, "Edmond and Estellia, today you will no longer be individuals, but one couple. Please hold each other's left hand." Estellia and Edmond reached out and grasped each other's hand. Donav spoke again as he wrapped the rope around their clasped hands. "From this day forward, everything you do, you do together. You go with the knowledge that your decisions and choices affect both of you."

Donav continued as he tied their hands together. "The gods have gifted you and bound you to each other from this day forward. This binding does not make one servant to the other. It is a sign of equal devotion to each other, that the two of you have become one."

Donav finished tying their hands with a knot on top. "This knot represents your love, always tight. A forever covenant never to be undone. It is a symbol of the choice you make. To forever treat the other with honor and respect. Cherishing and caring for one another till the end of your days."

Donav placed his hands around the handfasting. "Do you affirm you are willingly entering this covenant and promise that you will love each other unconditionally for as long as you both shall live? To always be faithful to one another, in all circumstances?"

Donav paused for effect before glancing at Edmond. Edmond looked into Estellia's eyes and smiled. "I do."

Donav turned to Estellia, who smiled back at Edmond. "I do."

Donav broke into a large grin and addressed the crowd. "They have agreed to this covenant in front of you as witnesses. Please bring forth the drink the two shall share."

Jocab, who had been standing by Edmond's side, grabbed two glasses of ale from a small table nearby, and proudly handed them to Edmond and Estellia.

Donav looked at the happy couple as he spoke to the crowd. "These two shall share a drink to symbolize their covenant with each other."

Estellia and Edmond locked arms and took a drink. They lifted their glasses as the crowd hooted and hollered. After the crowd quieted down, Donav announced, "Let the glasses be a symbol of fidelity. Never to be touched by another!" Edmond and Estellia threw their glasses, smashing them against a pile of rocks behind Donav.

They spent the rest of the day in celebration. Food, dancing, and contests of strength and skill went long into the evening. Revelers who could not attend the wedding joined later. Jocab guessed everyone from Settoo eventually found a way to the festivities. Eventually, and with great fanfare, they led Edmond and Estellia away to the honeymoon suite. Even without the newlyweds, the celebration continued.

Harlen waved at Jocab as he started in his direction. Jocab, with his arm around Ayleth, waved back. Ayleth asked, "Who's waving?"

"Harlen."

Ayleth smiled as she saw him approach. "Good evening Harlen, Settoo can put on quite a party."

"That they can. We do it up big once or twice a year."

Ayleth could hear the pride in his voice.

Jocab nodded as he looked around. "We might steal a few of your ideas for back home."

Harlen laughed. "Feel free."

Ayleth could tell Harlen had a question but was hesitating. "You have something on your mind."

"I do," he replied with a little trepidation. "I wanted to see if you'd join the team signaling the incoming ship?"

"We'd be honored. I didn't know you had everything worked out."

"I had two technicians test the laser yesterday. I need your help to verify we send the signal in the right direction. The laser has a narrow beam. There's little room for error."

"How soon are you thinking?"

"I'm hoping you can leave tomorrow?"

Jocab took a deep breath and let it out slowly. "I'm afraid not. Edmond's been doing all the math calculations. You will need him to help pinpoint the direction."

Harlen gave a weak smile. "I was afraid of that. Looks like we will have to wait for the honeymoon week to end."

Jocab smiled back. "Afraid so, Harlen."

"Will he go? I mean, he just got married. Will he be willing?"

Ayleth placed a comforting hand on Harlen. "I'm sure he will."

"Good! Please enjoy the rest of your evening," he said before wandering off among the crowd.

CHAPTER 33

Jocab wrapped himself in a thick outer coat as he prepared to exit the tent. He could hear the wind blowing loudly as it passed overhead. The low roof allowed him to sit up, but not much more. Jocab finished buttoning the coat and stepped out into the wind. They were on a flat surface near the top of the mountain. There was no protection from the elements. Small rocks dotted the landscape, but little else. Several more low-profile tents were scattered nearby for the rest of the party and their equipment.

He saw the two engineers breaking down the laser. They had spent the last two days sending the message toward the incoming ship. Jocab and Edmond had used the telescope to help determine where to point the laser. Since they had no way of knowing if they succeeded, they sent the message multiple times throughout the day and night to increase the chances of their success.

The strong wind continued to buffet Jocab, the beginnings of a upcoming snowstorm approaching. He shoved his hands in his pockets as he tried to tuck himself deeper into his coat. Jocab knew they would receive several feet of snowfall before the day ended. Ayleth, Estellia, and Donav waited at the base camp just below the tree line with Clancy and Garron. Jocab guessed they would arrive before sundown unless someone twisted an ankle again. Jocab smiled to himself, remembering how Edmond had sprained his ankle the last time they were in the mountains. Edmond had to push himself hard for them to keep ahead of the soldiers. Jocab wondered what had become of the soldiers after they made their escape. He was certain they would have eventually overtaken them if Garron had not intervened.

Edmond brought Jocab back to the present when he handed him a warm cup of tea. "Here, drink this. Then you can help us break camp."

Jocab put his hands around the warm cup. "You just want to get back to Estellia."

"Uh, yeah! I'd rather sleep next to her than you any day."

Jocab laughed, almost spilling the tea. "You got me there."

The sun was low in the sky when they finally arrived back at base camp. Exhausted and tired, Jocab was ready to just crawl into his bedding. Their packs were extra heavy with all the cold weather gear, telescope, and communication equipment, and seemed to get heavier with each step they had taken. The descent was extra slow, as they were careful to not injure themselves or damage the equipment. Garron, Donav, and Clancy helped them stow the gear and guided them to the fire, where Ayleth and Estellia gave them steaming bowls of stew. "How did it go?" Clancy asked.

Jocab took a bite before replying. "We sent the signal, hopefully they received it."

Clancy gave a low chuckle. "That's all we can do."

Jocab gave the stew his full attention. It wasn't long before he was scraping the bottom of the bowl. Looking up, he noticed he was not alone. Both technicians were already asking for seconds.

Ayleth reached for his bowl. "You want more?"

Jocab shook his head and stood. "No, I just want to sleep."

Ayleth took the empty bowl from him and leaned in for a hug. "You do that then."

Jocab hugged her back and headed for his tent. The last thing he remembered was successfully wrestling out of his coat and crawling into his bedding.

It was snowing as the team finished loading the wagons for the trip home. They had risen early and had a warm breakfast before breaking camp. Jocab slung the tent siding over his shoulder and dropped it in the wagon. It took two additional trips to load the last of his gear. Jocab was grateful for the wagons. It would have been impossible without them.

Edmond dropped more gear in the wagon. "You all packed?"

"Yup, everyone is waiting for you."

Edmond smiled. "Well then, I'm ready when you are."

Edmond turned to where Garron and Clancy were sitting and hollered. "We're ready."

Jocab and the others climbed aboard the wagons. Edmond and Estellia settled up front while Ayleth, Jocab and Donav tried to make themselves comfortable in the back. Jocab looked at the other wagon. The two technicians sat in the back while Garron and Clancy sat up front.

Kenneth ordered the church guard to fan out in a kilometer long line as they advanced slowly through the trees. He and Kenneth followed behind the line ahead of the wagons. It was slow going as the tracks they were following were just two thin lines meandering through the trees. Kenneth could see that very few wagons traveled this way since the ruts weren't very deep. They'd been moving through the forest for over a week, in a north-westerly direction. Solomon was very proud of what they had accomplished so far. They had swept up the "unfaithful" that had built their home among the trees, obviously trying to hide from the temple. "This is turning out to be a productive trip," Solomon thought to himself. "Capturing Jocab and Edmond will be the icing on the cake."

Solomon's mind was dragged back to the present when he saw two guardsmen pushing another "heretic" in their direction. Solomon and Kenneth reined in their mounts and waited. The poor lost soul had his legs bound at his ankles and his hands secured behind his back. His clothes, face, and hair were filthy. It looked like he had fallen into a swamp. The guards' boots and trousers, similarly stained, with a liberal application applied to their arms and faces, showed what must have been a messy capture.

Kenneth steadied his mount as he addressed the guards. "Looks like he gave you a little trouble."

"Not much, captain. He tried to run but couldn't keep his feet."

Kenneth smiled. "Good work, gentlemen. Toss him in the jail cart and get yourself cleaned up."

Both guardsmen nodded and pushed the prisoner toward the jail cart behind them.

Kenneth turned to Solomon. "How much longer are you going to do this?"

Solomon answered with a smile. "Until we apprehend our two misguided souls."

Kenneth kept his voice calm. "I am concerned our jail carts will be full long before then."

Solomon thought for a minute. "Then we can either send for more carts or cleanse their souls out here," his voice cold and hard.

Kenneth kept his composure as he fought back a shudder. "I pray to the gods it doesn't come to that."

Solomon gave Kenneth a sideways glance. "I'm sure the gods will rejoice in the removal of any heretic from this blessed land."

Kenneth chose not to reply. He was afraid his answer might put him in the jail cart, along with the others. Instead, he glanced around for something to change the subject. An approaching rider saved him. One of the advance scouts was returning. The scout slowed and reined in his horse before saluting. "We found them, Captain."

Solomon seemed to sit two meters taller as he grinned from ear to ear. He raised his hands in the air in worship. "The gods show fortune upon us."

The Captain gave a small smile. "How close are they?"

"Two days' ride, Captain."

"That close?" Solomon stammered.

"Yes, Your Excellency. We confirmed it was them. There are at least seven of them traveling in two wagons heading west."

"Did they spot you?"

"No sir. I heard them coming. I set up a lookout along their path and waited for them to pass before heading back."

"Who did you see?" Solomon asked impatiently.

"The two you've been looking for, a priest, two women, and four men I didn't recognize."

"Well done, Render. Get some food and some rest. You earned it," Kenneth replied, dismissing the guard.

Solomon sat in silence as he digested the information. He smiled at the thought of Jocab, Edmond, and Donav sitting in the jail cart. Athels would have no choice but to reward him when he returned.

CHAPTER 34

Harlen was sitting at his desk when his attendant burst through the door. A woodsman followed directly behind him. Harlen frowned at the interruption. "What is so important that you feel you must barge in?" he asked impatiently.

"Church soldiers are approaching," the woodsman announced. "Looks like a full company coming up from Liberty."

Harlen's eyes grew wide. "This is highly unusual. But these are unusual times." He stood and came around his desk, motioning toward the guest chairs in front of the desk. "Please have a seat, mister?"

The woodsman slid into a chair. "Jorge, sir."

Harlen took a seat opposite him. "Now, Jorge. What about these church soldiers?"

"A full company is moving up the main road and taking captive anyone in their path. A small group of refugees fleeing this way alerted us."

Harlen ran his hand across his brow. "How soon before these refugees arrive?"

"I would guess some might arrive later today, but more are certain to follow."

"You're sure it's a full company of soldiers?"

"That's our guess, but it will take longer to confirm."

Harlen thought things through before continuing. "A company isn't big enough to attack the settlement, but big enough to cause us trouble."

"Do you want us to engage them?"

"I'd like to avoid that, but we can't let them just arrest everyone either." Harlen pondered for a moment before continuing. "This was bound to happen one day. I just didn't think it would happen this soon."

Jorge sat in silence, not knowing how to respond. Harlen leaned forward in his chair and pushed a button on his desk. His secretary, Stephanie, entered seconds later. Harlen turned in her direction and spoke. "Please call an emergency session for the full council to meet in one hour."

"Yes, sir!" Stephanie replied as she hurried from the room.

Harlen turned back to Jorge. "Please notify the chief woodsman to send out a call. I want every man and woman ready yesterday. The longer we wait, the fewer options we have available to us."

Jorge stood, saluted, and headed for the door. Harlen called out to him, "I'll need you at the council meeting to answer questions too."

Jorge froze for a second before replying, "Understood, sir!"

Clancy pulled the wagon to a stop when he noticed two hooded archers had appeared in front of them. They seemed to materialize out of nowhere about twenty meters ahead. Garron stood and pulled his hood back.

The archers pulled their hoods down and smiled as they approached. The one on the right with curly black hair and broad shoulders said. "Garron, Clancy. Good to see you."

"Good to see you, Voren. You're a little out of your way."

"You got trouble ahead."

Garron pursed his lips. "What kind of trouble?"

"Church soldiers are sweeping the forest, arresting everyone they come across."

Clancy glanced back at the others briefly before asking, "Can we avoid them?"

Voren contemplated the question before answering. "Only if you ditch the wagons. They are just over the rise there," he said, pointing east.

"That's too close," Garron replied, frowning. "We won't make it. We have too many of us and only four horses. Do we have any hideouts nearby?"

"Sorry, Garron. They are already full."

Garron grabbed his pack and jumped down from the wagon. "Clancy, grab your stuff too."

Clancy climbed down and was pulling his pack out when Jocab walked up. "What's going on, guys?"

"Bunch of the church guard is sweeping the forest in our direction."

Jocab furrowed his brow. "That's not good. Any way we can avoid them?"

Garron shook his head. "Probably not. I'm hoping you can outrun them. Keep the wagons moving while we provide you some cover."

Jocab looked at the men. "Who's we?"

Garron motioned to Clancy and the woodsmen. "The four of us. You and Edmond each take a wagon and keep them moving. Drive them hard if you have to."

"We can do that," he said as he waved the others over. It took only a minute to fill everyone in. Garron and Clancy had pulled their bows out and strung them as the rest of them climbed in the wagons. Jocab and Ayleth sat up front in the first wagon. The two technicians rode in the back. Edmond, Estellia, and Donav took the second wagon. They urged the horses forward as Garron and Clancy faded into a thicket with Voren and the other woodsman.

Garron looked at Voren. "Things won't go well if we harm them."

Voren pursed his lips. "And they'll catch the wagons if we do nothing."

Clancy placed a hand on Voren's and Garron's shoulders. "I agree with Garron. Things could escalate quickly if we're not careful."

Voren, visibly upset, opened his mouth to protest when they saw the first guard crest the hill a kilometer away. They watched as the rider appeared over the rise and made his way toward them.

"Come on, I got an idea," Clancy said, motioning them into the trees.

CHAPTER 35

It wasn't difficult to get behind the line of temple guards. Voren could tell they were unaware of the ways of the forest. They had no training in this kind of warfare. Two guards rode past Voren without a glance. Had they looked up, they would have seen him and several others hiding in the branches. He was glad that they had chosen not to confront the guard. Voren didn't think he could kill anyone if they couldn't defend themselves. He waited silently for them to go about a hundred meters before he dropped to the ground. Three other woodsmen dropped around him and together they worked their way east.

An hour later, they stood behind a group of trees, watching the last of the support wagons pass by. It amazed Voren that they hadn't posted a rear guard. Without a rear guard, Voren could strike without fear of reprisal. "They're worse than idiots," Voren whispered to himself. "Who leaves the rear unguarded?"

"You say something?" Loki asked quietly.

Voren turned to Loki. Loki was almost one and a half meters tall and built like a brick wall. He had dark brown hair that was shaved on the sides and trimmed short on the top. "Just talking to myself. No rear guards."

"That'll make this easy," Loki said with a big smile. "What do you want to do first?"

Voren looked at the wagons moving away. "Let's get closer and see what we can do."

Both men slipped in behind the wagon. Voren was certain one of the two riders would turn around and notice them any second. It seemed like an eternity as they walked quietly behind the tailgate, inspecting its contents. Satisfied, Voren nodded to Loki, and the two drifted back into the woods, leaving the wagons to continue.

"I saw tents and sleeping gear," Loki said. "What did you see?"

"Same as you."

"What are you thinking?"

"We torch the wagon."

"How? Shoot flaming arrows into the back?"

"That stuff looks pretty thick and won't catch well. I think we need something more. Let's find some kindling."

Loki nodded and immediately started looking for small branches and twigs they could use. Soon they were hunched over behind the wagon again, tying kindling around the axle. Loki grabbed his knife and a piece of flint from a pocket while Voren produced a handful of tinder. It took a few tries to ignite, but after several attempts, Loki finally got the spark to catch. Voren immediately cupped the tinder in his hand and lightly blew on it. He kept his breath steady till the spark turned to flame before placing it on the axle. Voren watched as the fire spread to the twigs and branches. Satisfied with their results, they both abandoned the wagon and slipped back into the woods. They found a fallen log and ducked out of sight to watch their handiwork. Loki was snickering as the flames spread on the underside of the wagon, quickly engulfing the entire back end.

Seconds later, they heard a loud cry from the two occupants as they realized their wagon was on fire. They watched both men jumping off the wagon as it disappeared among the trees. "We better get out of here before they start searching for us."

Voren nodded, and they headed deeper into the woods. "I wonder how many of them will sleep under the stars tonight."

Kenneth sat behind a small desk in his tent. The sergeant was standing in front of him, giving his report. "We've pulled the wagons inside the perimeter, doubled the guard and expanded the parameter around the campsite."

"How long is one person on watch before being relieved?" Kenneth asked.

"I let them choose between two six-hour shifts or three four-hour shifts and they chose the four-hour shifts,"

Kenneth nodded before asking, "And what about sleeping arrangements since we lost the one wagon?"

"They will be hot swapping with those on guard duty."

"We have enough?"

"Yes sir, we have enough beds, but not enough tents."

"And how have you handled that?" Kenneth asked.

"They drew lots. I saw several claiming positions under the wagons."

"Creative…" Kenneth commented.

"Agreed. Anything else, sir?"

"Thank you, sergeant. That will be all."

Garron and Clancy stood behind a tree as they watched from a distance while the soldiers made camp. They had an unobstructed view of everything between the campfires and the bright lights of Avalon's moons overhead. "We going to do anything tonight?" Clancy asked.

Garron shook his head. "No, the moons are too bright, and they're on high alert. We will just monitor them tonight."

"Darn, I was looking forward to some fun."

Jorge waited inside the stable for a horse to be saddled up. He was happy to be done with the council meeting and was eager to engage the church guard. Jorge detested politics, and the long meeting the previous night only solidified his distaste. He answered question after question, giving the same answers repeatedly. It chafed him when they tried wording the question differently, hoping it would somehow change his answer to fit what they were looking for. He was happy when Harlen finally released him to rejoin his kinsmen and relay the council's orders. Slow the advance while they sent out the call to arms.

Jorge was pulled from his thoughts when the stable hand brought him a horse, saddled and ready to go. He gave a quick nod of thanks as he mounted up and rode out into the street. Jorge made sure the road ahead was clear before pushing his mount into a gallop. The horse lengthened his stride as it picked up speed, its warm breath creating a mist in the chilly morning air.

Leon was next to ride out of the stable. This was his first time as a messenger. He felt honored and excited to be picked. Three other riders still waited for their mounts as he took off toward the mining village and cave entrance. It would take a few hours of hard riding to reach the first village. Afterward, he would head north to the other villages that skirted the mountain range. He and three others would deliver the call to all the villages and mining towns.

The sun was halfway in the sky when Garron caught sight of the wagons moving along the road. Garron noticed several soldiers on horseback watching over the wagons after their loss yesterday. He signaled to Voren on his right. Voren and another woodsman were standing behind a tree several meters away. Voren returned the signal and began stringing his bow.

Garron strung his bow too and started unwrapping the tip of an arrow. He carefully nocked it, the front being heavy from the large sticky glob attached to the arrowhead. He turned to Clancy, who lit a small amount of tinder. Clancy blew on the spark and soon had a flame going. They placed their arrows over the flame and lit the sticky globs.

A quick glance at Voren confirmed he was ready. They raised their bows and drew back the strings. Garron took a deep breath and slowly let it out as he released the arrow. It shot into the sky a half behind Voren's. Both arrows reached their peak and slowly turned downward, gaining momentum before slamming into their targets below. Additional arrows dropped into several other wagons, wreaking havoc with the men and horses.

Garron and the woodsmen ran back into the woods, smiling. The shouts of the guard behind them got quieter as the woodsmen retreated deeper into the forest.

Solomon raged at the delay. "How can you let them do this?"

Kenneth kept his cool, ignoring Solomon's outburst. "We can discuss options afterward, Your Excellence." Turning back to the sergeant he said, "Please continue."

"We put the fires out quickly. There was only minor damage to a few of the wagons."

Kenneth nodded. "How about the contents?"

"Some food stores, extra gear, more tents and bedding, but nothing serious."

"Thank you, sergeant. Pull some of the guard from the front and have them cover our sides and rear."

"Already done, sir."

"That will be all."

As soon as the guard had spun away, Solomon said, "This is getting ridiculous."

"I expected they might try something like this."

"You're kidding me?" Solomon stammered.

"Not at all, Your Excellence. I would be surprised if they did nothing."

"Well, how dare they."

"We are invading their land, Your Excellence."

"Their Land?" he screamed.

"There are two wagons full of prisoners, and we have driven the rest from their homes as we advance. You cannot expect them to put out the welcome mat."

"You go too far, Kenneth."

Kenneth kept his voice flat. "I'm only stating the facts, Your Excellence, nothing more."

"What are you going to do about it?" Solomon sneered.

"Exactly what I am doing." He watched Solomon fume for a few more seconds before adding, "Plan on it getting worse, Your Excellence."

"What?" Solomon replied, his voice rising.

"Yes. The deeper we go, the more these encounters will occur."

Solomon looked amazed. "They wouldn't dare!"

Kenneth maneuvered his horse close to Solomon and leaned over in the saddle to talk privately to Solomon. "Your Excellence. They could consider this an act of war. The population in these woods do not follow the gods, nor do they recognize the temple's authority." Solomon raged inside, but held his tongue, much to Kenneth's amazement. Kenneth hoped and prayed the high priest would abandon this adventure before some of his men got hurt or killed.

It took Jorge two days to reach Garron. The temple guard was advancing, slowed by the harassment the woodsman was dishing out. He had arrived at the makeshift camp just as the sun was setting. There were a few tents set up and a couple of cooking fires spread about. Not knowing where Garron might be, he dismounted and secured his horse at a picket line with the other horses. Afterward, he headed toward the cooking fires. "Good evening. Can one of you point me to Garron?" he asked as he walked over.

Two men pointed toward the tent. "That way."

Jorge changed course in the tent's direction. "Thank you," he hollered over his shoulder. Both flaps were pulled back and several people were standing over a makeshift table. He reached it several strides later and called, "Garron?"

All eyes turned toward him. Garron stood and answered, "Yes, can I help you?"

"I'm Jorge. Harlen sent me."

Garron's eyes lit up. "Come in. Please, come in."

Jorge ducked his head and entered the now crowded tent. Garron turned and made introductions. "Your fellow woodsmen, Voren and Clancy. This is Clancy's brother Jocab and his friend Edmond."

"Nice to meet you," Jorge said as he shook everyone's hand.

"What did Harlen and the council have to say?"

Jorge glanced at Jocab and Edmond. He was apprehensive about sharing the news with strangers in their midst.

Garron nodded in understanding. "They can hear what the council decided. We believe the guard are after them."

Jorge took a few seconds to collect his thoughts. "The council has sent the call out to gather all the woodsmen. They instructed them to head west and join us immediately."

"That's good," Voren replied quietly.

Garron glared at him before turning back to Jorge. "Go ahead, please."

"The council also wishes to avoid bloodshed. We are NOT to provoke or initiate any conflict."

"What are we allowed to do?" Garron asked. "Did he give you any rules of engagement?"

"Yes, Harlen instructed us to use non-lethal actions to deter them."

Garron grinned. "Sounds like we will continue as planned."

Voren smiled back. "What happens when the rest of our troops arrive?"

"Non-lethal means non-lethal."

"They will overtake us tomorrow," Voren protested.

"I know. We'll make a stand in this meadow here." He pointed at the map. "There's a ridge here, and thick woods along here. We can set up a good defensive position and wait for them to arrive."

"So that's it then?" Voren asked.

Garron grinned from ear to ear. "Oh no, we have one last surprise for them tonight."

CHAPTER 36

Jorge followed Loki across the creek and up the other side. They stayed under cover, moving from tree to tree in the darkness. He had volunteered to go on this mission and had practically begged Garron to allow him. Garron relented with no genuine concerns, and Jorge was grateful for that. He wanted action. There was little glory in telling family and friends that he was just a messenger when the guard had invaded.

He stopped next to Loki and leaned over to talk in his ear. "How do you want to do this?"

"I think we do something more than shoot the fire arrows into their camp. I say we sneak in close, and when Patryk and Dominic shoot their arrows, we cut the picket lines and steal the horses."

Jorge smiled. "I love it."

"We better move. We have to get within their security perimeter."

The two of them wrapped their cloaks around them, using the darkness to hide their approach as they slipped closer to the horses.

Dawson sighed and rubbed his eyes. He was tired and couldn't wait for the changing of the guard. Fifteen minutes and he could go back to sleep. After tonight, he would have a night off from guard duty. Dawson smiled at the thought. He was on the back end of his four nights of sentry duty. Tomorrow would be his one night off.

A streak of light caught his eye. He turned and watched it fall into the camp. Several more followed closely behind. He watched as six flaming arrows struck the camp. He stood frozen for a moment before yelling, "Fire!" repeatedly as he ran toward the camp. Other guards on duty took the call up. Soon, those sleeping jumped up and started fighting the flames.

Knowing that he was still on guard duty, he turned and headed back toward his post. He was just a few meters away when a figure appeared in front of him, bow drawn, and arrow pointed in his direction. "That's far enough, my friend."

Dawson froze as another dark figure swung up on a horse and dug their heels into its flanks. A group of horses tethered together followed along behind the rider. He turned to the man who had spoken, only to find they had disappeared back into the darkness.

"The horses!" he yelled as he charged forward. "They are taking the horses!"

He was about ten meters away when he saw another line of horses head off into the darkness. Dawson finally made it to the horses and was glad to see the rest still attached to their picket lines. Dawson couldn't believe this was happening to him. Why him? Why did this have to happen to him?

"AHHHH. The gods be damned!" He screamed into the darkness, his frustration getting the better of him. He knew his fellow guard would haze him forever over this. The picket lines were his responsibility, and he'd technically abandoned his post when he ran to warn the others.

Kenneth waited in his tent for the sergeant to announce himself. It took just a few minutes to put the fires out. Kenneth smiled at the knowledge that one arrow landed in a water barrel. He took a deep breath and relaxed. He knew his guard could not take much more of this. One way or the other, this would have to end.

"Captain," a voice called from outside the tent.

"Enter," Kenneth replied.

The sergeant moved the tent flap aside and entered, snapping to attention.

Kenneth let out a long sigh. "At ease, sergeant. What's the damage?"

"Minimal damage. One side of a supply tent and one cooking station, sir."

Kenneth nodded. "Any injuries?"

"A few minor burns from fighting the fires, but nothing serious."

"And the horses?"

"We lost twenty-seven, sir."

"We were lucky. And who had security detail?"

"A new recruit," the sergeant replied. "He's beating himself up really bad. He knows he messed up and he should have maintained his post."

"I can assume you will handle that?"

"Yes sir. I'll make sure he is okay. Might bark at him so the men don't feel he's being pampered. Plus, it will help keep the rest on their toes."

"Do you think he'll be alright?"

"I think so. It was the luck of the draw. He was the unfortunate one to be on watch."

"Thank you, sergeant. That will be all."

Dawson was sitting, eating breakfast by himself. He was still angry at the loss of the horses. Several of the guard had already given him grief over having to walk instead of ride. He wished the gods would open a hole and just swallow him up. He took the last bite of his breakfast when he noticed a single rider advancing toward the camp. Dawson sucked in a breath to announce the rider when several guardsmen started shouting and pointing. The rider pulled up, dismounted, and stood waiting. His hood up and long cloak wrapped around him, hiding his features.

More and more guardsmen stopped to watch the rider when they heard the sergeant bellow orders, "Get moving, you sorry excuses. Quit standing around with you thumbs up your back-end gawking. Move it!" He headed toward the rider waiting in the distance when his eyes fell on Dawson. "Dawson. Go collect our guest. I'm sure he wants to see the Captain."

"Yes, Sarge!" Dawson acknowledged and hurried toward the rider.

Dawson strode forward, trying to show some confidence that he didn't have. He could feel his knees wobble as he fought the urge to throw-up. As he got closer, he was unsure of what to say. The woodsman helped him out. "Good morning friend, I would like to speak to your Captain."

Dawson swallowed and nodded, finally finding his voice. "Right this way, sir," he said as he turned toward the camp.

The rider stepped up next to him and they walked side by side.

"My name is Voren. What's yours?"

"Dawson, sir."

"A good strong name."

"Thank you, sir." Voren could hear the nervousness in his voice. The young man's hands were shaking, but Voren pretended not to notice. They walked silently through the camp toward a tent three square meters in size. The tent flap was open, and Dawson could see the sergeant and the Captain waiting patiently.

As they approached, the sergeant exited the tent. "Thank you, Dawson. I will call you when we finish."

"Yes Sarge," Dawson replied, snapping to attention.

The sergeant motioned toward the tent. "This way please."

Voren handed the reins to Dawson. "Would you be so kind as to care for my mount, friend?"

Dawson's eyes widened. "Certainly, sir."

Voren followed the sergeant into the tent before he pulled the flap down to give them some privacy.

The Captain stepped forward and held out his hand. "I'm Kenneth."

Voren nodded and shook his hand. "I'm Voren, Sir."

"Pleasure is all mine. What brings you to my camp this morning?"

"I bring word from Settlement Settoo. Your aggressive actions are an act of war. We are hopeful we can resolve things before they escalate any further."

Kenneth studied the man in front of him for a few seconds. "And how does Settoo wish to resolve this?"

"For us to meet and discuss terms."

"And where would you like this meeting to take place?"

Voren walked over to a map spread out on a table and examined it. "There," he said, pointing. "Follow the road until it parallels this creek. About two kilometers further up is a small meadow. We will wait for you there."

Kenneth stepped up beside Voren and was examining the map when Solomon thrust the tent flap aside and entered, his priestly robes flowing behind him. "What is the meaning of this?" he demanded.

Kenneth turned to Solomon. "This gentleman from Settoo dropped by for a visit,"

Solomon snarled. "Visit indeed! Why was I not notified?"

"Our guest just arrived, Your Excellency," Kenneth replied, his voice void of emotions.

"And what does this guest want?" Solomon sneered at Voren while placing an emphasis on guest.

"To meet with us, Your Excellency." Kenneth turned to Voren and smiled. "We'll try not to be late."

Voren gave a small node. "Thank you, Captain."

Kenneth turned to the sergeant. "Please show our guest out."

The sergeant snapped to attention, then pulled the tent flap aside for Voren. Voren gave Solomon a toothy grin as he exited. Once outside, he chuckled. "They really don't like each other."

The sergeant gave a small cough as he fought to keep his composure.

"Tell your captain he has impeccable patience."

"I will tell him you said so."

Voren accepted the reins from Dawson before leaping effortlessly into the saddle. "Thank you, Dawson. It was nice to meet you. Please stay safe." He turned to the sergeant. "You too," he said, before nudging the horse forward.

Both men nodded and watched as Voren rode off into the trees.

"I like him," the sergeant commented. "And I'm certain I wouldn't want to be on the receiving end of his bow."

Dawson's eyes widened at the unexpected comment from his superior.

They stood there in silence for a few seconds before the sergeant patted Dawson's shoulder. "Come along, Dawson. Camp won't break without us."

CHAPTER 37

The riders had picked up the fresh wagon tracks just after breaking camp. Kenneth had sent a message to all the guard to stay alert, and had set riders to scout ahead. Both he and Solomon rode closer to the front as the troops gathered on both sides. Kenneth brought his mount close to Solomon so they could talk. "The scouts say they've stopped at the small meadow a kilometer away. The men have orders not to approach."

"Why? It's still early in the afternoon."

"It is the place they chose. My guess is they realized they cannot evade us."

"Of course, they can't. The gods are on our side."

Kenneth sighed and struggled to keep his thoughts to himself.

The afternoon sun was at it's zenith when Kenneth and Solomon finally reached the tree line. Kenneth stayed in the shadows as he looked out at the meadow beyond. It was almost fifty meters wide and a hundred meters long. He could see two wagons in a defensive position, with tall trees directly behind them. Kenneth didn't see any woodsmen hiding in the trees. He knew they were there, ready to rain down arrows of death if needed. Kenneth focused on the wagons again, noticing a small opening between the two, creating a choke point. Any attempt to get inside the wagons would be costly. He looked around one more time before walking back to his waiting sergeant.

"They did a good job finding a defensible position, didn't they?" the sergeant said as he handed the reins to Kenneth.

Kenneth gave a small laugh as he swung his leg over the saddle. "They sure did," he answered, before riding over to Solomon.

Kenneth and Solomon led their small contingent of men into the meadow. Their horses pranced as they broke out into the sunlight and advanced toward the wagons. Kenneth watched two men step through the narrow opening between the wagons. Both stood relaxed with their arms across their chests, waiting for their guests. They wore their long brown cloaks, with the hoods up, hiding their faces. Each had bows strung, resting over their shoulders, a quiver of arrows on their back, and a long knife on their belt. Kenneth and Solomon reined in their horses a few meters from the wagons. Solomon's face wore a big scowl. Kenneth could hear his men take up their assigned positions behind him. Kenneth wished he could conduct the negotiations without the pompous priest beside him. He found Solomon's fanatic behavior unsettling. Kenneth believed there was something greater than themselves, but he didn't share the utter devotion that Solomon did. He leaned back in his saddle to take a quick survey. Two men caught his eye, and he recognized them as the ones they were looking for. Both were leaning against the wagons, watching him and Solomon closely. Further back were two women, several woodsmen, and a priest. Kenneth couldn't help but raise an eyebrow as he wondered what a temple priest was doing in their midst.

Kenneth refocused on the task at hand when the taller of the woodsmen stepped forward and pulled his hood back, revealing a narrow face and black wavy shoulder length hair. His broken nose and sharp gaze radiated self-confidence. Kenneth feared and admired him at the same time.

The man addressed the high priest. "My name is Garron. What can I do for you, Your Excellency?"

Solomon sat up straighter and jabbed a finger at Edmond and Jocab. "You can turn those two over immediately!"

"Why would we do that, Your Excellency?" He paused before adding 'Your Excellency,' as an afterthought.

Solomon took a deep breath to continue, but Kenneth spoke instead. "The high priest Athels needs their assistance."

Garron laughed aloud. "Assistance? You bring a small army, invade our lands, and arrest everyone in your path."

Solomon screeched. "How dare you question the will of the gods!"

"Will of the gods, be dammed, Your Excellence," Garron shot back. "I know the real truth. Just like you do."

Solomon raged but held his tongue. A wicked smile appeared on his face as he pictured this heretic screaming in pain as he burned at the stake. Solomon would see to it.

Kenneth knew things were going from bad to worse with every word Solomon uttered. "If you would give me a moment to speak to his Excellency?"

The leader nodded and leaned against the wagon.

Kenneth nudged his horse closer to Solomon. "You are not helping yourself one bit. Remember, every meal tastes better with wine than with vinegar."

Solomon snorted, but relented. Kenneth settled back in his saddle and continued. "What terms do you require before releasing them into our custody?"

"How do we know you will treat them properly?" the other woodsman asked, taking a half step forward.

Kenneth looked at Solomon for assurance.

"Enough of this," Solomon barked. "Hand them over now!"

Kenneth's shoulders dropped. People were going to die today if Solomon kept interrupting.

"Or, what?" the woodsman said as he slid the bow off his shoulder

Jocab surprised Kenneth when he pushed his way to the front. "We will go," Jocab stated, his voice calm. "But there are a few conditions."

"You're not in a place to make demands," Solomon sneered.

"And you are?" Garron replied as several archers drew their bows.

"We'll make your stinking life miserable all the way back to Liberty," the other woodsman stated.

"We outnumber you," Solomon stammered, trying to get the upper hand.

Garron smiled. "You don't know that. But know this, my first arrow is for you."

Kenneth dismounted and stepped out in front of Solomon's horse. He gave Jocab and Garron a warm smile as he removed his helmet. "I certainly do not wish to start a conflict. And I would like to hear your requirements."

Jocab stepped out in front of Garron and Clancy. "For starters, we go as guests and not as your prisoners."

Solomon cleared his throat to speak, but Kenneth spoke first.

"Done. What else?"

"You will release all of your captives. They've done nothing wrong except to be in the wrong place at the wrong time."

It was Kenneth who tried to speak when Solomon announced. "Absolutely not!"

Kenneth ground his teeth, taking a moment to collect himself. "Please give us a moment."

Jocab nodded. "Take your time."

Kenneth walked back to Solomon and gently led his horse off into the meadow. Kenneth stopped when they could talk privately without fear of being overheard.

"Your Excellency," he started. "We are not in a good position to bargain right now."

Solomon huffed. "We cannot let them control the terms!"

"We don't have much choice."

"We have an army behind us."

"And they have an army surrounding us. Believe me when I tell you that they will slaughter us."

"You told me yourself, that these are trained soldiers."

"Yes, they are the finest men I have ever commanded. But we cannot fight what we cannot see."

Solomon glanced at the trees, unable to see anything in the shadows.

Kenneth continued. "You can bet they have men behind every tree with an arrows pointed at us."

Solomon sat up straight. "We can still win."

"And how many faithful men do you wish to die for your victory? How many young boys and girls will never hug their daddy again?"

Solomon glared at Kenneth. Thoughts of his parents perishing in the fire threatened to overwhelm him. Solomon remembered the pain of that loss as if it were yesterday. Kenneth patiently waited him out. Eventually Solomon capitulated. "All right."

Kenneth relaxed, not realizing he was holding his breath. "Thank you, Your Excellence."

They both wandered back, Solomon scowling the entire time.

Kenneth nodded to Jocab. "We agree to release the prisoners."

"Thank you."

"Anything else?"

"You will fully remove your men from the woods. Settoo takes your actions as an invasion."

Solomon huffed. "Invasion!"

Kenneth frowned at Solomon's outburst. "There is no intention of staying after completing our mission."

Solomon sputtered. "We have every right to be here." He took another breath to protest further but was silenced when several archers raised their bows and drew at him.

Kenneth failed to hide his smile. He kept his back to Solomon and his voice neutral. "Anything else?"

Garron smiled back. "Nothing more."

And what of our horses?"

Garron leaned against the wagon. "They will be used to compensate those directly affected by your actions."

Kenneth thought about it for a few minutes. He wondered how many were driven from their homes as he advanced through the forest. He slowly nodded to Garron. "We accept."

Solomon raged as he sat quietly on his horse. "These men will pay, the Temple will be vindicated and these heretics will burn." Solomon was pulled from his thoughts when Jocab stepped forward, spit in his palm, and held it out. He sat in amazement as he watched Kenneth spit in his before they grasped each other's hand, giving them a hearty shake.

Afterwards, Kenneth secured his helmet, mounted up and led his men back into the woods on the far side. Solomon followed, praying to the gods for insight on how to avenge the temple.

Jocab leaned against the wagon as the guard retreated across the meadow. He watched as they marched back into the trees. Edmond came up beside him. "How soon do we leave?"

Jocab gave a small laugh as he turned to Garron. "Would you be able to spare a few woodsmen?"

Garron furrowed his brows. "What are you thinking?"

"I trust that high priest only as far as I can throw him. I'd like to have some friends to help keep him honest."

Garron glanced down at the ground while he mulled things over. "I'm sure we can get a few volunteers."

Within the hour, they had organized a small party to join them, packed their gear into a wagon, and sent a dispatch back to Settoo with a full report on the outcome of their negotiations.

Jocab, Clancy, and Ayleth rode in the wagon most of the way back. True to their word, the guardsmen released their captives and made a hasty retreat. It horrified Estellia when she found out Birgit had spent over a week in the back of a prison wagon. She was traveling to Liberty to purchase more bolts of cloth when the temple guard snatched her early on. The thought of Birgit being treated like a criminal inflamed Estellia. She made a point of glaring at Solomon every time she saw him. The three ladies had fast become friends, and it was no surprise that she continued her trip to Liberty.

Jocab and Clancy took delight in the guards' discomfort when they caught fleeting glimpses of woodsmen stalking them during their return. The guard almost broke ranks when they saw the edge of the forest ahead of them. Just before the guard exited, Clancy leaned toward Jocab and Ayleth. "Watch this."

As the first soldier left the cover of the trees, the woodsmen, over three hundred strong, lined the road in front of them. It was shocking to the guard to see such an obvious show of force. Jocab watched as it rattled a few nerves. Kenneth surprised Jocab when he called the guard to attention and had them salute the woodsmen. He had them hold the salute till every man and wagon had passed all the woodsmen along the road. Kenneth then high stepped his horse to the center of the road, stood in his stirrups, and bowed to the men before riding away.

Solomon rode at the front of the column as if he were a general leading his victorious forces home from battle. Jocab kept the group back with the wagons, avoiding Solomon as much as possible. He still didn't trust Solomon and feared what would happen on the second leg of their journey. Garron and Clancy mingled with the guard in the evenings. They would talk with the guardsmen for hours about everything from family to farming, and occasionally theology. Donav spent his evening making the rounds and ministered to their spiritual needs. Every night, Kenneth insisted one or two of them dined with him in the captain's tent. Jocab laughed when he overheard Solomon's displeasure of

Kenneth "dining with heathens."

Jocab and Edmond found they had an audience every time they set up the telescope. It became a nightly ritual to give others a peek at the heavens while they privately tracked the object. Jocab had just packed up the telescope for the evening when Edmond pulled him aside. He had spent the afternoon with his nose in the journal. "What is it?"

"The object has moved past us."

"Isn't it supposed to stop here?"

"That is what I thought. And it still might."

"What do you mean?"

"It is going slow enough that we'll catch up to it in about a week."

"I don't understand."

"Let me see if I can explain it better." Edmond grabbed a small stick and scratched some circles in the dirt. "This is our sun, and this is Avalon's path orbiting around the sun."

Jocab nodded in understanding. "Yeah, I know that."

Edmond drew a line across the outer circle. "This is the ship's path. At the moment, the object is moving faster than we are orbiting."

"I understand, go on."

"It should complete one more burn. At that point, it will be here, but going slower than our orbit. Avalon will eventually catch up to it."

"That makes sense. How soon?"

"If they continue to follow their existing pattern, it should be tomorrow night. That is why I've been busy all afternoon. I wanted to make sure my math was correct."

"Will we be able to track it?"

"I hope so. It will be tough, plus we'll have to move the telescope often to stay with it."

Jocab looked at the scattered clouds overhead and replied, "I hope the sky is clear then."

CHAPTER 38

Jocab had the telescope set up, hoping to get another look at the object. Broken clouds were drifting overhead, making it almost impossible. He wanted one last look before they left Liberty.

Ayleth came over and stood by him. "Not a good night for this, is it?"

"Not really. I'm hoping this cloud cover will blow over later tonight."

She leaned into him and wrapped her arms around his shoulders. "Maybe you should get a few hours of sleep then."

"Probably not a bad idea. Is Edmond going to stay up?"

Ayleth smiled. "Estellia and Birgit said they would. I'll probably join them and make it a ladies' night."

Jocab pulled her into a hug. "Well then. I will take my cue and get some sleep." Ayleth didn't let go, adding a kiss before releasing him. Jocab felt thoroughly hugged and kissed.

"Goodnight," she whispered.

"Goodnight," he replied as he tried to recenter himself.

Harlen walked out onto the top of the stairwell for Pod B and climbed the narrow ladder to the top of the pod. Once he reached the top, he straightened and looked around. A lone figure, Tory, stood about 30 meters away, looking through a telescope. Tory was about one and a half meters tall, with brown hair and a thin, well-trimmed mustache and beard. Harlen liked Tory. He was always trustworthy and didn't pull punches. Harlen knew he would always get a straight answer, even if it wasn't what he wanted to hear. Harlen hollered as he walked toward him. "Have you found anything, Tory?"

Tory jumped a little and backed away, rubbing his eye where it hit the eyepiece. "Dang! You made me jump."

Harlen smiled sheepishly. "Sorry about that."

"I'm fine," Tory responded while still rubbing his eye.

"You able to find it?"

"Not yet. According to that guy Edmond, the thing should light up in the next hour."

"Hopefully he is right, and we can see it."

"His math has been right on so far, so I trust it."

"You double checked it?"

"Oh, yeah. Spent the afternoon looking over his calculations. He's a brilliant mathematician. I ran some of it through the mainframe too."

"So where should we see it when it happens?"

Tory pointed toward the eastern sky. "It will be high on the horizon up there. You might see it with the naked eye."

"Really?"

"Yeah, it is really close now. If Edmond's right, it passed us by last week."

"I thought it was coming here?"

"It is. It was going too fast and needed to pass us. This is the last one for it to slow down. We'll catch up to it in a few days."

"Think we can send it another message?"

"Absolutely. Once it is in orbit, we can keep the laser on it every time it circles overhead."

"Any other way to communicate other than with the laser?"

"Not sure. Radio signals can't penetrate the atmosphere."

"Unfortunately, that's always been the case."

"I still think we should set up a bunch of the lasers between the towns," Tory said.

"I'd love that, but we don't have the raw materials."

"Like everything else, we have the knowledge, but no way to use it."

"It could be worse," Harlen teased. "You could live in Avalon and have the priests dictate everything."

"Not on your life." Tory replied sternly as he moved the telescope higher and peeked into the eyepiece.

Harlen looked to where Tory had pointed the telescope. He jumped when he saw a twinkling light appear.

"Is that it?" Harlen asked with excitement in his voice.

"Hot Damn!" Tory exclaimed as he quickly aligned the telescope. "It's brighter than I thought it would be."

Ayleth nudged Jocab gently. "Wake up, Jocab. The skies are clear."

Jocab opened his eyes and tried to focus. "How late is it?" he mumbled as he sat up.

"Just a little past midnight."

"Do we still have time?"

"Edmond thinks it should happen in a few minutes."

Jocab shook himself awake. "Are the clouds gone?"

Ayleth leaned in and kissed him on the cheek. "Yes, my darling. Come out and see."

Jocab quickly dressed before joining Edmond at the telescope. "Little cold tonight."

Edmond blew on his hands before replying. "What gave you your first clue?"

Jocab gave a short laugh. "And I was nice and warm in my bedding."

"So was I, but I'm not missing this."

"Where are we supposed to see it tonight?"

Edmond pointed eastward. "I figure it will be up that way."

Jocab loosened the knobs holding the telescope and aligned it where Edmond pointed. "Any idea how bright it will be?"

"It should be much brighter since its closer, but I don't really know."

Jocab looked into the eyepiece, trying to locate the object. "How come we can't find it?"

"The technician in Settoo said the flame was an engine slowing it down. If that's true, then the engine is facing away from us right now."

Jocab pondered his words while he continued to look. "I guess that makes sense. We wouldn't see the normal glow then."

"Exactly. But we should see it when it lights up."

"I wonder what the priests will do."

"I've been thinking the same thing. Temple doctrine's going to fall apart real soon."

"That's what worries me."

"Why would that worry you?"

Jocab sighed. "People need something to believe in and something to hold on to. That is going to change drastically and not everyone will handle it well."

"Do you think the priests knew all along?"

"That's hard to say. But they knew enough. I don't know why they let it get this bad."

"Only the gods can answer that."

"It's going to be out of their control soon."

Edmond was about to say something when a twinkling light appeared. "There it is," he said as he pointed toward the heavens.

Jocab aligned the telescope and stuck his eye up to the eyepiece. "Wow, that is close!"

Edmond continued to stare at the object while Jocab watched it from the telescope. "I didn't think it would be this bright."

Jocab stepped back from the telescope as Edmond took a turn and watched with renewed interest.

They were three days out of Liberty and Jocab could see the morning light making its way into the tent. He took his time getting out from under the warm bedding while trying to avoid the chill still lingered in the air.

Ayleth gave him another nudge. "Come on, Estellia already has water boiling for tea."

"All right," Jocab said as he grabbed his shirt from within his bedding and pulled it on.

"I don't understand why you do that. You get it all wrinkled that way."

"This way, I always put on a warm shirt."

"Men," she commented as she left the tent.

Once outside, Ayleth handed Jocab a cup hot of tea. The sky was clear, and everyone bundled up to keep warm, their hands wrapped around their steaming cups. He glanced around at their small campsite. Estellia was pulling bacon out of the frying pan as Ayleth added more wood to the fire. Jocab noticed the crew from Settoo missing.

"Where's Garron and Clancy?"

Donav blew on the top of his tea to cool it before replying. "They are saying goodbye to the guard."

"Yeah, they are heading back to Liberty." Edmond added.

"They said a unit from Avalon will arrive this afternoon."

Jocab raised his eyebrows. "Now, Solomon doesn't get his grand entrance?"

Edmond snickered. "I think that's why the Captain's leaving now."

"I would have paid a lot of coin to see Solomon's face when Kenneth told him."

Edmond laughed aloud. "Forget that. I would have sold tickets."

Solomon chose not to break camp until the guard from Avalon arrived. Ayleth commented it was because he had no one to do his bidding. It was an odd sight, seeing the high priest's tent alone by the side of the road. Donav became the de facto servant, bringing him lunch that Ayleth and Estella had made.

They were just finishing lunch when the guard from Avalon finally arrived. They watched from the side as Solomon ranting at the sergeant about being late and attending to his needs. While the sergeant received his tongue lashing, his men were quick to get organized and set up camp.

Later that evening, Jocab set the telescope on the tripod and carefully tightened the knobs that held it in place. He and Edmond could not find the object since they had left Liberty. It was no longer visible in the night sky. Once it completed its last burn, it had gone completely dark, making it impossible to follow. The two of them hoped to watch it as it closed the distance to the planet. Jocab pointed the device in the direction Edmond suggested. "This might take a while," he grumbled.

"Yeah, it will. But it's necessary if we want to find it again."

"It's like trying to find a coin in a barn full of hay."

"If we break the sky up into a grid, it should be easier. We can each cover a different area."

"I'm not sure I agree, but sooner started, sooner finished," Jocab said dryly.

After an hour of searching in vain, Edmond groaned as he stood back from the telescope. "I'd rather muck stables than do this much longer."

"My turn anyway. And the stables are that way if you're serious." He pointed down the road toward Liberty.

Edmond laughed and hit him in the arm. "How does Ayleth put up with you?"

Jocab jumped back as he tried to avoid Edmond's blow and bumped the telescope, almost knocking it over. Both men grabbed the tripod, keeping it upright.

"That was too close," Jocab said, relieved.

"Sorry about that," Edmond replied.

"My fault too," Jocab said as he aligned the telescope to where they were to search next. "How many more squares do we have left to search?"

"We are halfway there."

Jocab was peering through the eyepiece when he gasped. "By the Gods!"

"What is it?" Edmond asked.

"It's lit up!" Jocab replied, still looking through the telescope.

"You found it?"

Jocab stood back, his eyes wide. "No. The wheel overhead. Uh… The ship that brought us here. It's lit up!"

Edmond stepped forward and looked for himself. Small points of light emanating from the center of the wheel. "This changes everything," he whispered.

"You think?" Jocab replied, keeping his voice low. "Do we tell Solomon?"

"Certainly not!" Edmond hissed. "Let's talk with Donav before we do anything."

Jocab and Edmond carefully broke down the telescope and put it away while trying not to draw attention to themselves. They joined the others afterward and after a short and quiet conversation, decided not to share their findings until they arrived in Avalon.

It was three days later when Jocab heard a rider fast approaching from behind. A temple guard, pushing his horse hard, hurried past their wagon and stopped next to the high priest.

Clancy leaned over to Jocab. "Should we be concerned?"

"I'm not sure," Jocab replied. "Let's wait and see."

They continued to watch the rider as he spoke to Solomon. It was obvious they were the center of conversation, as Solomon would occasionally glance in their direction. Shortly after, the rider switched horses and headed back to Liberty while the rest of them continued toward Avalon. Jocab, Edmond, Clancy, and Garron had their heads together in the back of the wagon while keeping an eye on Solomon and the sergeant.

Garron fidgeted in his seat. "They are going to try something. I can feel it."

"What do we do?" Edmond asked.

Clancy locked eyes with everyone before speaking. "We do nothing till we break for the evening. Garron and I will take the horses and go hunting. You guys set up camp and have the ladies make a quick dinner. They can pretend to go to bed and disappear into the woods after dark. Have them stay together and try not to leave a trail."

"It's going to be cold tonight."

Clancy smiled that annoying smile. "Tell them to dress warmly."

"That's going to slow them down."

"They'll be fine," Garron said. "We'll keep them safe."

"What about us?" Edmond asked.

"You're going to let them take you," Garron replied, his voice like cold steel.

"You think they are going to arrest us?"

Garron nodded firmly. "Without a doubt."

"Then what happens?"

"We'll get the ladies to safety and come back for you."

Jocab looked at Edmond for a few seconds. "Can you think of anything better?"

Edmond pondered. "Not really."

"Then we go with that."

They all settled back in the wagon as Jocab shared their plans with Donav, Ayleth, and Estellia.

CHAPTER 39

Jocab was unsure if the guards noticed they had set their tents a little further from the camp and closer to the trees. While the groups camped separately, they were always close enough for a guard member to join them around the evening fire. Tonight, though, both sides mysteriously stayed away. Garron and Clancy rode east with their bows across their back, pronouncing they were going hunting and would be back after dark. Estellia and Ayleth prepared a quick meal over the fire as the sun disappeared into the distance.

True to their prediction, the evening turned out to be a cold one. After dinner, Ayleth and Estellia headed off to bed, only to slip into the woods unnoticed. Donav, Jocab, and Edmond huddled around the fire, talking as the night grew colder. They finally retired to their tents after both moons were high overhead. Donav said a small prayer for everyone's safety as they said goodnight.

Jocab wasn't sure if he could sleep as he waited alone in his tent. He smiled when he heard Edmond snoring from the tent next to him. "Well, one of us can," he murmured to himself. Sometime later, rough hands grabbed him, waking him as they pulled him from the tent. He could hear Edmond and Donav being pulled from their tents too.

Once outside, they dragged Jocab next to Edmond and Donav. Jocab watched Solomon in his flowing robes, directing things like a conductor leading an orchestra. He saw a feral smile cross Solomon's face as their eyes met. "You thought you could keep things from me?" he hollered.

Jocab kept quiet.

"Well, you can't," Solomon sneered. "I know what you've been hiding and now you'll pay for it." His voice rising to a shrill pitch.

Donav shrugged off the guard holding him. "We are unsure of what you speak of, Your Excellency."

Solomon raged. "They're here and you know it!" He pointed at a guardsman. "Search their belongings. I want proof they knew."

The guard saluted and started rummaging through their gear before holding up the journals and Jocab's metal box.

"Bring those to me!" Solomon commanded. The guard quickly handed them over. Solomon shoved them in a saddlebag as he addressed the sergeant. "We leave immediately."

"The others..." the sergeant started.

"Now!" Solomon shouted. "I don't care about anything else."

The sergeant nodded and started barking orders. "Stick them on a horse and let's get moving."

Minutes later, they sat tied to their saddles, with a contingent of guardsmen surrounding them.

The sergeant tried one more time. "You sure you don't want to wait till the morning?"

"No! We ride tonight," Solomon stated.

"The camp, Your Excellency."

"Leave a few men to deal with it. We don't have time."

Garron watched from the trees as they herded the three off into the darkness. A few minutes later, he had worked his way back to the others. "They're heading to Avalon tonight."

Ayleth pursed her lips. "You were right."

"I'm not taking any pleasure in it either," Garron said dryly.

"So, what next?" Estellia asked.

"Clancy and I will take turns watching over the camp tonight. We'll see what the guards leave behind in the morning."

Clancy chuckled. "I hope they leave a wagon."

Ayleth smiled. "That would be nice. You think we'll be safe tonight?"

Garron thought for a minute before answering. "I think so. It was Jocab and Edmond they wanted."

"Do we follow them?" Estellia asked.

"I thought we'd head to Settoo," Ayleth replied.

Garron shook his head. "No. We need to follow them if there is a chance of rescuing them."

"They'll have a good head-start," Clancy said.

"That can't be helped," Garron replied. "We need some food and some of our gear first."

"We only have two horses."

Garron grinned broadly. "We'll grab a few from the guard when we catch up to them."

Clancy watched and waited for the last of the guard to leave. Once they were out of sight, he signaled to the others. Garron and the two ladies appeared moments later. They worked their way toward the remains of camp and their belongings. The guard had picked through their things and helped themselves to whatever they wanted. It surprised Ayleth they didn't take more. They cobbled together a few rations, some bedding, and a dented pot for cooking, before tying them to the horses. Clancy climbed into the saddle and offered Ayleth a hand up while Garron helped Estellia on the other horse.

Estellia settled in behind Garron. "They won't hold up to this for long."

Garron nodded. "We won't ride them too hard today. Just enough to stay close to the wagons."

Clancy grinned from ear to ear. "We can grab fresh mounts from them tonight."

Later that evening, Ayleth and Estellia waited next to a fallen log as Clancy and Garron pulled on their cloaks. They both waved to the ladies before disappearing into the woods. Some of the light from one of Avalon's moons found its way through the clouds, creating additional shadows among the trees. "They just vanish like magic," Ayleth commented.

"It's scary how they do that," Estellia agreed.

Clancy followed behind Garron as they made their way toward the camp. Both men silently moved from tree to tree, keeping focused on the campfires in the distance. Fifty meters out, they both settled back against a tree to watch and wait. Garron was the first to speak. "Four wagons and twelve men," he breathed.

"I see two. Over there and there, on the edges of the camp," Clancy said, pointing.

"There are only two tents," Garron observed. "Some must sleep under the wagons."

"We'll find out when they change the guard."

"True," replied Garron. "See if you can spot anything else."

Clancy nodded, and the two let the silence surround them as they continued to observe.

Garron stood, waking Clancy. "It's time."

"What's your plan?" Clancy asked, as he let Garron help him to his feet.

"You gather the horses and I'm going to steal some food."

"Sounds good. I'm hungry."

"Me too," Garron said before drifting off into the shadows toward the wagons. Clancy pulled his cloak around him and made his way to the horses. It took only a few minutes to gather the horses and wait. He turned toward the camp when a shout rang out. "You! Stop right there!"

Clancy spotted Garron running toward the guard with a large sack in one hand. He watched as Garron swung the sack at the guard's face. The guard ducked under it and thrust his spear at Garron. Garron slipped sideways, getting inside the range of the spear, and slammed his elbow into the guard's face. Clancy knew it landed hard when the guard toppled over backward with his hands going to his nose. "Ouch. That's gotta hurt," Clancy said, smiling to himself.

Garron kept running as the guards' cries woke more of the camp. Clancy whistled, high and shrill. Garron changed direction as he kept running. A guard grabbed his spear, pulled his arm back, and launched it at Garron. "Spear!" Clancy yelled. Garron immediately adjusted his course as he continued forward. In a few heartbeats, Garron flung himself on a waiting horse. Both men dug their heels in and raced away, leading the rest of the horses with them.

Garron asked. "You took all of the horses?"

Clancy smiled. "Yup. Figured we would switch horses often, so they don't tire as quickly."

"Good thinking," he replied. "We'll make better time."

Minutes later, they linked up with Ayleth and Estellia. Both women emerged from behind a tree. "Look, Ayleth, we get our pick," Estellia said, smiling at the horses.

Ayleth laughed as she retrieved their belongings. Garron quickly distributed the gear among the four of them. They headed into the woods afterward, with both moons lighting the way. After an hour of riding, Garron pulled up and gathered the others near him. "I think we need to split up."

"What are you thinking?" Clancy asked, surprised.

"We send the ladies to Settoo while we ride after the others," Garron said firmly.

Estellia opened her mouth to speak when Clancy spoke, "I think it would be safer to have them with us."

"We have to get word to Settoo that Solomon double-crossed them and that they are in danger."

"But we can't go back through Liberty," Ayleth said. "The Temple Guard will catch us."

Estellia smiled. "I know a way around Liberty. There is a canyon that takes us further west."

"Really?" Clancy commented. "That's good to know."

"It's how we got past them last time on the way to your family farm."

"I wondered how you did that."

Garron cut in. "We need to hurry. They have a day's head start."

"Sorry," Clancy replied. "Let's split the gear up so we can go." It took them a few minutes before they were ready to part ways.

Ayleth hugged Garron and Clancy. "You bring my husband back safe, all right?"

"I promise," he replied.

Estellia hugged the two men. "Bring mine back too. And also that priest that married us."

"Two husbands and a temple priest," Clancy said, grinning. "Did I forget anything?"

They all shared a laugh before they headed off in different directions. Ayleth and Estellia led their horses deeper into the woods while Garron and Clancy raced off down the road.

The sun was beating down on them when they stopped for lunch. They had ridden hard for two days, sleeping, and eating little. The sergeant had finally gotten Solomon to rest, but only after a horse became lame from the brutal pace they had set. Solomon spent the time holding court. He had the three dragged in front of him like common criminals. The three men stood before Solomon as he sat on a pile of blankets. Jocab watched as Solomon stabbed a small knife into bite-size pieces of cheese before sliding them into his mouth with the tip of the blade. After several bites, Solomon washed the cheese down with some water before acknowledging them.

Jocab ignored his hunger pains as he waited patiently. Their last meal had consisted of a small bowl of oats the night before.

Solomon fixed his gaze on Jocab. "You three will tell me what you know. Right now!"

Jocab held his gaze. "Is there anything specific, Your Excellence?"

"When did they arrive?"

"I would have to check my journal, Your Excellence."

Solomon turned to a guard standing nearby. "Bring me his things." Solomon went back to eating as the guard fetched the items.

It was all Jocab could do to not roll his eyes as Solomon flaunted his authority.

The guard returned quickly and placed the contents in front of Solomon.

Solomon gazed in amazement at the small metal box, forgetting his previous questions. "Where did you get this?" he demanded.

Jocab kept his voice level. "A family heirloom, Your Excellence." For the first time, he feared Solomon.

"Intriguing," Solomon commented as he pulled the box closer to him. The three men stiffened as Solomon opened the lid and peered inside. "Well, well, well. What have we here?"

Jocab shared a sideways glance with Donav and Edmond but stayed silent. Solomon's hand shook as he picked up the journal and focused on the embroidered letters. He studied the words on the front before looking back at Jocab. "You said, family heirloom?"

Jocab struggled to keep his voice calm. "Yes, Your Excellence."

Solomon stared at Jocab in amazement. "Let me get this straight. This is a family heirloom? You are claiming to be related to Leah?"

Jocab took a deep breath, knowing the weight of his words. "Yes, Your Excellence."

The three of them jumped when Solomon barked out a laugh. "Did you hear that, everyone?" Solomon said as he stood. "This urchin claims to be the direct descendant of the gods!" Solomon sauntered over. "Son of a god, huh?" he said, scoffing at Jocab.

Jocab stood tall and kept his gaze forward.

"Look at me!" Solomon shouted. "I'm the high priest here and I carry the god's authority, Not you!"

Jocab flinched but kept his eyes straight ahead.

Solomon stood in front of Jocab and smiled. "I said you were dangerous. Even told the council you were. I just didn't know how much." Jocab didn't like the malice that hid behind Solomon's smile. He could see both Donav's and Edmond's nervous postures as they stood on either side of him. Solomon locked his gaze on Jocab before continuing, "Now, the council must decide what to do with you, and your family connections."

Jocab clenched his jaw. His gaze bore into Solomon's while the high priest sized him up again. "You're pathetic," Solomon said, spitting in his face. "You are nothing but a common villager. No way are you the descendant of a god. Least of all, Leah." Solomon turned to the surrounding guards. "If he were a descendant," he shouted to them. "He would have their power to stop this." He drove his fist up and under Jocab's rib cage.

Jocab doubled over, a look of astonishment and pain written across his face. He slowly sank to his knees as he tried to suck in much needed oxygen, his diaphragm paralyzed by the blow.

"If you were a descendant, you would see that coming too," Solomon said, striking him again, bloodying his nose.

"Besides," Solomon laughed. "She is the goddess of beauty, and you lack those features." He struck again, knocking Jocab to the ground.

Solomon looked triumphant as he raised his hands, shouting toward the heavens. "This man admitted blasphemy, and for that he will pay!" Solomon kicked him in the ribs and spit on him again. Finally, the high priest seemed satisfied and sat back down. "The temple will hold these items for safekeeping."

Jocab surprised Solomon when he spoke, his voice loud and clear. "You will not confiscate that."

Solomon raised an eyebrow as Jocab struggled to his knees. "You think you can dictate terms here?"

Jocab swayed back and forth as he spoke. "It is wrong for the temple to take what is not theirs. And… for a high priest to beat his followers." Jocab looked at the guard before continuing, "Is this how the temple operates? Is it now acceptable to beat the people you claim to serve?"

Solomon noticed the guard watching intently, hanging on to every word. Several of the men looked uncomfortable. "Perhaps you are right," Solomon acknowledged before a big grin swallowed his face. "But that's for followers, not heretics."

Jocab's head dropped to his chest as the full meaning of the high priest's words sunk in.

Solomon held out the items for the sergeant. "Hold these. They will be evidence at their trials with the high council."

The sergeant took the items and gave a brief glance toward Jocab before he hustled away.

"And take these heretics out of my site." Solomon commanded, as he waved his hand dismissively.

CHAPTER 40

The three huddled close to each other as they ate their bowls of oats and honey. The darkness slowly descended on them as they talked among themselves. "What next?" Edmond asked. "Are we going willingly to our execution?"

Jocab looked at Edmond with his one good eye. The other was swollen shut. "We have to make a break for it tonight."

"You've got to be kidding," Edmond said. "You're in no condition to run. I think you have a cracked rib or two."

Jocab looked at both Edmond and Donav. "I'm serious. We will be dead in a week if we don't. We are getting out of here tonight."

"If we get away," Donav replied. "They'll be on our heels the whole time."

"I didn't say it would be easy."

"If they catch us, they'll kill us," Edmond commented.

"It will be worse if they turn us over to the jailer in Avalon," Donav added solemnly.

Jocab winced in pain. "That's why we are going tonight."

Avalon's second moon, Acrobba, was high overhead when Jocab sat up. He lost his balance as he stood and fell across the sleeping forms of Edmond and Donav. Both sleeping men groaned loudly. "I'm so sorry," Jocab replied as he struggled to his feet.

The sentry standing nearby walked over to investigate the noise. Jocab gave an embarrassed smile. "I tripped over my bedding."

"And where do you think you are going?" the guard asked.

Jocab grinned sheepishly. "Nature calls. I can't wait till morning."

The guard nodded. "Make it quick."

Jocab shoved his feet inside his boots and headed for a nearby tree. "Thanks," he called over his shoulder.

The guard was watching Jocab step behind the tree when a muscular arm wrapped around his torso, pinning his arms to his sides. He opened his mouth to yell when he felt a sharp point dig into his neck. Edmond whispered into his ear. "You will do exactly what I say, won't you?"

The guard nodded, his eyes wide with fear. Edmond smiled. "Let's go for a little walk then, toward the horses."

Jocab hustled from behind the tree and helped Donav gather their belongings before joining Edmond and the guard. Edmond was steering the guard along the edge of the camp, limiting their exposure while keeping alert for any signs of movement. Jocab caught up to them and asked, "Where are my things?"

The guard shook his head. "I don't know. I think the sergeant has them."

"Where is he?"

"On the far side of camp, near the cooking fire."

Jocab scanned the camp, his eyes settling on the remains of the cooking fire and the men sleeping around it. "You better be right," he said, before moving toward the sleeping men. He leaned over each of them as he searched their faces, trying to identify the sergeant. Finding him, Jocab looked around for the box and journals. He spotted the bag they were in next to the sergeant's boots and reached over the sleeping form and grabbed the bag. He lifted it, slowly separating it from the rest of the gear when the contents in the metal box shifted.

A hand shot out and seized his wrist. Jocab almost fell backward in surprise. The sergeant and Jocab stared at each other silently for several heartbeats. Hopelessness descended upon Jocab, as he knew the sergeant had him. There was no escaping the iron grip. The sergeant held his gaze a few more seconds before letting go. "Go quickly," he whispered before turning and pulling his blanket around him.

"Thank you," Jocab whispered, before hurrying back toward Edmond and the horses.

Donav and Edmond had bound and gagged the guard to a nearby tree. "You have your items?" Donav asked quietly. Jocab held up the bag and smiled.

Edmond smiled. "Good, let's go."

The three men climbed into their saddles and prodded the horses forward. They brought them to a gallop once they were safely out of earshot. Jocab was still wrestling with his thoughts, knowing that the sergeant had let him go.

CHAPTER 41

Jocab watched the road as Edmond and Donav attended to the horses. He still couldn't see out of one eye from of the swelling. He favored his left side as leaned against a tree, still recovering from where Solomon had kicked him. They had stopped to rest the horses as they stayed ahead of the soldiers. They had ridden them hard and the poor beasts were exhausted. Edmond used a watering bag while Donav searched for handfuls of choice grass. Jocab rested his head against the tree and closed his good eye for a second, craving sleep. His body jolted him awake as he almost toppled over. Jocab moved away from the tree and looked down the road. His vantage point allowed him to see for several kilometers before the road disappeared into the distance. He guessed they were a half a day's ride ahead of the guard, and he wanted to keep it that way. Jocab knew they were fleeing for their lives this time. He hoped they could find refuge some place or make it to Settoo. Jocab recognized they would never be safe anywhere the temple exerted their control.

Edmond whistled, causing Jocab to jump. He took one last glance down the road, half expecting to see Solomon racing after them any second. He wondered how long they could continue with this pace as he headed back to the others.

Clancy gently shook Garron's shoulder to wake him. "I hear riders approaching."

Garron sat up and pulled his hood over his head. It amazed Clancy that Garron could sleep soundly one minute and be wide awake the next. Clancy looked at the sun high overhead. They had ridden through the night and early morning in their quest to rescue Jocab and Edmond when they decided a rest was necessary. Garron had taken the first watch while Clancy slept through the morning. They had shared a lunch before Garron laid down and dozed off. Clancy felt bad waking him. Garron had just slept for two hours. He watched as Garron found cover near the road when the riders came into view. Clancy observed three horses thundering down the road, their coats glistening in the afternoon sun. Garron called out in surprise as his eyes settled on the riders.

Clancy heard his cry and grabbed his bow. He had already strung it with an arrow as he stumbled out of the trees. His jaw dropped when he recognized Jocab, Donav, and Edmond reining in their mounts.

"Well, it looks like my little brother doesn't need rescuing after all," Clancy announced.

Garron laughed. "I think you're right. Although, it looks like they're in a hurry."

"You guys in a hurry?" Clancy called out.

"You might say that." Edmond replied.

Clancy grinned. "I say we get our horses and join you."

"Great idea," Garron replied. "I'll be right back."

Garron reappeared with the horses a minute later.

"Where are the ladies?" Donav asked, surprised.

"They are heading toward Settoo. Estellia said they'd follow a canyon that will help them bypass Liberty."

Edmond smiled. "Box Canyon."

"We should do the same," Jocab replied.

Donav frowned. "How long ago was this?"

"Just the other day. They said they would keep to the woods and stay off the road."

"That will slow them down."

"True, but they will avoid the guardsmen that way."

Clancy caught sight of Jocab. "What happened to you? Looks like you fell out of the ugly tree and hit every branch on the way down."

Jocab laughed and winced as he favored his ribs. "The high priest was not a fan of our family tree."

"What's wrong with our family tree?"

Edmond looked surprised. "You mean you don't know?"

"Know what? You're holding out on me, little brother."

"Pa gave me a family heirloom. Said his dad passed it down to him."

Clancy's eyebrows shot up. "I'm listening. Is that where you got the torchlite you were talking about earlier?"

"Yup, and some other things."

"Like a journal," Edmond interrupted, unable to contain himself.

"Spill it," Clancy said in exasperation. "You're taking the long road to get there."

Edmond laughed. "You and your family are direct descendants from the gods, Clancy."

"What?"

"Yup," Edmond continued. "Did you know that Leah and Lipinski were married?"

"No, the scriptures never mention that."

"The high priest didn't like it either," Jocab replied.

Clancy frowned. "That's not good."

"Yeah, it was straight to the gallows for us. Seems we are all heretics now."

"Including Donav?"

"I'm afraid my lot is with them," Donav replied. "The high priest was in a pretty foul mood at the time."

Edmond chuckled. "That's putting it lightly."

The conversation dropped off as they mounted up and headed north.

Solomon squirmed in his saddle, trying to get comfortable. The last several days were taking a toll on him. Any change he made just caused him to hurt in other areas. He cursed under his breath before his impatience got the better of him. "What is it?"

The guard looked up. "Looks like they stopped to feed and water the horses."

"How long ago?"

"Several hours," the guard replied.

"We still have some daylight left. Let's keep moving."

Everyone was too tired to hold a conversation when Garron spoke. "We are about a kilometer from where we stole the horses. The guard may still be there with the wagons."

"How many guardsmen were there?" Donav asked.

"There were six."

"Yikes," Edmond commented. "Let's go into the woods and circle around them."

Jocab shook his head. "We can move faster on the road."

"But we will be safer in the woods," Edmond countered.

"The road, and that's final," Jocab stated.

Garron nodded. "Let's give the horses a break first,"

"Great idea," Clancy agreed. "That will give me a chance to scout ahead." They all agreed and dismounted to walk their horses while Clancy jogged ahead.

Jocab walked with the others as his eyes wandered to the telephone poles along the road. Edmond caught him gazing at them and commented, "Was a lot of hard work, wasn't it?"

Jocab smiled. "It sure was, but it gave us the cover we needed. I wish we had that now."

"You helped put this up?" Garron asked, surprised.

"Yeah. Jocab helped the contractor fix their voice communicator on our way to Avalon. He hid us among the crew when we escaped later."

"We ended up having to be part of the work party," Jocab added. "That was until we reached the trail to the canyon."

Edmond smiled, remembering. "It was perfect. We hid in plain sight."

"The contractor even paid us for our work," Jocab said, laughing.

Garron shook his head in disbelief. "Now that's funny."

They spotted Clancy moments later jogging toward them. "I saw four of them camped out with the wagons. No sign of the other two."

"How long did you watch?" Edmond asked.

"About ten minutes. I didn't want to stay too long and risk you guys coming up behind me."

"Any idea about the other two?"

Clancy shook his head. "Sorry, no idea."

Garron got a crooked smile. "Let's hope they are walking back to Liberty for more horses."

Clancy nodded. "Yeah, that's a lot of gear to just abandon."

Garron looked at Jocab. "Your call. Rest here till sunset, or go now?"

"Now," Jocab replied. "I'm worried Solomon will appear behind us any minute."

"How far are we from this canyon you guys used last time?" Clancy asked.

"I think a good day's ride."

CHAPTER 42

USSF CALYPSO

"All right, let's go over the details once more. This time, we will record it for the ship's record." Steven nodded and pressed the record button on the console in front of them.

"This is Captain Danielle Yasser and First Officer Steven Collins. After a successful journey, we are orbiting the planet. We have been reviewing the ship's logs while monitoring the planet below. Our observations show no heavy industry or large-scale production at any of the known population centers." Danielle paused and took a sip of water. "Satellite images show pre industrial age population centers with fishing and agricultural farms in the surrounding areas."

"Since we have no way to monitor, communicate, or remotely gather any meaningful intelligence, I have determined we must take a shuttle down to the planet."

Danielle looked at Steven. "Do you wish to add anything?"

Steven shook his head. "I'm good."

"Thank you," she commented before continuing. "We will enter the atmosphere over the ocean here." She said as she placed her finger on the console. "This will limit our exposure as we come through the upper atmosphere. Afterward, we will stay within the cloud cover till we arrive at the landing site."

Danielle paused when Steven signaled with his hand.

"These two weather systems can help hide our approach."

Danielle smiled. "Thank you. Let's time our entry, so we land in the dark of night. That will help minimize the risk of being seen."

Danielle leaned over and stopped the recording. "That's it. Now, how soon can we leave?"

Steven grabbed his tablet. "Optimum orbital insertion is in three hours."

AVALON

Ayleth was kneeling down, tending to a small fire, when she heard some motion to her left. She turned, thinking it was Estellia returning from relieving herself, when a male voice spoke. "She's right here Hans."

Ayleth whipped around to see a guardsman smiling at her, a spear in one hand and a knife in the other.

He approached her, balancing the spear expertly. "You and your stupid friends caused us a lot of trouble."

Behind him, Ayleth saw another guard holding a knife to Estellia's neck. "This is our lucky night," Hans replied. He had Estellia sit with her back against a large rock. "Bring her over here, Clinton."

Clinton motioned with his spear for Ayleth to join Estellia. Ayleth considered her options for a heartbeat before sitting beside her and pulling her legs up to her chest. Clinton smiled. "That's a good girl."

"You keep an eye on them while I get something to tie them up."

Clinton waved his spear back and forth. "First one of you that tries anything gets this in their gut."

Ayleth leaned into Estellia. "You all right?"

Estellia nodded. "Yeah, they caught me by surprise." She said, keeping her voice low. "I found myself in a choke hold with a blade at my throat."

"Shut it, you two wenches," Clinton barked.

Estellia glared at the man but kept silent.

Hans appeared a short while later with some leather straps from their packs. He made quick work tying their hands and feet while Clinton stood guard, spear in hand. Once secured, Hans wandered over to their small fire to take inventory.

"Any good food?" Clinton asked, still standing guard.

"A little cheese and some dried meat."

"I was hoping they bagged a rabbit."

Hans handed Clinton a slice of meat while he stuffed a few bites into his mouth.

"So, what do we do with these two?"

"We will have to take them to Liberty."

"But we're riding the horses," Clinton replied. "They can walk."

Hans leered at the women. "Maybe we ride something else tonight."

Clinton took an appraising look at the two ladies. "I like what you're thinking."

Both women glared at the men. Estellia was about to speak when Ayleth elbowed her to keep silent.

Hans shoved a piece of meat in his mouth as he leaned down next to Ayleth. Brandishing the knife again, he lifted her chin with the blade. "I just need to decide who I want first."

Both women could sense each other's fear. Clinton kept his spear ready. "Don't take too long figuring it out. They're both fine young things," he replied, stretching out the word fine.

Hans moved to Estellia's side and leaned in, slipping the blade under the laces of her shirt. With a quick flick of his wrist, he cut the laces.

Estellia lunged forward with all her might. Her head slammed into Hans. He fell backward with a grunt, his nose gushing blood. "That was a mistake," he growled, getting back up. She tried to draw away from him but froze as his icy blade dug into the side of her neck, just breaking the skin.

"You stay right there," Hans hissed in her ear. Turning to Clinton, he announced. "I want this one."

Clinton smiled, thrust his spear into the ground, and pulled Ayleth to her feet. "You're mine then," he said, groping her.

"Get your grubby hands off me!" she snarled, spitting in his face. He backhanded her, knocking her to the ground. "So that's how you want to do it," he replied as he grabbed his spear.

Ayleth rolled away as Clinton drove the spear into the dirt, missing her by a few centimeters. He didn't slow as he stepped forward and kicked her below the ribs, knocking the air from her lungs. She curled into a ball and gasped for air. Clinton stood large over her with rage in his eyes. She watched helplessly as he raised the spear for another thrust. Ayleth, still unable to breathe, made a feeble attempt to roll away. She waited for the jabbing pain of the spear when she heard a whooshing sound come from behind her, followed by the shaft of an arrow protruding from Clinton's neck. Fear and surprise shone in his eyes as he made a gurgling sound before collapsing at her feet.

Hans jumped up, his trousers sliding down around his ankles as he tried to use Estellia as a shield. He looked around frantically as an arrow found his eye, burying itself deep in his brain. He crashed to the ground, dragging Estellia with him.

Ayleth scrambled away from Clinton as the ground soaked up the blood spilling from his neck. Estellia screamed as she tried to untangle herself from the corpse beside her.

Jocab and Edmond ran to their wives, holding them gently as the two women processed what had just happened. Ayleth glimpsed Garron and Clancy exit from the trees with a bow in their hands before she passed out.

"In the eye, huh?" Clancy said.

"I wanted him to see the error of his ways," Garron joked. "I noticed you shut your guy up right quick."

"I take no pleasure in killing a man."

"Neither do I."

"But they cease being men when they force themselves on a woman."

They retrieved their arrows and cleaned them with the shirts of the two dead men.

Edmond and Jocab had untied their wives by the time Garron had quivered his arrow and looked around. "Sorry to be so callous. But we need to get going."

Voren led the group to the bottom of the canyon. Two dozen woodsmen silently disappeared down the canyon wall, leaving the farms of Liberty behind them. They had been hurrying south for two weeks now, ever since they received private message from Kenneth. The Captain of the guard at Liberty had sent a rider advising of possible treachery from the High Priest Solomon.

Not only did he give Voren the early warning, he had also

provided instructions on how to bypass Liberty without being seen. This canyon provided Voren with the means to shave off some valuable time unnoticed.

Once at the bottom, they ate a quick meal while enjoying the late afternoon sun.

Danielle maintained an altitude of six kilometers above the surface. She kept her eyes on her instruments while maneuvering through the cloud cover. The display screen provided a contour map of the world below. A small marker tagging her landing site blinked in the upper corner.

Steven broke the silence in the cockpit. "Two minutes out."

"Got it. Can you give me any thermal images?"

He leaned into the console. "Sure, coming up."

Thirty seconds passed before Danielle asked, "You having a problem?"

Steven was busy swiping and pressing buttons on the screen. "Sorry, Sar. Thermal and infra-red imaging were damaged during entry."

Danielle frowned. "That's not good. Can we detect if the landing zone is clear?"

"Maybe, but we'll have to be right on top of it."

"Great," she replied, drawing out the word.

"I'll let you know if I see something."

Solomon pushed his horse forward. Even he could see that the tracks were less than an hour old. Finding the dead guardsmen still warm told him they couldn't be too far. The men, enraged, drove their horses at a maddening pace, eager to catch the killers and enact retribution for the deaths of their fellow guardsmen.

The moon crested the canyon walls, providing some additional light to see by. The woodsmen men glided across the canyon floor while blending into the surrounding rocks. They moved with the grace of a hunter stalking their prey. Their brown cloaks camouflaged their movements and hid their features. Voren held up his hand when he noticed movement on the rocks ahead of him.

Each of the men slowly knelt down, blending into the surrounding terrain. Voren slowly made his way forward, observing the two guardsmen blocking his path. He thought about his options when he heard one of them speak. "I wish they would get here."

"So do I," the other responded.

Voren recognized the second voice. He stood in the middle of the path and walked forward. "Dawson, is that you?"

Both guardsmen jumped at the sound.

"Who goes there?" the first guardsmen called into the darkness.

Voren appeared, lowered his hood and smiled. "Dawson, it's Voren."

"Voren?"

"It's me. I wasn't expecting any of you."

"Yeah, the Captain marched us out here a few days ago. He said to keep an eye out for you."

"I can see that. Just not sure why."

"He said to invite you all in when you arrived. He's been waiting for you."

Voren pondered Dawson's words for a few heartbeats. "Give me a second to let the others know."

"Sure thing," Dawson replied.

Voren disappeared back into the darkness. A few seconds later, Dawson heard the hoot of a night bird. Several seconds later, he heard another hoot further away. Voren reappeared with a warm smile on his face and held out his hand. Dawson accepted, and they shook. "Good to see you," Voren said.

"And you too, sir." Dawson stammered.

"Who's your friend?"

"This is Neil," Dawson replied, quickly.

Neil accepted Voren's handshake. His eyes bugged out as he saw the woodsmen appearing out of the surrounding darkness.

Voren sensed the men behind him. "Since we are all here, lead the way."

"Uh, yes, sir," they replied, and hurried back down the trail.

They had walked a few hundred yards before coming upon the rest of the guard, relaxing in the darkness. They all started to get up when Dawson and Neil guided the woodsmen into their midst.

Voren immediately spotted the Captain rising to his feet. Voren knew you could always spot a captain. The presence of command surrounded them. "Captain," Voren said.

"Hello, Voren. I'm glad you could make it."

"This is unexpected, Captain."

"I agree, but I think it will be necessary. And please call me Kenneth."

"Thank you for the escort, Kenneth. It will make moving through the area much easier."

"My thoughts exactly." Kenneth turned toward his men. "Alright, let's shake off the dust and get moving."

Voren watched as the guard quickly gathered their belongings and mounted up.

"I have horses for your men," Kenneth said.

Voren's eyes widened in surprise.

"I thought that speed was another necessity."

CHAPTER 43

Edmond kept an eye out behind them as they made their way toward the canyon. The trail snaked back and forth as they gained in elevation. They had abandoned the horses a short way back, having pushed them to exhaustion. Jocab felt they would be safer on foot. Jocab also figured they would have a better chance of hiding if they didn't have to worry about their mounts.

Garron insisted they leave their gear and go. He wanted as much distance as possible between them and the dead guardsmen. Ayleth walked next to Jocab, using Clinton's spear as a walking stick. She glared at Jocab when he suggested they leave it behind. Estellia was struggling from her encounter as well. She walked in front of Edmond, cocooning herself in a blanket as she tried to withdraw from the world. Jocab knew they were still processing what had happened, but he also understood they needed to deal with the trauma soon to avoid any long-term emotional damage. He wished he could just take Ayleth, hold her, and make her pain disappear.

The trail ahead leveled off for a hundred meters before dropping further into the canyon. Edmond gave one last look over his shoulder before the road disappeared from view. "Oh, no." Edmond exclaimed as his eye spotted movement below.

"What?" Estellia asked.

"I think I see the high priest."

Estellia stopped to look at where Edmond was pointing. "I see them too. We better warn the others."

"I am over the landing site," Danielle stated. "Any thermals?"

"Nothing, Sar." Steven replied.

"All right," she said grudgingly. "I'll have to make a quick drop to limit our exposure."

"Ready when you are," Steven replied.

"Here we go," she said as the shuttle dropped straight down. The darkness obscured the ground as they fell like a rock. Steven called out their rate of descent as he watched the altimeter. His stomach almost revolted when Danielle slowed their descent at three hundred meters. "Landing gear deployed," he said as he collected himself again.

"Two hundred meters, one hundred meters," he continued. "Fifty meters, ten meters."

He felt the gear absorb the weight as the shuttle touched down.

Voren and Kenneth rode together, letting the horses pick the speed. Minutes later, a powerful gust of wind hit them as it blew through the canyon. They tucked themselves into the wind and urged the now nervous horses onward.

"That wind sure spooked them."

"And unexpected," Kenneth replied as he looked at the clouds overhead. "Clouds don't seem to match the wind, either."

"Is that common in this canyon?"

"Not really."

They pushed onward, the wind dying down just as fast as it had started.

Clancy was in the lead, hurrying toward a large group of rocks. The rest followed at a slow run, knowing the high priest was gaining on them. "If we can get to those rocks, we can set up a defense."

Garron nodded. "Sounds good to me."

They tried to pick up the pace when a strong wind buffeted them, surprising them with its ferocity. They leaned into it as they made their way forward.

Danielle's hands danced across the console in front of her. "Shutting down all engines. Do we have any thermals now?"

"No, Sar. Visual only."

"I can't see anything between the canyon walls and the pile of rocks we are hiding behind."

"We should be safe. Satellite Images showed this canyon is not used often, if at all."

"How long did you monitor it?" Danielle asked as she stood up.

"Several weeks," he replied as he released his straps to stand beside her.

"There they are," the guard shouted, pointing at the small group running several hundred meters in front of them.

"After them," the high priest yelled, pushing his horse forward. The guardsmen surged forward, gaining ground by the second.

Ayleth slipped and stumbled, slamming her knee into the ground before crashing hard on her right side. Garron reached down to pull her up when he noticed two guardsmen overtaking Edmond in the rear.

"Clancy," Garron yelled. "Bow, Now!"

Clancy grabbed his bow and strung it as he spun around. He was reaching for the first arrow when Garron shouted, "Get the lead horses!"

Clancy let loose an arrow. It flew through the night and buried itself deep in the horse's chest. The horse stumbled and went down, throwing the rider. The poor soul didn't stand a chance. His momentum carried him forward, dashing him into the rocks where he started twitching. Garron pulled back the string to fire at the other guardsman who had zeroed in on Edmond, his spear poised to throw.

"Spear!" Garron yelled as he let his arrow fly.

Edmond dove for the ground, the spear missing his back and cutting into his arm, leaving a deep gash across his bicep.

The arrow reached the guardsman a second later, digging into his thigh. He slid sideways from the saddle as he clutched his leg.

Edmond jumped to his feet and resumed running. Jocab and Ayleth passed Garron, who was helping Estellia while Clancy stood nearby with another arrow ready to fly.

The other guardsmen pulled up short to avoid being Clancy's next target and milled about, just out of range. "Get them!" Solomon yelled as he tried to urge the men forward.

"Dismount and fan out." the sergeant ordered. "Shield yourself with your horse and move in."

The two dozen riders followed orders and created a skirmish line as they advanced.

Clancy held them at bay till Garron yelled to him they had safely reached the rocks. Then he too bolted in their direction.

"Don't stay too bunched up," the sergeant shouted. "Half of you work yourselves to the right and cut off their retreat. Four of you work up the sides," he said, pointing to the cliff walls.

Solomon stayed seated on his horse a few meters behind the line and watched the men advance. "They have the height advantage up there."

"Yes, Your Excellence, they do. And in this darkness, we won't be able to see their arrows till it's too late."

"Then charge them," the high priest demanded.

"And lose half my men?"

"Have them charge now," Solomon snapped. "Or I will brand you a heretic and find myself a new sergeant."

The sergeant's eyes went wide. "Yes, Your Excellence."

Voren pulled up and cocked his head to the side. "Did you hear that?"

Kenneth stopped beside him. "It sounded like yelling."

"We should spread out then," Voren replied. Kenneth and Voren signaled for their men to spread out as they pressed forward.

"We need to fall back," Garron commented.

Clancy walked backward, keeping his eyes on the guardsmen in front of him. "I agree. They are trying to put men on the canyon walls."

"Which way?" Donav asked.

"Let's get closer to the walls over there," Jocab suggested. "There are some large rocks and boulders we can take cover behind."

"You guys go first. We'll keep them honest," Clancy replied.

"Don't get hurt," Jocab replied. "I don't want to tell Ma any bad news."

Clancy smiled. "I promise Bro, now get moving."

Clancy watched them disappear into the darkness as they headed toward the canyon wall.

Steven met Danielle in front of the airlock. "So how do I look, Sar?" he asked.

"Like the natives."

Steven felt the fabric on her shoulder. "Is that cotton or wool?" he teased.

She spun around, showing off her outfit. "Wool. Do you like it?"

"Very nice, Sar."

Danielle laughed as they both entered the airlock. "I want no hostilities. If we shoot, it is to disable, not to kill."

"Got it, Sar." Steven said, smiling. "Unconscious, not dead."

Danielle rolled her eyes as they entered the airlock. It took a minute to cycle through it before they could enjoy the cool night air.

"Get ready," Clancy said. "Here comes the first charge."

"Wait till they are close enough that you can't miss," Garron instructed. "We have a limited supply of arrows."

"Please, don't remind me."

They watched as a dozen mounted men readied for a charge. It was too dark to see anything more than their silhouettes in the distance. All at once, they charged, holding their spears at the ready as they galloped forward.

Clancy and Garron waited as the horses drew closer. At about thirty meters, both men pulled and let loose. In a smooth motion, they fired again and again, and again. Half of the men fell from their horses in a flurry of arms and legs. Several of them threw their spears before wheeling their horses around and galloping away. Clancy and Garron had to stop firing and take cover as several spears landed where they had been seconds earlier.

"This is like hunting chickens in a barn," Garron commented.

"I think that's enough, don't you?"

"Yeah, I've used up half my arrows."

"Then let's go," Clancy said, sprinting away.

Garron followed, hot on his heels.

Jocab and Donav came to an immediate stop as they rounded the corner. Edmond and the ladies collided with them, almost knocking everyone to the ground.

They stared in awe at the silhouette of a large metal craft occupying the darkness in front of them. Standing in front of a closing door were two individuals.

"By the Gods," Ayleth whispered.

Voren strung his bow. "That's fighting I hear up ahead."

"Let's not rush into things," Kenneth cautioned.

"Agreed. I'll send some scouts ahead."

"I was just going to offer that," Kenneth replied.

"No offense, Kenneth. Your men are as quiet as a pig at a feeding trough."

Kenneth laughed. "Compared to your woodsmen, I have to agree."

"What was that?" Solomon raged. "You call that a charge?"

"No, Your Excellence. That was my men being sent to their deaths."

"They don't have enough arrows to kill all of us. Send some more men and finish this," the high priest demanded.

"I need to retrieve the wounded before we do anything else, Your Excellence."

Solomon fumed. "You can get them after," he replied. "You will do this my way, or I'll burn your family as heretics in front of your eyes."

The sergeant blanched before he hurried away, barking orders.

"So much for not being detected," Steven commented under his breath.

Danielle frowned. "This is not going to plan."

Steven snorted. "And their English sounds funny."

CHAPTER 44

Solomon followed in the rear as the guardsmen charged forward. They brought their horses to a quick gallop, hoping to reduce the time an arrow could strike them down. They reached the rocks where Clancy and Garron had made their stand and found it abandoned. The soldiers milled about, looking this way and that when several more men fell from their horses, the shafts of an arrow providing evidence of their plight. "Keep moving," the sergeant yelled.

Garron looked at Clancy. "I'm out of arrows."

"Me too. Let's catch up with the others." Both men ran into the darkness toward their next rendezvous point.

"That way!" Solomon screamed, pointing into the darkness. "They went that way."

The guards adjusted their course as they maintained their pursuit.

The two woodsmen returned shortly, gasping for air. "Temple guards are chasing some people and one of them looks like Garron."

"That's not good," Voren said aloud.

"Did you see the high priest?" Kenneth asked.

"Too hard to tell in the darkness. Although Garron and someone else were giving the guards a whooping."

"Explain," Voren replied.

"They dropped a guard with every shot. That is until they ran out of arrows."

"We need to move then," Voren replied.

Kenneth turned to the men behind him. "Now we ride, men. The high priest is using our own guardsmen to hunt down innocent people. They are being hunted, not because they are heretics, but because of their knowledge. You were all handpicked for this mission because you saw with your own eyes the misdeeds that were carried out in the forest. You saw the evil works of Solomon and his fanatical beliefs. Tonight, you ride to protect the innocent from the temple's injustice. You ride to protect your friends." He spun his horse around before shouting, "Let's ride!"

Both guardsmen and woodsmen dug in their heels and rode into the night.

Clancy and Garron rounded the corner at a dead run. Their eyes bugged out as they spotted the craft just meters away. Garron was the first to recover his wits, the urgency of the situation overriding his amazement. "That crazy priest will be here any minute."

"Quick, find cover." Edmond yelled. The group scattered, ducking behind trees and rocks, looking for some way to become invisible in the darkness.

Danielle and Steven pulled their weapons and powered them up. The two took refuge next to their forward landing gear, keeping out of sight.

"We stay out of this," she commanded. "This isn't our fight."

"Yes, Sar." Steven replied. "And if they target us?"

"Neutralize them," she commanded.

"But no killing," he acknowledged as he ducked down beside her.

Voren looked at Kenneth. "We are going to be too late."

Kenneth could see the grief in Voren's eyes. "We can only pray," he said as they galloped forward. They could see the riders below gaining ground as his friends scattered to hide.

"Do you see that?" Kenneth asked.

"See what?" Voren replied.

"There's a dark shape down there."

Voren scanned the darkness where his friends were hiding. "I think I do."

A dozen guardsmen rounded the corner on horseback, spears ready to take down anyone standing in their way. Upon seeing the strange craft, they pulled up and milled around, not sure what to do.

One guardsman shouted, "The gods have returned."

"The gods," another replied as they spotted Danielle and Steven. Several dismounted and fell to their knees.

Solomon arrived a second later and almost fell off his horse at the site of the craft. He watched the soldiers falling over themselves to kneel in front of the craft. "What is the meaning of this?" he yelled.

One of them answered. "The gods have returned."

Another voice spoke up. "They came for one of their own."

"It's true," another replied. "We've been chasing the children of the gods."

Jocab and Edmond looked at each other. Edmond did everything to keep from laughing aloud. Jocab frowned and wrinkled his nose at him before mouthing, "Don't even."

Edmond failed to contain himself and fell back against the rock, muffling his laughter. "You're up, god boy."

Jocab slapped him on the shoulder before exiting his hiding spot. He yelled to Solomon. "They've arrived, Solomon. And your men have seen them now."

Solomon turned toward Jocab's voice and saw him emerge from the darkness. "That changes nothing." he screeched, his voice lacking the confidence it once held.

Jocab continued forward. "Yes, it does. It changes everything. The temple will have to adapt and recognize the truth."

"No, it won't!" the High Priest bellowed.

"Oh yes, Your Excellence. You knew all along. You knew one day this would happen, but you chose to continue the lie. Now you're unprepared. Now you must deal with it, because it won't go away."

Kenneth and Voren lost sight of the situation as they drew closer, the rocks and vegetation blocking their view. They dismounted, spread out, and approached quietly so as not to give away their position. He was thankful the fighting had stopped but could still feel the tension in the air. Something was happening, and he needed to see what it was.

"Look at your men," Jocab continued. "They think the gods have returned. They think that because the temple told them how to think."

"We provide spiritual guidance," Solomon huffed.

"They need that guidance," Donav cut in. "And they will continue to need that guidance, but it must be within the confines of the truth." Donav continued as he joined Jocab. "We must embrace the truth first."

Solomon sunk back in his saddle, a look of confusion on his face. Everything he had worked for, believed in, was unraveling in front of him. Donav walked toward him, arms open at his sides. Donav could see Solomon's distress. He recognized how vulnerable and dangerous Solomon was at this moment. Donav knew he had only one chance to talk him off the ledge. "The world still needs us. They've placed their spiritual lives in our hands. They will listen to you, a High Priest of the Council. You have the wisdom and the knowledge, the keeper of the ancient relics. They will need Solomon, the High Priest, more after today than any other day, because you were here with them." Donav finished.

Solomon looked stunned, his confidence crumbling. "But, the gods," Solomon stammered.

Solomon's eyes darted between the ship, Donav, and Jocab.

Donav slowly walked up to Solomon and rubbed the horse's neck, all the while keeping his eyes on Solomon. "Please help us, Your Excellence. You are a vital part of what happens next. Be a spokesperson for your people and embrace the situation. Show the world the best the temple has to offer."

Solomon gave a slight nod, hypnotized by Donav's words. "I can do that," he replied, more to himself than those around him.

"Thank you, Your Excellence," Donav said, bowing his head for the high priest to bless him. Solomon reached out to place his hand on Donav's head when he froze, the spell broken. Donav looked up, confused to see Solomon frowning. He turned to see two more people coming into view.

"What are you doing here?" Solomon asked, surprised.

Kenneth snapped to attention and saluted. "We came because we thought you might need help."

"But you're with him," he said, stabbing his finger at Voren.

"Yes, Your Excellence, we came together."

"He's the enemy," venom dripped from his voice.

"He is our friend."

"He harbored heretics."

"They are not heretics, just men who stumbled upon a discovery."

"A discovery that threatens the gods and the temple."

"It doesn't have to," Donav said from beside Solomons' horse.

Solomon had forgotten all about Donav. He had forgotten about all the guardsmen watching the events unfold. He hadn't forgotten about Jocab. Something inside him snapped. It was all clear now. This was all Jocab's fault. He brought all this upon him. It was Jocab who was destroying the temple. He was responsible. He claimed to be a descendant of the gods. Heresy, all heresy. The voice of the gods spoke to him. "The descendant of Leah must die."

Solomon whispered to himself. "Yes, Jocab must die!"

He heard nothing after that. Conviction and self-righteousness surrounded him. Solomon spurred his horse, knocking Donav to the ground. He screamed, "Jocab must die!" as he snatched a spear from a stunned guardsman and charged.

Jocab viewed the next series of events in slow motion, small flashes in time. He heard Solomon's scream of rage. Jocab remembered being paralyzed in place, unable to move as the high priest charged, spear in hand. He watched Solomon stand tall in the saddle and draw back his arm. Unable to turn away from the oncoming spear, Jocab cried out as a sudden spasm of pain gripped his side, the spear digging deep into his liver. He felt himself falling sideways as he watched an angry Ayleth throw her spear at Solomon with all her might. Jocab hit the ground and lost consciousness, but not before witnessing the look of surprise on Solomon's face as he slid backward off his horse with Ayleth's spear firmly planted in his chest.

CHAPTER 45

Jocab slowly opened his eyes and looked around, blinking several times to clear his vision. He could tell he was resting on a cot in a tent, the light streaming in from the openings between the flaps. Jocab tried to move but stopped when he felt the pain in his side and a heavy weight on his chest. He gently lifted his head to see Ayleth's form slumped over him. She sat in a chair beside him with her head and arms resting on his chest.

He smiled as he looked at his wife, appreciating her beauty while she slept. He softly ran his hand through her hair, enjoying the moment alone. Ayleth stirred and made a small "Mmmm" sound before her eyes shot opened, realizing he was awake. "Hello beautiful," he said, softly.

She sat up quickly. "You're awake," she squealed, hugging him fiercely. "I was so worried." Jocab hugged her back, ignoring the pain. "I have to tell the others!" she exclaimed as she stood.

Jocab grabbed her hand. "They can wait a few minutes. Let it be just us for now."

Ayleth's grin grew bigger. "Of course," she replied as she sat back down.

"So, what happened? What have I missed?"

Ayleth took the next hour to explain how she watched helplessly as the travelers removed the spear and treated his injury. She explained how the travelers used a special medicine and special bandage on his wound that would speed up the healing process. That Garron and the Woodsmen were leaving tomorrow to carry a message to Settoo. How Kenneth and the travelers were waiting for Jocab to heal before they traveled to Liberty and that some would stay behind to guard the travelers' craft. That Kenneth would contact the High Priest in Avalon using the voice communicator upon their arrival.

"They are proposing a diplomatic summit at Liberty. It's the halfway point between Settoo and Avalon," Ayleth finished.

"So why is everyone waiting for me?" Jocab asked, confused.

Ayleth barked out a laugh. "Are you kidding?"

"No," he said. "I'm serious."

"Oh, my dense and loving husband. You are the center of this whole thing."

"I am not," Jocab insisted.

"Stop being so silly. Your humility won't work here."

Clancy and Donav interrupted any further conversation when they poked their heads through the tent flaps. "We thought we heard you talking," Clancy said, smiling.

"Yeah, Mister Dense here can't understand why we are waiting for him to get better."

Clancy laughed as they entered. "That's my little brother for you."

"Was he always like this?" she teased.

"Always. Sometimes we had to hit him with the reality stick."

Jocab frowned. "I'm not that bad."

"Nope, quite the opposite. You are the man of the hour."

"How?"

Ayleth leaned over and kissed him. "Everyone wants you and Donav to head up this diplomatic meeting in Liberty."

"What?" Jocab stammered.

"Both sides agree that the two of you will do the best job mediating," Clancy added.

Jocab looked confused. "Both sides?"

"Yeah, it was Kenneth's idea, and both Voren and Garron agreed. I think the travelers were going to insist. You impressed everyone when you and Donav tried to reason with Solomon."

Jocab reached for his side, feeling the bandage. "What happened to him?"

Donav bit his lip. "He died from his wounds."

Jocab closed his eyes and murmured a silent prayer, the image of Ayleth throwing the spear caught in his mind.

Clancy read his thoughts. "If it helps, there were already multiple arrows in his back before he stuck you with the spear. That's why he only got your liver."

Jocab looked at Ayleth. He could see the pain in her eyes. She wasn't proud of it, but Jocab knew she would do it again without hesitation. She was protecting the one she loved. "I'm glad," he replied, grabbing Ayleth's hand.

They spent three uneventful days traveling to Liberty. The travelers joined them but refused to answer any questions. "In the right time," the Captain, Danielle, reassured.

Once they arrived, Jocab and Donav spoke by wire to the High Priest, Athels. They agreed to have Solomon's body transported to Avalon and laid to rest with full religious honors. Athels also appointed Donav as an interim High Priest, giving him the authority needed to conduct the summit, and promoted Kenneth to Supreme Captain over all the temple guard.

All parties agreed to convene a summit in six weeks, thus allowing time for all sides to send representatives.

It was their second week in Liberty when Danielle knocked on the door of their guest house.

"Please come in," Ayleth said, opening the door wide.

Danielle entered. "Thank you."

Jocab stood. "Hello, Danielle. To what do we owe the honor?"

"We are heading back to our shuttle tomorrow morning."

Jocab nodded. "I appreciate your stopping by to let us know."

Danielle smiled. "That's not why I stopped by."

Jocab raised an eyebrow. "Oh?"

"Steven and I wanted to extend an invitation for you to join us."

Ayleth's face lit up. "I think we'd love to."

"That's great," Danielle replied. "Please make sure your brother Clancy joins us."

After some more small talk and a few hugs, Danielle left. Ayleth smiled as she wrapped her arms around Jocab. "We're going on a spaceship."

Thank you for reading the first in the Avalon Found series.
(A review would be greatly appreciated!)

Visit online at emhanzel.com

Want to be notified when new episodes are published or learn
about the author?
Please join the mailing list!
at https://emhanzel.com

Made in the USA
Monee, IL
11 March 2024

54352282R00144